TODAY I REMEMBER

TODAY I REMEMBER

MARTIN L. SHOEMAKER

WFP
WordFire Press

EBook ISBN: 978-1-68057-026-7
Trade Paperback ISBN: 978-1-68057-024-3
Hardcover ISBN: 978-1-68057-025-0

Cover design by Janet McDonald
Cover artwork images by Adobe Stock
Kevin J. Anderson, Art Director

Published by
WordFire Press, LLC
PO Box 1840
Monument CO 80132
Kevin J. Anderson & Rebecca Moesta, Publishers

WordFire Press eBook Edition 2020
WordFire Press Trade Paperback Edition 2020
WordFire Press Hardcover Edition 2020
Printed in the USA

Join our WordFire Press Readers Group for
sneak previews, updates, new projects, and giveaways.
Sign up at wordfirepress.com

CONTENTS

DEDICATION

The following stories are more than just some of my favorite of my works: they're important to me because of who I wrote them for. Each story in this book was inspired by or written in memory of someone who made a difference in my life. These are my tributes to those people; and so I am honored to share these stories with you.

—Martin L. Shoemaker

INTRODUCTION TO
TODAY I REMEMBER

This story is a companion piece to "Today I Am Paul" (found later in this book). To see the connection, you'll have to read my novel, Today I Am Carey, *available from Baen Books.*

My father, A. John Shoemaker, was good at so many things I'm bad at: construction, welding, electrical work, auto mechanics, camping ... I could go on. And my worlds of writing and programming were equally foreign to him. But one thing I got from him was his love of the circus, sheer amazement at people doing what no person should be able to do.

And so, I was thrilled in my teens to discover the early works of Barry B. Longyear, whose first published stories told of a world settled by a circus troupe lost in the stars. Those stories made me a lifelong Longyear fan. He was the first author whom I saw develop from the start of his career, and he made me believe that maybe someday I could be a writer, too. I still aspire to live up to his standard.

So, this story is dedicated to the memory of my father, A. John Shoemaker, and to Barry B. Longyear. Life with the circus is one long uninterrupted deeeeelight!

TODAY I REMEMBER

Today I remember. I hate days like this.

But the show must go on. What would old Greasy Pete think if I sat around wallowing in my memory? Memory's a *gift*. The reason why I got the damn implant.

But it's experimental, they say. It only does so much, and some days it doesn't do much at all. Some days I forget more than I remember. Forget ... what I've lost.

But good day or bad, you gotta do your act, Pete says in my head. That I almost never forget, not even before the implant. The doctors can never explain why some memories are stronger than others, even on the bad days. They say it's just part of how things are stored, whatever the hell that means.

And they also said it was getting worse, that I was forgetting more and more. And that the implant might help with that. They said that without it, I was going to lose ... everything. All the older memories, everything I'd grown up with. I was going to lose Pete. Lose ... Eric, and Anna. Lose the show.

And that was why I'd agreed to be a trial subject for the implant. Somebody has to remember the circus.

No wallowing! I get out of bed, throwing off the thin white covering. I'm still competent enough take care of myself, damn it. I'm not like some of the folks in Creekside Home. I can dress myself and feed myself.

And take care of myself. Gotta keep in shape. I turn to the battered old dresser next to the curtain. On the other side of that curtain Bo lies snoring. He sleeps most of the time these days, and I worry about him. How long will he be around?

That's one problem with remembering: I can't forget my roommates, none of them. Bo, and before him Leon, and before him ... Curtis. That's right, Curtis. He was one of the good ones. Curtis got better, good enough to move out of Creekside Home and into assisted living across the street. He still comes to visit, some days. Which is more than I can say for Eric.

Damn it. Don't remember Eric. Don't remember how many months it's been since he's visited. *It's work, Papa,* he says. *I have to go where the job is. And besides ... the home can take care of you. Better than ... better than I can.*

I remember the shame on his face. I miss my boy, but I don't miss making him sad like that.

I pull out clean clothes, and I start to change. I'm standing there, bent over, bare ass in the air, when the door opens. Nurse Cindy says, "Excuse me, Luke!" and she shuts the door.

I chuckle at that. She's still new, still embarrassed at a patient running around naked. What kind of nurse gets embarrassed by that? Not like old Nurse Ratched, who doesn't even blink when she walks in on me. Nor when I make a joke about it.

I put on my shorts, and then I sit on the bed to pull on my socks. I don't have to. My body's as good as ever, my reflexes almost still good enough for the show. But I make the nurses twitch. So many of the folks here in the home are fall risks, and they treat us like we all are. They give us these damn socks with the no-slip bubbles on the bottom; and they watch like hawks, waiting for us to do something dangerous.

I pull on my sweatpants and a T-shirt, and I open the top drawer and look inside.

The sack is missing.

"Nurse Ratched!" I storm out the door. "Nurse Ratched, where are my damn balls?"

Nurse Cindy rushes out from Mrs. Carruthers's room next door. "Mr. Tucker—"

"I want my balls! Nurse Ratched said I could keep my balls; keep juggling, if I didn't try to do any acrobatics. I haven't done a single handstand! Where is Nurse Ratched?"

"It's Nurse Rayburn, Mr. Lucas," a voice says behind me, "and I have your balls."

I turn and look at the senior nurse, young and kinda pretty, with that white uniform and the blue sweater and the dark hair tucked under the cap. Today I remember her real name; but I also remember how much it annoys her when I call her Nurse Ratched. And annoying her is some of the only amusement I get around here.

"May I have my balls, please?" I hold out my hand, and she hands over the old burlap sack.

"Carlos was washing them," she says. "They were pretty muddy after last time. You really shouldn't go outside when it's wet."

I look at the bright sunlight shining in through the window at the far end of the hall. "It's dry today," I say with a grin. "Oh please, Nurse Ratched, pretty please, may I go out and juggle today?"

She grins. She's in a good mood today. "Yes, Mr. Lucas, go ahead and juggle. But be careful!"

I feel the three hard plastic balls through the fabric of the sack. Geez, they're too light to hurt anybody; but I suspect that I pushed her too far for today. "I'll be careful, I promise."

Then a small, fragile voice speaks from the door beside mine. "Luke, can I come watch?"

"You'll have to ask Nurse Ratched, Mrs. Carruthers," I say.

Nurse Ratched turns to Nurse Cindy, who answers, "She's finished her breakfast."

From the room, Mrs. Carruthers adds, "I ate in my chair today, Nurse Rayburn!"

"Is she dressed?" Nurse Ratched asks.

"Yes, I am." Cindy nods in agreement.

Nurse Ratched nods in response. "All right, when Cindy's done with her rounds, she'll wheel you out to watch Mr. Lucas rehearse."

"To hell with that," I reply. I tuck the neck of the sack in my waistband, and I squeeze past Cindy and into the room. Mrs. Carruthers cackles as I grab the controls of her wheelchair, spin it around, and wheel her towards the door.

"Beep, beep!" Mrs. Carruthers says, and Cindy bolts out of the way. I wheel the chair out into the hall as fast as it will move.

Behind me, Nurse Ratched shouts, "Not so fast!" But Mrs. Carruthers laughs, and I join her.

Maybe not such a bad day after all.

I don't really have to push the chair, of course. Even a bargain-basement facility like Creekside can afford chairs that run themselves, on voice control or a little stick thing you push. They're smooth and can travel over bumps and curbs in just about any terrain.

But Mrs. Carruthers is rated as a high fall risk. Her chair will go anywhere she wants in the home, but not outside. Not unattended. So, when I take the handles, it knows she's got company, and it won't stop at the door. *And* it'll let me override the speed controls: an attendant sometimes has to get a patient someplace in an emergency, after all.

The parking lot is empty. I remember that today; but on my bad days it's a surprise that the lot is always empty, that few of us ever get visitors. The temporary cases get them a lot, the folks with head injuries who will be in here for a couple of days, a couple of weeks, maybe a month or two. Their families come all the time, sometimes every day. Sometimes a whole batch. Patients even bring them to dinner, joining everyone in the big dining hall. That delights the rest of us, giving us new people to talk to—when they'll talk to us.

But most of them stop attending dinner, eventually, when they realize we tell the same old stories, over and over. Some leave because their loved ones have gone home. And some stop showing up when they realize that their loved ones aren't leaving. That their loved ones ... that we are what their loved ones are going to become eventually. Memory patients, forgetting most stories, and constantly retelling the ones we do remember.

That's when they get discouraged. That's when the visits get farther and farther apart.

That was when Eric stopped coming. I remember now. That last fight, he felt so awful, so guilty. And I ... I was in no mood to make it easier on him. If I had ... If I had gotten mad, too, I could have ... driven him away. He would've had that as an excuse, that we just didn't get along anymore.

But I was cruel. I hadn't realized it then, only later. I was quiet, understanding, accepting. Eric was moving away, he had to. I ... I made him. Well, not me, but the cost of my care. The home ... Even with Medicare, even with my small policy that Anna had scrounged and saved for ...

Anna. I missed her. She'd always been the smarter one of us. She'd had to remember things like finances and planning. Show folk didn't often have insurance. Oh, I know what the law says, and if anybody checked our books, it would say we were in compliance. But the show takes care of our own. We don't rely on the rubes and the grifters and the slick gentlemen to tell us how to run things. We take care of our own.

And they do, a little. I still get a check every month. The show folded long ago, not many years after my accident. Oh, not because they lost me. I was always a minor act between the big draws. The show must go on, even when it loses an acrobat. And while the show was a going concern, the checks had been bigger.

But even today, the checks arrive, every month. A small amount from Governor Kilgore. He's gotta be paying that out of his own pocket, bless him.

And bless Eric. He had a chance for a job in Dallas, for more than twice the money he could make here in Michigan. He had to take it to pay for my care. And he works so hard, so many hours, and has so few days off. So, he comes here when he can—but that's not often.

I look around the parking lot at all the cars that aren't there. Every one of them has their own reasons. It's not that they've forgotten us, not most of them. I'm sure that every one of them has realized that the show must go on. That they have to keep going with their lives, that they can't be stuck here just because we are. That they can visit, but they can't be trapped with us.

Understanding doesn't make me any less sad. Maybe more so. Our damn injuries and diseases, they afflict our whole families.

Damn. On days like this, I regret getting the implant. I almost hope the experiment's declared a failure, and they turn the damn thing off. Memory's a gift ... and a curse.

I wheel Mrs. Carruthers under the big maple tree. The leaves have just started to bud, so there's not a lot of shade; but she likes the warmth of the sun on her skin. Anyway, it's too early in the year to worry about sunburn.

Then I estimate a safe distance away. She's not likely to get out of that chair, and it's going nowhere out here without someone to guide it. So, I only have to worry about me and the balls; and I trust that still I know what I'm doing, that I won't hurt her. So, I step three steps away, close enough that she can see well even with her weak eyes.

Nurse Ratched would not approve. Screw her.

I set the old burlap bag down at my feet. In the show, I had a fine silk sack to carry my pins and balls; but I lost track of that years ago. Even with the implant, I might never remember where. Almost, but ...

Nurse Ratched wouldn't let me have pins, anyway. But I still have light practice balls in the old brown sack.

I start stretching out, chatting with Mrs. Carruthers as I go. We speak of the nice weather, and of the birds coming back and singing in the trees. She tells me stories of spring on her farm, so far back. She isn't regressing, not like some of the residents. She knows exactly how old she is. She just has long gaps in her memory, stretches that will never come back. Like many of us, she remembers the oldest years best. "We had two dogs," she says. "Well, we had lots of dogs through the years, but two were the best shepherds you ever did see. Those two could work together as if they were talking and planning. They could herd the sheep anywhere you wanted, and they seemed to *know*. Yes, they took commands, but often they ..."

I wait. She has lost the word. I can guess what it is but filling it in can upset the patient. So, I wait.

Finally, she says, "... anticipated. As if they anticipated what you wanted."

"I suppose they did," I say. "If they had the same routine,

day after day, they could learn it. We had dogs in the show that knew their act as well as their trainers did. Horses, too."

"You're right, Luke," she says. She has a faint smile as she remembers. "Those dogs learned the routine, figured out what to do, kept those sheep in line. They learned really well."

But then her face falls bit. "They sure were smart. I wish ..."

I don't want her thinking about what she wishes. It might be to have the dogs back, and they were surely dead thirty years now. Or it might be that she could learn like they did. Neither was going to happen. I really could use more stretching, but Mrs. Carruthers needs a distraction.

So, I bend down again, dump the red and green and blue balls onto the grass, pick them up, and straighten up. "Here we go!"

Mrs. Carruthers focuses on me, and I start the routine. First the simple toss, all three balls in the loop. The day I can't do this routine in my sleep, well, call the undertaker. I'd learned this from my Papa so long ago.

Thanks to the implant, I still remember details of those lessons. Or maybe it's just an old memory, one of the ones we keep. I was ... Six? Seven? Yes, seven. Before that, I had just done tumbling. I'd taken to that right away, and I was part of the kids' act before I turned five. The natural flexibility of youth, plus blood will tell. Tumbling and acrobatics always came easy to me. I wish I could do a few rolls and leaps and cartwheels now, just for the pleasure. Maybe make Mrs. Carruthers smile. But Nurse Ratched would restrict me if she caught me at it; take away my balls.

In my teens I would return to acrobatics, ever more elaborate acts. I even mastered the Wheel of Death, a giant spinning wheel that rotated on a long axis, driven only by my own momentum and balance. But that day, six years old, I had begged Papa to teach me to juggle. And so, I had started with the red and green and blue plastic balls. Not these I toss lightly in the air today, but close enough. He started me with one and spent that whole first day getting me so I could toss it and catch it without having to even look at it. I had been impatient, of course. I *was* only six. But Papa had been firm: *Three is easy, Lucas. One is hard. When you can throw one and catch it with your eyes closed, you can juggle three. You must do one until it is part of yourself.*

And that skill I remember, even when I can't remember the lesson itself. Even before the implant, it was ... a different kind of memory, in a different place. A place not broken by my injury. Muscle memory, but more, integrating my senses into one grand sense. On my skin, I feel the motion of the air, reading where wind comes from. With my ears, I hear how strong it is, so I know what to compensate for. In my muscle sense, my awareness, my body tells me exactly how fast and hard to throw each ball, closer than any computer could calculate. And my experience tells me how fast and how far it will rise, and how far it will travel as it rises and falls. So, my left hand throws it up, and my right hand is there to catch it. I don't have to look, sometimes not even with peripheral vision. It's as if I feel where the ball is.

And Papa was right: once I know where one ball is, knowing where three are is not much more difficult. I've done four, sometimes five. When I was young and prideful, I'd occasionally done six.

But three is the magic number. When I have all three balls in the air, there's a natural rhythm. Throw in time to catch in time to pass in time to throw in time to catch in time to pass in time to throw in time to ... I almost think I *could* do this in my sleep. It's relaxing, familiar. As if I were back in the show. Back in the day ...

Back in *that* day ...

And suddenly I am. It's that day. Even with the implant, up until this moment, that day has been lost to me. The doctors had said that I would never get it back, that the injury had prevented ... What did they say? Prevented transfer into long-term memory. That I had experienced it, but never processed it. So, there was nothing to recover.

But they were wrong. Somewhere, the memory has been buried. Or ... the implant has reassembled it somehow. I'm on the lot. Greasy Pete is beside me, in full costume: the orange wig, the white greasepaint with the big black brows and the giant nose and the red lips. The fright mask he calls it, and he laughs when he does. Pete is my best friend, but sometimes he's a sadistic bastard. He loves to make the little kids laugh; but he also loves that some people, even some grown-ups, are afraid of clowns. And he gets a kick out of trying to draw those folks into the act. I love him like a brother, but sometimes his sense of humor is low. There's no art in practical jokes, if you ask me.

We walk through the lot. It's a slow night, like too many of them recently. Sideshow Lane is half empty, and even Main Street is looking sparse. The only serious noise and activity comes from Robot Row.

"Damn VR," Pete says.

I don't answer. It's an old conversation, so there's really nothing more to add. Governor Kilgore had added Robot Row, a bunch of carny games and VR sets and such, in what he'd said was simple self-defense. *Kids these days aren't interested in watching, they want to do.* Their parents still have nostalgia for the show, but the kids are harder to drag away from their video games. So, we gave them more things to play.

That wasn't proper. A show might have a *few* games, but shows are *acts.* They're performance. Art. Not that carnivals aren't ... you know, *respectable* ... but they're not the same.

But a show that can't make its nut isn't a show for long. A circus needs money. And like it or not, Robot Row seems to be working. The Row is crowded, and the other two lanes are busier than they've been in months. We have more butts in seats now with Robot Row there. We can't deny the gadgets are working: wheels and carousels, the old reliable rides; and now laser galleries and arcades and headset games. They draw crowds.

But they make us feel ... dispensable, you know? Like we need the robots, but do they need us? Do robots *need* anything?

I glance at Pete's face. Beneath the greasepaint, I see a frown. That won't do! How's a clown supposed to cheer somebody up when he's sad?

In an effort to lighten the mood, I throw him a punchline. "You don't understand ... I *am* the great Pagliacci."

Pete knows the old joke, and he chuckles. "Leave the jokes to me. You tell it poorly."

"Better than you juggle," I reply. "Show me how, Pete. Let's entertain some rubes." I grab Pete's baggy sleeve and pull him over to a knot of people: five children, two men, and a woman. They talk animatedly, and Pete falls easily into the old shadow routine, standing behind a tall, heavyset man in a brown T-shirt. The man talks with his hands, big motions, a perfect target. Pete stands behind the man, imitating and exaggerating every gesture, every wave, the hands, every nod. The children watch and start to laugh. Soon the man stops, looks at them, realizes that they're looking behind him, and turns to look.

Pete immediately falls into his pose: one hand on his chin, tapping as he stares at the sky, the other arm across his chest, lips pursed in a silent whisper. He's the picture of white-faced innocence. The man glares, and Pete looks at him and raises his greasy eyebrows. The children laugh—especially the youngest, a blond-haired little boy in coveralls as blue as his eyes. That one rolls on the ground, holding his sides.

I can see that the act will continue for a while, and that the children's laughter is cheering Pete up. He doesn't need a juggler, so I fade back.

And I back right into a RoustaBot, one of our labor robots. A recorded voice comes from the robot: "Excuse me." It pauses until I step out of the way, and then it continues on its path.

I watch it go. I suppose having robots keeping the lot clean is a good thing. They have their place. But I can't imagine a robot ever telling jokes and doing mime like Pete. Or juggling. I smile at the thought of a robot learning to juggle.

I continue down Robot Row—although the Governor has dressed it up in fancy lights and music and dubbed it the Galactic Zoomway. The barkers call from the ticket stands, pointing out different attractions. "Come enter the Laser Legion!" "Can you solve the Mystery of the VR Bandits?" "Come ride the Sky Cycles!" That last, positioned outside the main Robot Row to give it some space, is a combination of VR and robotics: enclosed "cycles" zip up and down a wall draped to look like a mountainside. They're safe, with passengers closed inside, but they move fast enough to give the feel of real loops and climbs, and in the closed interior, simulator screens show the riders that they're in a star fighter flying high into space and then zooming down among asteroids at insane speeds.

I've ridden it. We all have. I wasn't that impressed, but I understand. In a way, it's just another act, a very mechanical *artiste*. And half the secret to an act is that the rube *wants* to believe, wants to see a miracle. Wants you to show them something they've never seen anywhere else. They do half the work. After you've got your routine down, even something like the Wheel of Death becomes second nature to you.

Almost effortless. Boring. But put on just a little razzle-dazzle, add some music and lights, and finally add an audience, and *then* the magic happens. The audience is the key. They don't understand how routine it is, and so they see magic.

And in those moments, it's still magic for me. I remember six-year-old me, watching Papa and Mama up on the Wheel, and how my mouth dropped open and I gaped. They were so beautiful, flying through the air as if gravity were optional. They taught me how, eventually, to the point where I forgot the magic. But through the audience, I remember.

And speaking of six-year-olds ... A blond blur in blue coveralls staggers into me and bounces off. Behind, exhausted, runs his mother. "Danny, slow down," she gasps. But he shows no sign of hearing as he veers around me and heads toward Clownapalooza, a holographic clown game. He slides right under the safety rope as his mother hurries behind, apologizing and handing a ticket to Ripper Ripatti. Ripper smiles and takes the ticket, and the virtual clowns appear and start dancing with the kid.

I look back to the entrance to the Row. The remaining four kids are running in, the two men in tow. Pete stands behind them. I catch his eye, and he shrugs.

Pete turns away. I amble out, come up behind him, and clap my hand on his shoulder. "Sorry, Pete."

He sighs. "What are ya gonna do? Kids these days ..."

"Kids these days ..." I reply. "Hey, you know what Eric wants to be when he grows up?"

"Huh?"

"A computer programmer." I half turn and wave at Robot Row. "He wants to *make* those things."

Pete's mouth narrows. He pauses in thought. "It's a good career, Luke."

"I know, but ... He's his mother's son. She always ..." I choke back a sob. "She always understood numbers and stuff."

"I know." Suddenly it's Pete's hand on my shoulder. "And she'd be proud of him."

I take a breath. "She would. But he and I ... With her gone, we have less in common every day. He's not interested in the act anymore. At all. If I try to get him to rehearse ... it always ends up in a fight."

Pete smiles. "Sons fight with fathers. You think my dad was happy I joined the clowns? 'We're an animal act,' he said. 'We've always been an animal act.' But here I am."

"I know." And I do. Eric's smart. I *am* proud of him, even if I can't understand half of what he says. So, what's wrong with me?

As if reading my mind, Pete says, "But even as a clown, I was still in the show. You're afraid Eric will leave, join the rubes."

"I am," I admitted. "No, more than afraid. I *know* he will. It's his dream. He likes you all, but ... he doesn't like this life. I've always known it. He wants to leave it behind. Forget it."

"No, he doesn't."

"He does! Just like ..." I wave my arm toward the main gate. "Just like the rest of the world. We're just a nostalgia trip today. The world's gonna forget us. Forget the circus."

Pete has no answer. He just walks beside me. It's an old discussion, and with no new answers, just the same conviction: *Somebody has to remember the circus.* So, we just wander toward the back lot. Soon the show will wind down for the night, and we can have a few beers and get some sleep. Tomorrow the show must go on.

But before we can go a hundred feet, I hear a woman scream, "Danny!" I turn back, looking for trouble.

It takes several seconds for me to make sense of the scene.

The woman is running across the lot, panic-stricken. So that tells me where to look for the kid.

I turn toward the Sky Cycles. "Damn!" I hear Pete say, but he's far behind me, I'm already running. Somehow the damned squirt must've snuck under another guard rope, straight into the ride itself. My juggling sack slips from my waistband and rattles on the hard pavement of the lot; but I don't have time to worry about it.

I don't have time to think, just run. I don't have time to wonder how the kid got tangled up in the machinery and lifted into the air, just tumble over the safety rope. I don't have time to plan, just bound into the air and onto the nearest cycle. It's just routine, just my act. Just like climbing into the Wheel.

If the Wheel of Death were a damn robot, climbing and diving and doing its best to buck me off.

It's just an act. I steady myself, refusing to fall. *Just an act.* I spot the kid on a cycle nearing the top, and I leap to the rail supporting the cycle above me. *Just an act.* I grab the rail, flip, and land on my feet on the next cycle. *Just an act.* One more bound, and I alight on *his* cycle—in time to see his coveralls rip during an upswing.

Just an act. He tumbles upward.

Just an act. I leap for him.

Just an act. I catch him in midair.

Just an act. I look down. Nothing to stop my fall, but I've taken worse. I know how to fall.

But the kid doesn't.

I have to twist, get under him, cradle him loosely in my arms, cushion the impact, take the fall on me, not on him.

Just—

Some clouds in the sky. When did those get there? And why am I ... laying on the grass?

"Is he all right, Daniel?"

"Another seizure, Mrs. Carruthers. I don't think it's worse than the last one."

My eyes turn from the clouds to the face that hovers over me. With the light behind him, I can't make out details. Blond hair hanging down. Not Eric, wrong hair color. The worry lines are too deep for such a young man ... Maybe in his twenties? Who is he?

And ... "Why am I laying here?"

supports my back. "A seizure. I've had them since ..."

"Since the accident," he says.

I nod as if I remember. *Accident?* "Help me up." Then I shake my head. "No, I can get up myself. Don't want Nurse Ratched to see me down here. She might take my balls away."

I grin at the kid, and he grins back, as if sharing an old joke. "Can't have that," he says. He stands beside me.

If I felt better, I would spring to my feet, just like always. But I'm shaky. Uncertain. So, I carefully kneel, and then test my left foot. When it seems steady, I rise and try my right.

I'm standing. From her wheelchair Mrs. Carruthers looks at me, her forehead furrowed.

Then Nurse Ratched calls from the main entrance. "Oh, Daniel, you're here! Is everything all right?"

The young man looks over and nods. "Yes, Nurse Rayburn. Everything's fine. Luke's giving us a show." He turns to me and hands me my juggling balls. "Aren't you, Luke?"

I look deep into his blue eyes. "Do I know—" But then I shake my head. Doesn't matter. "Sure thing, son. Pull up a patch of grass."

He sits on the lawn beside Mrs. Carruthers's chair, and they both look up at me, smiling in encouragement. I start tossing the balls into the air.

The show must go on.

INTRODUCTION TO IL GRAN CAVALLO

I have no particular artistic ability, but I enjoy art; and I especially enjoy sculpture. All kinds, from classic representational to modern abstracts and more. I can spend hours wandering Frederik Meijer Gardens and Sculpture Park, one of the world's best sculpture parks right here in West Michigan. And the centerpiece of Meijer Gardens is The American Horse *by Nina Akamu, inspired by Da Vinci's* Horse. *Frederik Meijer commissioned this 24-foot bronze horse, along with an identical horse for Milan. The* American Horse *is my muse, my inspiration—and my companion during my recovery from diabetes and an infection that almost killed me.*

So, this story is dedicated to the memory of Frederik Meijer, and to Nina Akamu. Thank you for adding to the beauty of the world.

IL GRAN CAVALLO

[First letter abridged and adapted from *The Notebooks of Leonardo da Vinci*]

Letter from Leonardo da Vinci to Ludovico Sforza, the Duke of Milan, Applying for a Position, 14 Luglio 1482

Most illustrious lord: having seen and considered the experiments of all those who pose as masters in the art of inventing instruments of war, and finding that their inventions differ in no way from those in common use, I am emboldened to acquaint your Excellency with my own expertise in these arts.

I can construct bridges which are very light and strong and portable, with which to cross trenches; I can cut off water from the trenches and make pontoons and scaling ladders and other similar contrivances; and I can demolish every fortress if its foundations have not been set on stone. I can also make a cannon which is light and easy to transport, as well as armored wagons for carrying artillery to break through the most serried ranks of the enemy and so open a safe passage for your infantry.

When it is impossible to use cannon I can supply in their stead catapults, mangonels, *trabocchi*, and other instruments of admirable efficiency; and if the fight should take place upon the sea I can construct engines most suitable either for attack or defense, and ships which can resist the fire of the heaviest cannon.

In time of peace, I excel in the construction of buildings both public and private, and in conducting water from one place to another. In painting, I am a master surpassed by none who walks this Earth; and I can further execute sculpture in marble, bronze, or clay. In your service, I would undertake the commission of the greatest sculpture of this or any age: a bronze horse, *Il Gran Cavallo*! It shall bring immortal glory and eternal honor to the auspicious memory of your father and to the illustrious house of Sforza.

Letter from Leonardo da Vinci to the Most Gracious Patron, the Duke of Milan, On the Subject of Greek Fire, 13 Maggio 1490

Your most generous Excellency, I must confess that my progress on Greek Fire has been slow. After studying the works of Pseudo-Geber, Bacon, and Magnus, I had a promising recipe: a pungent-but-potent mix of charcoal of willow, saltpetre, sulphur, and pitch, with frankincense and camphor and hemp, and other diverse ingredients in proper amount. This mixture so desires to burn that its flame clings to timbers even under water.

But I learned through most dangerous trials that this mixture sticks to almost anything devised by mind of man. It proved impractical as a weapon, for it was more like to burn the wielder than his opponent. Whether in catapult or cauldron, any attempt to cast it upon foes was in vain. I fear young Salai was quite burned in one trial before we could scrape the substance from his skin. You recall Salai, my headstrong young student? He will survive, I think, but my remorse at his suffering is deep. The boy is a thief, a liar, stubborn, and a glutton, but he is a good lad for all that. And after he has suffered this wound in my service (and yours), I shall be forever in his debt.

So, I fear this mixture shall be of no use to you should Alfonso of Naples prove treacherous, as you suspect. The only surface to which it does *not* cling tenaciously is bronze, particularly when hot. Perhaps I may construct bronze missiles with which to launch it, but as Salai can attest, it is not easily handled. Danger is always near. I shall endeavor to find some other use for this inflammable mix. It has already proven a most efficient fuel in heating my workshop in Castello di Varzi.

Meanwhile, should it prove necessary to defend against Alfonso, you might better trust alliance over alchemy. Courtiers tell that Charles l'Affable remains a true friend of your Excellency, and he has a strong army if the need arises.

On the subject of bronze, I was by no means boasting when I told of my plans for *Il Gran Cavallo*. A lesser artist would surely be boasting if he vowed to make a twenty-four-foot bronze horse sculpture. But I am Leonardo! I do not boast, I plan and design and sketch and research; and then when I am sure of success, *then* I announce what I shall do.

Oh, I have as yet made little progress on this tribute to your illustrious father; but I have requisitioned sufficient bronze for the work. I have made good progress on a clay model; but my research and work on your engines of war is always my highest priority. And now I must plan floats and clockwork entertainments for your impending nuptials. (I think you shall be pleased with my new clockworks, which mime movement as if alive.) I know this project has put a strain on the Milanese treasury; but rest assured, I shall make good use of the stock of bronze as soon as other projects permit. I think you shall be surprised when my work surpasses even the designs I have shown you. This statue shall be larger than Donatello's or Verrocchio's, and more lifelike than any!

Letter from Leonardo da Vinci to the Duke of Milan, my most magnanimous benefactor, 22 Ottobre 1491

As your Excellency has required, my students and I are removing our researches to your country estate in Varzi. I think this shall be all for the good, as your enemies shall have no chance to learn our secrets, and the Castello shall make a most excellent workshop for *Il Gran Cavallo*.

And of course, this shall prevent occurrences like the unfortunate incident of two nights past. I do hope Giovanni the vintner shall rebuild his delightful establishment even better than before. I am most saddened by the loss of his stock, as he always had the most excellent wines, and also saddened by my part in the fire, no matter how small. I still cannot determine how the Greek Fire mixture leaked from my workshop, across the street, and into his cellar, nor how it was ignited.

As for Giovanni's suggestion that Salai deliberately set the fire as a distraction to steal from his stock, I find that most implausible. The lad has a positive fear of the mixture after his accident. Still, if anything could tempt him to dare the fire, it would be Giovanni's finest. I shall be watchful, and if I see him with any of the vintner's wares, trust that I shall confiscate it. For his own good, of course.

Letter from Leonardo da Vinci to the Most Fortunate Groom, the Duke of Milan, On this Happiest of Days, 8 Gennaio 1491

Excellency, I must apologize that on this, your most blessed day, I cannot be present to see to the final details of your nuptials. Please trust that Salai has my utmost confidence and shall carry out my plans to the letter. (But please count the silver when he is done! If any should turn up missing, you have my word that I shall take it out of his delicate hide.) As long as you remind him to keep the clockworks wound, your parade shall include the most ingenious mechanisms to delight the revelers.

I know that under ordinary circumstances my absence from your wedding would be a breach of etiquette so egregious as to sever our relationship; but please understand that I am on a mission with only one purpose: to please you with a fitting tribute to *Il Sforza!* Last night I pored over the works of Avicenna and Persian Geber; and suddenly I was struck with a vision from our Heavenly Father! I *knew*, as I have never known before, that I had all the pieces at my fingertips and could create a work beyond any we had imagined. When I am through, your name will echo through the ages.

So, I have repaired to the southern hills, to your remote estate at Varzi. There I pursue a course both hazardous and secretive, applying my newfound knowledge to *Il Gran Cavallo*. If I have not gone a step too far, if I have not brought your generous patronage to an end, then I hope that you and the lovely Duchess Beatrice can join me when your celebrations are complete. What I will show you will be well worth your time, and I think shall please the Duchess as well.

Letter from Leonardo da Vinci to the Duke of Milan, and to the Duchess Beatrice, Fairest in the Land, 29 Gennaio 1491

Excellencies, I thank you again for your words of superlative praise. What I have done, I have done in your service, and could not have accomplished without your support.

Duchess Beatrice, you honor me more than words can convey, and you are most perceptive: the giant horse head is indeed motivated by some of the same devices as the clockwork angels in your parade. And be assured, moving the head is only the beginning!

To the Duke Ludovico: I have taken your command to heart. While *Il Gran Cavallo* shall be my greatest of inventions, I have taken steps to make it secret from the world. The Castello di Varzi is a most private place to work, and I have taken pains to erase all traces of the work from any records man might read. I have rewritten my journals and tampered with my recipe for Greek Fire, so that any who chance upon it shall create a flammable, adhesive sludge, but not the blindingly hot mix that powers the engines that drive the horse. And I have erased any mention of my clockwork miracle, mentioning only the great clay model I used for my casting. To the world, that shall be *Il Gran Cavallo*, and my attempts at casting a great bronze horse shall be seen as a failure. Indeed, that great loud-mouthed fool Michelangelo has already slandered me, telling all that I shall never finish this work. Let him talk! When you are ready, the world shall tremble at my genius, and at your power. In my long long-ago letter of introduction, I promised you "engines most suitable either for attack or defense." With *Il Gran Cavallo*, I shall deliver the greatest engine of war the world has ever seen.

Letter from Leonardo da Vinci to the most beneficent of patrons, the Duke of Milan, 3 Agosto 1492

As your Excellency has urged extreme secrecy in the matter of *Il Gran Cavallo*, I shall henceforth write all letters in mirror script, a minor skill of mine. When Salai delivers this message, he shall also deliver a fine silver mirror which I have crafted for the Duchess Beatrice. When she is not using it to admire her incomparable beauty, you might use it to read these reports from the Castello. (If by chance Salai should *not* deliver the mirror, I trust that you shall beat him firmly until he reveals its whereabouts; but I entreat you not to be *too* harsh, as I have grown quite fond of the lad despite his larcenies.)

This report must be brief, for I have much to understand about the clockworks inside *Il Gran Cavallo*. You might think that I as the designer would understand all that moves within that bronze shell, but I lack the omniscient eye of the Creator, and so I cannot see all the ways in which the works can combine. There remain many details to work out, but I wanted you to know that today, the statue took its first steps across the courtyard!

Letter from Leonardo da Vinci to the Duke of Milan, the Greatest Friend of the Arts, 15 Maggio 1493

Again, I must ask your Excellence for your forgiveness for the brevity of this letter. Time slides inevitably past, and my tasks grow ever more numerous. So, to the point: today the beast fairly *pranced* around the courtyard!

Yes, I called my creation a beast. True, it is a mechanism of clockwork and Greek Fire. Like the fabled stallion of Troy, it has a hatch in its belly through which I can crawl to tinker with the gears and cables and coils within, maintaining and even improving the mechanism. I do not delude myself that it is anything but my greatest clockwork, but still, it *moved* like a beast! Indeed, it looked like nothing less than one of your father's stallions on parade ... albeit a stallion five times the height of a man. Were I not your humble servant, I might very well burst with pride at my accomplishment, so close to life is it in manner.

But unlike any beast, this horse of bronze veritably *thunders* as it runs. The whole Castello shook as if in a quake. If the armies of Charles do not intimidate the treacherous Alfonso, then surely this greatest of war beasts shall strike fear into his black heart and rout his army as a horse scatters a pile of leaves.

Letter from Leonardo da Vinci to the Duke of Milan, the Very Soul of Understanding, 17 Dicembre 1493

Excellency, I word this letter with extreme care. I do not wish in any way to imply that I question your wisdom. You are, after all, the patron, and I but your humble inventor.

But I find myself compelled to ask: do you really think that a twenty-four-foot-tall bronze horse *needs* to breathe fire as well in order to intimidate your foes?

I do not ask merely from some mad desire to disappoint my

Duke. Rather I must tell you: this would be a surpassingly difficult task to accomplish.

Still, if such is your will, I can only apply myself to this task with renewed diligence.

Letter from Leonardo da Vinci to the Duke of Milan, the Very Spirit of Forgiveness, 21 Dicembre 1493

Most honored Duke, please be assured I have no wish for your patronage to come to an end! Again, I do not question your commands, I merely seek to understand them correctly so that I may properly carry them out. I am merely an inventor and not a diplomat, and I fear I failed in my message. If you want *Il Gran Cavallo* to breathe fire, then I shall find a way, though I cannot foretell what that way may be. I shall renew my researches into the works of Grosseteste and Zosimos of Panopolis. Perhaps they and the Good Lord shall guide me to fulfill your wishes.

Letter from Leonardo da Vinci to the Duke of Milan, he of the Most Marvelous Library, 11 Febbraio 1494

Excellency, the volumes you provided from your library have been of great assistance. Salai delivered them all, with only two missing. After I used the lash to impress upon him my displeasure, he divulged the two missing volumes, which he had not yet had time to sell.

After poring over these tomes, I have a recipe to render the Greek Fire more liquid without diminishing its potency. With a most ingenious rotating blade, I have spun this sludge into a burning mist that blows like breath—though with a brimstone stench at which even Lucifer might blanch.

These ancient formulae, forgotten by most and disbelieved by the rest, have two curious side-effects. The first may lead to some expense, I fear: the new mixture is a *hungry* fire. I know of no better word for it. It must be fed constantly. I have redesigned the beast's internal clockwork yet again just to ensure that the flame remains kindled. Even with the redesign, you would have to dedicate two men to refueling the beast after every sortie. Salai collapses in exhaustion each night from gathering fuel for the horse. This is most impractical, so I am at work upon a modification that may reduce the labor of maintaining *Il Gran Cavallo*. But the fuel shall still be costly.

Yet the other unexpected outcome shall make you glad of the expense, I think. This new recipe produces a most curious waste product (and in a fit of amusement, I designed the workings such that the waste emerges where you would expect a horse's wastes to emerge). Though this Greek Fire is fed by various oils and vegetation, the *excreta* that results from that alchemical stew is an exceptional alloy of *bronze*.

I know that this is most difficult to believe. I encourage your Excellence to come see it in person. This bronze may serve Milan in many ways, but in one especially. My skill in mimicking the patterns of life is such that the *excreta* emerges from the cooling channel in the precise shape you might expect from a horse: a nearly perfect sphere. As miraculous as this is to say, your great war beast excretes bronze cannonballs.

Alfonso shall not know what hit him!

Letter from Leonardo da Vinci to the Most Perceptive Duke of Milan, 27 Febbraio 1494

Thank you, Excellency, for honoring me with your visit and the company of the divine Duchess Beatrice. Your praise would be the highest possible reward for my work, save that her delight at seeing *Il Gran Cavallo* in canter was higher reward still. As to her concerns, please assure her that the creature is entirely under my control. I have inserted a clever locking mechanism which looks like nothing more than another wheel within the clockworks; and through that I alone can motivate the horse.

I am deeply sorrowed that your lordship has proven correct: the *excreta* of the beast is too large and irregular for proper cannonballs. I shall endeavor to redesign the alimentary channel to produce a better *bolus*. Until I do, your smiths must recast these nuggets to better fit the cannon bore.

Letter from Leonardo da Vinci to the Duke of Milan, Most Wise of Leaders, 8 Settembre 1494

Excellency, I have solved the fueling problem! The solution is at once both obvious and ingenious: I have modified the creature's "mouth" so that it may refuel itself. Through this opening it may intake grain or grass or even brush and tree branches to feed its internal furnace. As a further benefit, this approach allows it to be more regular in its *excreta* (if I may be permitted a coarse jest), producing bronze spheres of a more predictable size and shape. I trust that you are pleased with the cannonballs included with this message. (If Salai has not delivered the cannonballs, no doubt he has pawned them. In that instance, I hope your lordship will remember that the boy serves you well on most days, but still is tempted by his larcenous past. I suggest a whipping, but I would appreciate if he remained fit enough to help in my work.)

This new fueling technique has had another effect. Sometimes at night when I look upon *Il Gran Cavallo*, I swear the creature wants *more*: as if the ancient recipe has kindled a fiery spirit within my creation. Sometimes the eyes, mere plates of bronze, seem to glow from the heat within.

Perhaps I work too hard. These visions haunt my nights and leave me weary. Though I know they are mere fancies, I find myself checking thrice nightly to ensure that the tarnished silver wheel is in place, immobilizing the creature until I can supervise its actions.

Letter from Leonardo da Vinci to the beneficent Duke of Milan, 20 Settembre 1494

Your Excellency is correct: though I am loath to admit weakness, I am most tired by my labors in your behalf. Even pleasant tasks wear upon a body after hours such as these. Your suggestion of a holiday is exactly what I need. If I can get away for a week or so of rest, I can attack my problems with renewed vigor. I shall visit a friend near Genoa. Salai and the others can maintain the Castello until I return.

From Leonardo to Duke Ludovico, 24 Settembre 1494

I have no time for my customary pleasantries, as I must hurry to Varzi. Through travelers I learned that your false friend, Charles the Deceiver, did not stop with driving off the armies of Alfonso, but has now *himself* besieged Milan! I hope that my courier may deliver this through the siege lines, and that these words may give you comfort: *Il Gran Cavallo* shall soon gallop to your rescue!

Letter from Leonardo da Vinci to the most beauteous and charitable lady in all the land, Duchess Beatrice di Milano, 28 Settembre 1494

My lady, with a heavy heart I write to you and presume upon your kind spirit, pleading with you to intercede with your husband, the Duke Ludovico, that I might remain—if not in his good graces—then at least in his employ. For in this hour when the treacherous French camp upon the very slopes of his foothills, I have failed him.

When I learned of the French betrayal, I set back for Varzi in order to rouse *Il Gran Cavallo* and set the creature loose upon them. One night I was but a few miles from the Castello, almost in sight of the farmlands, when it seemed a mighty storm lay beyond the last mountain. Though stars were clear overhead, thunder echoed through the vales, and light flared behind the peaks.

But soon I heard that which struck fear to my very marrow: there was a *cadence* to the thunder. And worse, it was a *familiar* cadence: galloping hooves the size of wagon wheels!

I scrambled through the valley and up the pass to the Vale of Varzi. It took three hours to crest the ridge. In all that time, the drum of hooves and the infernal light drew nearer and farther in no particular pattern. Eventually, they faded.

I steeled myself for what I would see; but even the mind of Leonardo could not imagine the devastation. *Il Gran Cavallo* had run free across the valley, but that was just the smallest of the calamities before me. The horse's ravenous internal flames had driven it to consume all that had lain in the fields awaiting harvest. What the beast had not consumed, it had ignited with its flaming breath or trampled with those tremendous hooves.

Before I could climb down to inspect the wreckage, a hand snaked out from the darkness and grabbed my arm. "No, *maestro*," said a voice I recognized as that of a local peasant farmer. "Do not approach. *Il Diavolo* roams the night!"

It was with difficulty that I teased out the rest of the story, for fear had nearly robbed the man of his senses, but I had already guessed most of it. *Il Gran Cavallo* had somehow broken free and laid waste to the valley. The peasants had tried to defend their fields. They saw only a large shape, its full size hidden in the darkness until it got close, and so they thought some bear or other creature was upon them. Only when it started trampling their hovels and igniting thatch roofs did they grasp its gigantic nature. And then they saw the glowing bronze eyes, and they fled screaming, leaving the fields to the beast.

As a scholar and the beast's creator, I was doubly bound to learn the full story of that night. I set off into the valley, shaking off the peasant's protecting arm. I was unconcerned with safety, only knowledge.

As fast as I dared in the darkness, I followed the road to the Castello. Dawn had not arrived when I stumbled on unexpected rubble. By the light of the stars, I tried to make out the obstacle, and slowly I realized that it was the sundered walls of Castello di Varzi, brought to ruin by the blow of massive bronze hooves.

I sat upon a block, awash in despair. How had the beast gotten free? How did it move without command? And had Salai or any of your loyal servants survived its assault?

But in that moment, I suddenly worried less about their fate and more about my own; for I heard a loud rasping, and I smelled the foul brimstone and hempen odor of the beast's breath. I turned round, and *Il Gran Cavallo* loomed over me, those bronze eyes glowing red as they glowered down upon me.

In that moment, I, the great Leonardo, knew fear of my own creation, for it had done the impossible: it had exceeded my designs. Perhaps those ancient alchemists had an even greater secret than turning pitch into bronze: the secret of turning fire into *anima* itself! For I knew with an utter certainty that this beast had become some strange new form of life. How did I know? My answer is indelicate, my lady, to a degree I would not normally discuss with one so gracious as you; but please forgive me, I must be plain here. The beast eats, it breathes, it moves, it excretes. It needed but one more organic function to be alive in the eyes of scholars, that of reproduction; and that pre-dawn, though I had given it no means for that function, the means had somehow grown without my design. *Il Gran Cavallo* was, finally, truly a stallion. And it was ready for a mate.

And that was exactly what it wanted from me, and what I dared not give it: a mare to equal it in fire and stature. I could see both its lust and its cunning in those bronze eyes, but I could not set such a new species loose upon the world, even if the cost of refusal was my life. Still I was not eager to pay that price, and I hoped it would do me no harm so long as I was useful to it. So, I slowly stood and backed away; and when it started to move to cut me off, I dove into the rubble and sought cover.

The next two hours were a most fearsome game of cat and mouse. I hid among the ruins while *Il Gran Cavallo* tried to flush me out. For the first hour it took care to keep me unharmed; but eventually it grew impatient at my evasions, and it started smashing down obstacles. Finally, I think it must have grown completely enraged and forgotten its desire for a mare, so intent was it on punishing me. And so, it began spewing its flaming breath.

I wish I had been some brave hero to stand against the monster, instead of cowering for hours; but at that moment I was at least a scholar, and smarter than my creation. I realized it could not maintain its flaming breath forever without fuel, and it had already consumed most of the fuel for miles. So, I performed the bravest act of my life: I stood out, called the beast's attention, and waited for it to breathe flame at me, whereupon I again sought cover. And I repeated this time after time, until at last the flames grew weaker. Soon they were mere gusts of warm air, and I had no need to dodge.

I had hoped to taunt the beast into consuming its fuel entirely, freezing it in its gigantic tracks so I could regain control; but it retained too much diabolical cunning for that. The bronze eyes were dimmed but not dark as it stood there, glaring at me. We were at a standstill.

At last Il Gran Cavallo acknowledged defeat, at least for that day. It turned and headed across the valley. As the sun came up, I saw it slowly climbing the far ridge, and then descending behind it. And where it went after, I cannot say. I have not seen my wayward creation since; and if the Good Lord is kind to me, I never shall. I pray that it suffers a breakdown in the wild or fails to find sufficient fuel to go on, and my calculations tell me that this is the most likely event. But at night my dreams are haunted by Il Gran Cavallo, hiding in the mountains, and awaiting some chance to force me to comply with its desires.

Though I lived, I could hardly call my battle a victory. Castello di Varzi, once one of his Excellency's strongholds, is no more. The fields which should have fed Milan in the coming siege are laid waste. The unending source of bronze which I had promised his lordship is nowhere to be found, and after his lordship invested much of the bronze of the city in that project. More than bronze, much of his treasury has been devoted to this, funds that might better have been spent on Swiss mercenaries.

So, I send this letter by a courier who swears he can deliver it despite the growing war. I pray that this reaches you so that I may throw myself upon my lady's mercy. Though I have failed his Excellency at the last, it was not through lack of fervor and skill. I put all I had into his service, and I came very close to success. I still hope that in some way I can aid in the defense of Milan. I shall endeavor to make my way to our beloved city. I shall travel in the guise of a simple peasant, hoping that any soldier I cross will think the man on the donkey is just a man on a donkey, and not the great Leonardo, finest engineer of war in this or any age.

And if by chance Salai still lives ... And if by chance he also returns to the city, and you should find upon his person a small, tarnished silver wheel ... Then I entreat you to have him beaten, but not *too* severely. He is a good lad, after all.

INTRODUCTION TO UNREFINED

My first entry in the Writers of the Future Contest was a Finalist. It wasn't one of the three winners for that quarter; but contest administrator Joni Labaqui told me that judge Jerry Pournelle loved my story. I looked at my bookshelf, saw all of Pournelle's books there, and realized, the Writers of the Future Contest is a big deal. *Up to that moment, I had been ready to give up on writing; but after that call I resolved to give up giving up.*

Three years later, I was at risk of selling enough stories that I would be disqualified from the contest. I knew that this story had to be special. I had a vague idea about an asteroid- mining family, working the asteroid belt, trying to bring home a load after the death of their head. But before I could even start writing, Jerry Pournelle's voice was in my head, quoting from his essay, "Those Pesky Belters and Their Torchships." In there he proved mathematically that the asteroid civilization made popular by many writers (including his friend and partner, Larry Niven) was impossible. It's cheaper to go from any asteroid to Earth and back than to go from any asteroid to another distant asteroid. My idea was shot down before it started —shot down by one of my heroes and mentors.

But Pournelle didn't just ruin a whole subgenre, he showed another approach: "So we can end on a cheerful note, saying Goodbye to the Belters, but also making ready to greet the Minister Plenipotentiary and Ambassador Extraordinary from the Jovian Moons."

I happily adopted that solution. I set this story in Jovian space, a region I dubbed the Pournelle Settlements. And a year-and-a-half later, I stood on the Writers of the Future stage as Larry Niven handed me my third-place trophy for a not-a-Belter mining story.

So, this story is in memory of Dr. Jerry Pournelle. Without his encouragement, I would have given up writing. Without his influence, I wouldn't have written this story. Without him, you wouldn't be reading this book.

UNREFINED

I f this had been a vid, there would've been a computer voice
over the comms: "Thirty minutes to containment collapse."
At least I hoped like hell that I had thirty minutes left. I might
need every one of them.

But when you're facing a cascade failure across your
computer network, there are no automated warnings, no count-
down. I just had to move as fast as I damn well could and hope
I could get to Wilson and get us out before the fusion reactor
blew out the end of Refinery Station.

As Leeanne brought the flitter in toward the Tube—the
half-klick tunnel of girders that connected Habitat Module to
the Reactor and Refinery Module—I hung from its frame and
peered ahead, looking for the airlocks into Habitat's Control
Deck. If Wilson wasn't there, I wouldn't know where to look
for him. There were nearly three million cubic meters in Habitat. And in R&R ... but I stopped that thought. I'd rather not get
that close to a failing fusion reactor.

Refinery Station was the first of Wilson Gray's megastruc-
tures, massive artifacts in space that were half constructed, half

grown by Von Neumann constructor bots. At one end hung the Habitat Module, still mostly unfinished. At the other end of the Tube was the giant fusion ring.

The reactor provided power for Habitat, but the real reasons Wilson had built the station were the two structures on the far side of the reactor: a giant refinery utilizing the reactor's raw heat for metallurgy, and the two-and-a-half kilometer mass driver that would launch refined metals from the Jovian system back toward Earth. Wilson had invested his entire fortune into the station, and he had convinced a number of other entrepreneurs to sign up as well. Now all those investments were poised to fail, all due to an unexplained computer crash.

Finally, we got close enough that I could make out the airlock hatches between the girders. I was glad one of the best pilots in the Pournelle Settlements was flying. As Leeanne neared the closest approach point, the retros fired, bringing us almost motionless relative to Habitat. She had timed it perfectly—less than five meters, Leeanne was *good*—so I leaped.

For a moment I floated in empty space. Jupiter hung off to my right, half in shadow. The sunward side showed the giant cream-and-brown stripes, as well as an excellent view of the famous Red Spot. Closer to me but still dwarfed by its primary was Ganymede, our closest orbital neighbor. Its dark, reddish-gray surface was dotted with ancient impact craters, evidence that the Jovian system was a treasure trove of valuable rocks. Under other circumstances I would've enjoyed the sight, but I couldn't waste time sightseeing. I paid close attention to the task at hand, and I grabbed for a girder.

Contact! My gloved fingers wrapped easily around the girder, a synthetic carbon crystal rod five centimeters across. I grabbed another and arrested my flight. The girders sparkled in my suit light. Their lattice tied the two modules together even in the face of the minimal tidal force we experienced at this distance from Ganymede. The VN bots had spent over a month assembling this giant structure out of carbon that had cost Willy a small fortune to collect; and now, at any moment, it could all be shattered by the explosion.

"I'm on, Leeanne."

"Don't waste words, Sam! Go get Willy. Please!"

Wilson was Leeanne's husband. Nerves of steel were another trait that made Leeanne a top pilot, but hers were strained near their limit. "I'll get him. You just be ready to pick us up."

Leeanne and I had been hauling batteries from the magnetosphere generators back to Gray City, the collection of ships and small habitats that housed Wilson's team as we built Refinery Station. Until the fusion reactor gets up to full output, the generators were the most reliable source of electrical power in Jovian space, converting the radiation in Jupiter's magnetosphere into electricity and then storing it in batteries. These were one of our most successful products: half the towns in the Pournelle Settlements and a good number of the independent miners bought their power from Gray Interplanetary. But the generator output was too variable, and hauling massive batteries around used too much fuel. With the reactor, Wilson hoped to get a more steady power source for the refinery and the mass driver.

In another organization we could both have pulled rank to get out of such routine work: the boss's wife and partner and the boss's Executive Officer drawing a routine transport run? Ridiculous! But not when Wilson Gray was the boss: "Everybody gets their hands dirty" was one of his top rules to keep us in touch with our crew.

And this particular run ... Well, it was my fault, really. I had had another fight with Mari Brasco, Chief of Eco Management. It was the same dumb argument that had cropped up since we started dating: her claiming I ran our relationship like I ran a project, me trying to explain myself, and her saying I was proving her point. But this one had been bigger. Maybe she was stressed from all her contract work, I don't know, but we really blew up. She had told me to choose: boss or boyfriend? Before I could answer, she had stormed out. So, Wilson had sent me on the battery run to get me away from the station and give me time to cool off. I suspect he had sent Leeanne because she's a good listener and he had hoped she could talk me through my troubles.

When we'd heard the news of the computer failure on Refinery Station, though, my dating woes went out the hatch. We'd dumped our cargo in a stable orbit, and Leeanne had grinned and uttered her favorite words: "Hang on, Sam!" We blew most of our reaction mass getting back to Gray City to render aid if it was needed.

The work crews had evacuated before environmental systems could fail completely. It had fallen to Kim Stone to break the bad news to Leeanne: Wilson had refused to leave; he was trying to get the system under control and save the station.

At that news, I glanced over at Leeanne. I was sure she was thinking the same thing I was: *If only we had been there* ... And *I* was the reason we were gone, me and my stupid fight with Mari. If I blamed myself, surely Leeanne would blame me, and I expected an angry glare. But she wasn't looking at me at all. She stared straight ahead out the view port, her normally dark face turned ashen with worry. Flying usually put a broad grin across her round, friendly face; but the grin was gone, replaced by a grim line that turned downward as Kim continued.

The computer failures had spread, so comms to the station were out. Wilson was still on board, and no one wanted to get trapped in there looking for him. But I wasn't leaving my best friend, and Leeanne wasn't leaving her husband. Her face had turned steely, and she had flown us to the station at a reckless speed and then had pulled four gees as she brought us to a halt.

The girders were spaced to allow a suited person to climb between them. I did so, pushed toward the airlock, and grabbed the hatch ring to stop myself. The computer display on the hatch was useless: letters and numbers scrolling by too fast to read, occasionally interrupted by a complete screen wipe or random pixilation.

I ignored the screen and opened the lid to the manual controls. I twisted the lever, and the *Cycling* light lit up.

When the lock was in vacuum, I lifted the lever. The hatch opened and I pulled myself in and closed it behind me before cycling the far hatch. My audio pickups gave me the sound of air whistling in. I popped into the Control Deck annex.

I had been inside Habitat enough during construction, so that I knew my way around pretty well. The annex was right off the main cabin of the Control Deck: a bowl shape, thirty-meter-radius by ten deep, filled with a triple ring of monitor stations along the surface of the bowl so a supervisor could survey all stations from the center.

I pushed to the door and opened it. Immediately my senses were overloaded, light flashing through my visor and sound overloading my audio. Every computer at every station flashed data, buzzed alarms, called out gibberish warnings, and strobed bright and dark.

I blinked and looked away. "Wilson!" I shouted over the din, but with no hope that I could hear a response even if he made one.

"He's not here." Leeanne watched through my comms. Another person might have sounded frantic, but her control didn't waver. "The motion sensor's flaking out from all the signal noise, but there's no firm signal."

"We can't be sure. Let me get a better view." I pushed off toward the supervisor harness, a set of straps in the center of the bowl, and I looked around.

I didn't want to make Leeanne anxious, but I was sure she was right: Wilson wasn't there. Unless he was jammed behind a workstation where I couldn't see, he was nowhere on the Control Deck. That didn't make sense. Where else would he be?

"Sam!" Leeanne called on the comm. "The power monitor station. The panel's open!"

Sure enough, an open panel led into the guts of the workstation. I dove over. Wilson had to have opened it to trace a data feed. I could tell because he had left his network analyzer there, still tied into the juncture box. The readout on the analyzer made me sweat: *Fusion Deck*.

Leeanne's whisper on the comm lacked her usual steely control. "S-Sam. Don't do it."

"What?"

"You know where he went, Sam. We're gonna lose him. We can't afford to lose you, too."

But it wasn't until she said that that I realized: Wilson had followed the signal to the Fusion Deck. He was less than fifty meters from a glowing ring of fusing hydrogen plasma that was just waiting for containment to fail so it could escape.

Fusion reactions are so difficult to sustain that they can't go critical like a fission reactor. When something goes wrong, the reaction just collapses, destroying the reactor but not posing a threat outside the immediate area. The station was designed so that Habitat Module would be safe in the event of a collapse— but the Fusion Deck and the refinery would surely be destroyed.

So, despite Leeanne's warning, I was going after Wilson. "We're not losing him."

"Sam!"

"We are *not* losing your husband, Leeanne! Don't waste time arguing. Just get your ass over to the far end and wait for us."

I went back out through the airlock and into the Tube. There were elevators between the modules, but I crossed the distance faster on my jets.

My rad meters didn't change appreciably as I came to a halt at the far airlock. The radiation from the reactor was contained by shielding except where it was used in the refinery, and what escaped the shielding was barely above background radiation from Jupiter itself.

I had selected a lock near the control center. At least I hoped so. I was so used to the computer answering questions like that, but I feared to trust my suit comp. It hadn't been compromised yet, but if I tied it into station information, it might be. I didn't need my suit to fail me now!

When I got inside, I wished I had trusted the computer. I wasn't in the control center; I was in a darkened room. Flickering lights through a thick window in the far wall showed part of a giant torus, fifteen meters on the short radius and ninety on the long. The fusion reactor! I had entered in a service room off the main reactor chamber, and that room was *hot!* I checked my meters: not hot in the radiation sense, or at least not dangerously so, but the temperature was over 30 °C. Any warmer and it would start to tax my cooling system. I could hear the cooling fans whirring up already.

I looked around the darkened room. The flickering showed no light switches, just a bank of storage cabinets, a row of work pods, and a wall of monitors—malfunctioning, of course. Once my eyes adjusted to the flicker, I picked out two hatches. One led into the reactor chamber. I pulled open the other, exited the service room, and sealed the hatch behind me. Immediately my cooling fans grew quiet, and my temperature began to drop.

I still sweated, though. It wasn't from the heat.

At least I knew where I was going now. I floated along a large transit corridor; and in this part of R&R, all corridors led to the control center. The corridor was in darkness, but my suit light showed a hatch about forty-five meters away. That was my destination.

I checked my comp timer. Despite moving as fast as I could, it had been more than ten minutes since our approach to the station, and thirty minutes had been just a best guess. How long did we have? I broke several safety regulations by using my jets to race through the corridor.

When I got to the control center, I entered a room designed almost as a mirror to Control Deck: a giant bowl with three rings of screens. And just as in Control Deck, most of the screens displayed gibberish. The one main difference from Control Deck was my target: the suited man working inside the panel of one of the stations.

"Wilson!" Suit comms couldn't penetrate station shielding, but they worked fine in the same room.

Without pulling his head out of the panel, Wilson answered, "Sam? Good! Hey, buddy, gimme a hand. Need you to jettison the mass driver, and once that's done, cut us loose from the Tube."

"Boss!"

"We're gonna lose the reactor, Sam. No hope, I can tell. Refinery, too. We just have to salvage as much of the station as we can."

Typical Wilson, worrying about assets and losses while his dream disintegrated around him. He could be passionate when he sold an idea; but when it came to implementation, he was a cold-blooded numbers guy.

And as usual, he made sense. There were months and fortunes tied up in the station. If any of it could be saved, we had to save it.

I flew over to the superstructure controls. These weren't part of the main computer network, so maybe they weren't corrupted. Maybe.

If they were, our ploy was already doomed.

But if this was so important to Wilson ... "Boss, what are you after in there?"

Wilson answered tersely, "Evidence." He went back to work, cursing as he did. When he started swearing, I knew better than to interrupt until he'd solved the problem.

I studied the superstructure controls. They were clean, or at least not flashing gibberish like all of the others. These were part of the construction network, not the station operations network. When the time had come to hook all the systems together, Wilson and the network guys had debated whether it made sense to tie construction in. I'd never paid attention to the outcome, but it looked as if Wilson had decided to isolate the system.

I'm not a computer guy, but I'm a competent engineer and physicist. I understood the basics of the controls, but it was designed to make it difficult to accidentally cut the station into pieces—like I was trying to do.

I worked through the layers of safeguards and confirmations while also figuring out the process. There were rocket engines on the mass driver and the R&R Module. Explosive bolts would cut the mass driver loose, and the rockets would burn on a preset trajectory. Then I could do the same for R&R.

But first I had to choose the trajectories, feed them to the rockets, double check everything, and confirm everything one more time, all while trying to learn an unfamiliar interface.

I knew that I was taking too long. My suit timer showed

twenty-two minutes when I finally felt the station tremble. If it had been the reactor, it would've been a lot more than a tremble, so it must've been the first explosive bolts.

I watched on the screen and confirmed that the mass driver was drifting away from the station, picking up speed as the rockets began to burn. Over ten minutes to figure out the controls.

I hoped I would move faster on the second set.

But I didn't have to. Wilson nudged me aside and handed me a clear bag containing a computer board. "Sam, I've got this. Get that board out of here."

I looked at Wilson through his suit visor. His face, darker than Leeanne's, nearly always wore a smile. It wasn't from humor—though Wilson had a great sense of humor—it was friendliness and confidence. Wilson Gray was happiest when we had a challenge to tackle. So, when I saw that his smile was gone, I grew even more worried. "Boss, I'm not—"

"*Now*, Sam! This wasn't an accident, and the evidence is on that board. Get it off this station!" And Wilson turned to the superstructure controls, hands moving twice as fast as mine.

Despite Wilson's orders, I hesitated. He pushed me away, and I tumbled through the air. Wilson didn't need my help and he wouldn't be dragged away and arguing would only distract him. Whatever that board held was important to him, so I had to get it out, like he had ordered. I cycled through the nearest airlock and hoped that he would not be too far behind me.

Just as I pulled myself out of the lock, I felt the whole station *shudder*. Somewhere inside the big, disk-shaped module, the magnetic fields had passed a critical point of imbalance. The laws of physics took over from there: on the one hand, the delicate fusion reaction snuffed itself out harmlessly in the first microsecond; but on the other hand, the cooling system failed and the high-pressure coolants escaped and damaged the ring structure.

In a chain reaction, the massive magnetic coils that had taken person-years to assemble and fit into place suddenly broke free from their blocks and ripped themselves to shreds— giant, fast shreds that tore through shielding, tore through bulkheads ...

And tore through the hull!

I fired my jets at max throttle, getting me away as far and as fast as possible. I barely escaped the flying shards of tin and aluminum and carbon compound.

Wilson hadn't cut the modules apart. The shudder propagated up the girder tunnel, causing it to twist and flex dangerously.

Some girders nearest the R&R Module snapped entirely, something I'd never seen carbon girders do. The lattice structure absorbed the shock, but I had to fly over a hundred meters before I felt it was safe to cross between the rods.

Then I just hung outside the girders, looking back at the wreckage that had been R&R. My best friend's greatest dream, and now his destruction. I floated silently and waited for his widow to pick me up.

Life in the Settlements didn't give us a lot of spare time, not even to grieve.

I assembled a crew, and we went into the shattered husk of R&R to retrieve Wilson's body.

I remembered his last words: *This wasn't an accident....*

I still didn't know what he meant, so I recorded everything for ... well, for evidence, I guess. The scene was horrific, his corpse filleted by the fast-moving shrapnel. I locked down my recordings. No way would Leeanne see these if I could help it.

Then I had to get ready for the funeral. It took me a while to find my cabin in Habitat, since I still wasn't familiar with the new station. Before, I had only visited my quarters before long enough to stow a small kit bag with clothes and essentials. When I found my hatch, I went inside and sealed myself in.

And then, for a few scarce minutes alone, I cried. Wilson Gray was dead, and people needed me to carry on, but I needed … I needed Wilson. If only I had been here sooner … But that thought led me to a dark vortex I might never escape, so I wrenched myself out of it.

I had to find something to do, some activity to anchor myself. So, I opened my kit bag, unzipped the toiletries pouch, and pulled out my razor. I set it for a short trim, just enough to even out my goatee and mustache. As the blades spun and the vacuum sucked away the bristles, I stared at my eyes in the mirror. They were red against pale skin that bagged around them. I wished I had some water to rinse them, but Habitat didn't yet have water to the residence decks. I would have to live with the red. And with the patches of white in my beard and scalp. When had those appeared? When had my hairline receded so far? This project had made me old, but that day I felt the impact all at once.

I combed my hair, put on a fresh pair of coveralls, and pushed out of my cabin and into the half-completed corridor. Many of the wall panels were missing, exposing conduit and tubes and electronics. There were no signs and no obvious way to navigate, but I didn't need them. I just followed the other stunned, red-eyed faces as they floated their way to the recycler.

As per his will, we gave Wilson a small ceremony—I spoke, and Kim did, as did a few others as Leeanne floated in tearful silence—and then we fed him to the organic recycler. New crew from Earth had trouble with this concept, but the recycler is our version of the natural order of life and renewal. New recruits understand this on an intellectual level, but it still creeps them out. After you've been through a few funerals in the Settlements, though, you start to feel it: Wilson Gray was gone, but his essence would be with us forever.

Most of Gray City attended the service in person or by tele-visit. The only ones who couldn't attend were the crew I had assigned to stabilize Habitat. We also had visitors and televisitors from across the Pournelle Settlements, the collection of independent towns and stations inspired by an early aerospace pioneer who was the first to describe the energy efficiencies of mining colonies in the Jupiter system. The Settlements were loosely affiliated in trade and support alliances, but most of them prized their independence. It had taken all of Wilson's incredible charm and diplomatic skills to unite them in the Refinery Station project. Some had openly called it Wilson's Folly. They had the good taste not to mention it on that day, but the phrase would soon come back, I felt sure.

By chain of command, Leeanne should've directed the ceremonies and the aftermath, but my steely-eyed pilot had finally given in to her human side. She had watched her husband and her future all shredded in an instant. She had made my pick-up like a pro, but after that she had just stared at the wreckage, her eyes sunk in her suddenly hollow face. She had barely mustered the energy to answer simple questions since. I had had to take the ship's controls, and since then everyone just turned to me as if I were in charge of the entire city. Maybe I was.

I never signed up for this, Wilson. I wasn't the decision maker. I was the guy who carried out the decisions. That was my part in our triad: Wilson had the wild dreams and sold them to the world, Leeanne was the practical one who told him when his dreams were *too* wild, and ol' Sam Pike led the grunt work to make the dreams come true.

Now I had to hope that I could remember the lessons Wilson had taught me as I stepped into his role. That included something that always came natural to him, something I could never be comfortable with: leading meetings.

Immediately after Wilson's service, as Kim led Leeanne back to her cabin, I called an emergency meeting. Even limiting it to department heads, there were still thirty people gathered in the Atrium of Habitat, and six more by televisit. That was too many for an effective meeting, but I couldn't guess which department might have a handy miracle or two. We needed every miracle we could scrape up.

The hubbub in the Atrium was more uneasy than I'd ever heard it. Even in the darkest can-we-do-this hours of station design and construction, the department heads had all been on board, drawn in by Wilson's enthusiasm and quick answers to any problem.

Now I saw them clumping into worried groups, bobbing in the air as they talked among themselves. The faces I saw ... Some looked almost as haunted as Leeanne's. I needed to get them all on task—whatever the task would be.

I pushed off to the chairman's harness in the center of the atrium, but I didn't strap in. It just felt too soon for that, and I was still kicking myself for not being at the station when Wilson needed me. So, I strapped into my harness next to his.

Then I raised my voice, but not so much as to echo off the walls. "All right, people. Come to order." Somehow it was easier there in *my* harness. I could pretend that Wilson was just "away," and I was running things in his stead as I had done many times before. So, I followed our usual routine. "Status reports, people."

I looked at Hank Zinn from structural engineering, but he hesitated, staring at his hands. Before Hank could answer, the tumult broke out again. This time I did echo: "*People!*"

They dropped silent again. "Okay, we can't pretend we're not shook up. When you get out of here, you all have my permission to panic for an hour. But Wilson Gray hired *professionals,* goddamn it, and I expect you to start acting like it! Or none of us are gonna last long out here."

More tumult. Mari's voice broke over the rest. "We're not going to last anyway!" There were shouts of agreement.

I looked at Mari: a petite woman with golden skin, red-brown curls, and usually a confident attitude that fascinated me. Even now, stressed and grieving, confidence in tatters, she still appealed to me. She was still the fireball I had fallen for. We had dated for several months before our latest fight, and I really hoped we weren't over. I hated to turn on her, but I had to put this down *now.* I tried to sound cold. "If you believe that, Mari, there's the hatch. I need a united team. If you're giving up on us, hitch a ride to Walkerville or Callisto One or Earth, for all I care. I'll comp the transit costs in your last check. Is that what you want?"

Mari glared at me, and I was coldly sure that our last date had been our *last* date. But she shook her head and bit her lip. I gave her a second in case she wanted to add something, then I continued: "If we're going to come out the other side of this, it will be by following Wilson's troubleshooting protocol: tally our assets and status, define the problem, refine it into a solution, assign tasks to our assets, and design the process and build whatever new assets we need. So, it's tally time, people. Hank?"

Hank turned to me, his voice was steady and calm. Maybe I had handled that right. "We're in bad shape. Not fatal, but bad. Habitat still has a slight wobble." We could see that just by looking around. The walls occasionally flexed as a slow standing wave passed through the structure. "We'll have that under control in a couple hours. But the Tube took serious damage at the reactor end. We can salvage the material, but it's going to take a month. R&R is worse. The debris is orbiting with us in a cloud, but some of the material is not recoverable at any reasonable cost. The mass driver is safe, but its orbit is unstable in the long run. We have maybe three months to boost it to a stable orbit before it draws too close to Ganymede and tidal forces pull it apart. We can do that, if you're willing to spend the fuel."

I nodded. Wilson had given his life in part for the driver. We wouldn't give it up now. I turned to Mari. "Eco?"

Mari's voice was bitter. "As I tried to tell you, we're screwed in the long term. We have consumables enough for now. We can scavenge some, and we can barter with other settlements. There's still demand for our batteries, right?" She looked at Sissi Sneve from power management, and Sissi nodded. "But our loads from Earth ... Well, we've got twenty months in the pipeline, and that may be it. My buyers back on Earth say it was already difficult to get credit before. Sellers doubted Mr. Gray's plan. Now that the news is out, that credit is drying up. We'll see gaps in the pipeline twenty months down; and four or five months after that, the pipeline will *stop*."

I tried to sound conciliatory. "Can we conserve enough to make the difference?"

"Maybe ..." But her expression didn't look convincing, a combination of a glare at me and a trembling frown.

Discussions broke out again; and for the first meeting in over a year, I resorted to the air horn.

The shriek echoed off the walls, and some put their hands over their ears. When the echoes died, I continued as if nothing had happened. "Then we'll find another answer, like always. Power?"

Sissi summarized the generator status and the power market—the two bright spots of the meeting—and I moved on to the next topic. By the time most of the departments had reported, I noticed a flash of short platinum hair at the nearest hatch. Kim had returned to the meeting. Her face was even paler than usual, and her delicate face showed—no, not sadness, fury! *Oh, shit, what now?*

Kim gently squeezed through the crowd to join me, sliding up to my side while trying not to draw attention. She handed me the computer board from the reactor, and she pushed a report to my comp. While I listened to the status reports, I checked Kim's data.

Oh, shit, I thought again. This was bad. It might be the last straw. Wilson had been right; it hadn't been an accident. This could break our spirits.

Or maybe ... As the last status report completed, I surveyed the room. "Thank you. That's what I expect from you all: your best effort as professionals. And we need that." I held out the computer board. "I thought we were dealing with an accident. But it turns out we have a whole different problem: sabotage." Immediately the room broke into shouts, and I had to use the air horn again. "I'm pushing Kim's report to you all. It won't stay secret, so I won't try. This circuit board that arrived from Earth six months ago has a very clever, invasive virus hard-coded into its core. Ladies and gentlemen, somebody tried to stop us. Maybe kill us."

This time I let the shouts play out. I *wanted* them shouting. I wanted them *angry*. And amid the shouts, I heard two words more than any other: "Initiative" and "Magnus." Magnus Metals ran an Earth-orbit refinery that sapped much of our profits in refining fees, and the System Initiative were the bureaucrats who thought *they* ran space from cushy offices in

Rio de Janeiro. Between their regulations and more fees and fines, they sapped much of the rest of our profits.

Refinery Station had been Wilson's giant middle finger to both of them: we would do our own refining, and the Initiative were welcome to fly out to Jupiter to try to enforce their regulations where the laws of physics were the only real authority. Either might be our saboteurs, maybe even both. I didn't need to work out who, yet. It was enough to know that the two things Settlers hated most were the government squeeze and the corporate squeeze. This news had unified the department heads more than anything I could have said.

But Wilson had taught me: some messages are more effective from "the troops" than from the boss. So just as Wilson had often done to me, I tapped out a message and pushed it to Kim. When her comp buzzed, she looked at it. Then she nodded and gently pushed out until she was in among the others, shouting and talking like the others. And as a lull hit, she shouted over the rest. "They tried to kill us!"

The echoes were louder than the air horn. "*Yeah!*"

"Are we gonna let them stop us?"

This had been one of Wilson's simplest motivating questions; and the answer this time shook the walls worse than the standing wave. "*Hell, No!*"

Right then, I knew: I had my team again. We would survive.

Now I just had to figure out how.

That's what I *thought* I would do; but I had no idea how my time would actually be spent. I had never appreciated what Wilson had done all day. More meetings. More soothing of frayed nerves. More reviews of plans and schedules. More calls back to Earth, pleading with creditors and suppliers not to cut us off until we regrouped.

More calls to our business agents, too, to try to track down the source of the virus. Yeah, like that was ever gonna happen. Whoever did it had covered their tracks too well.

There was so much to do, and every day the list grew faster than I could whittle it down. I started sleeping in my office, when I found time to sleep at all. No matter how hard I tried, the work piled up. Maybe Mari was right, maybe Gray Interplanetary was dead like Wilson, and we were just waiting for it to stop breathing.

And Leeanne ... Leeanne might've been walking dead herself. For the first week, she didn't come out of her cabin, and she barely ate the food that Kim brought her. Then she started coming out for a few hours at a time, but she spoke little. Her eyes were still wide and red, her face muscles slack and expressionless. One look told you she was still in shock. People tried to engage her, but the conversations always trailed off into uncomfortable silence. Over time she started wandering into the middle of work areas, sometimes talking but mostly watching. People complained to me. They couldn't say it, since legally she was now the top boss, but they wanted me to keep her out of their hair. As if I didn't have enough problems. I added that to my list, but not near the top.

Three weeks after the funeral, though, Leeanne pushed herself to the top of the list, floating into my office as I went over power management reports late at night.

She waited for the hatch to close, then for the first time in weeks she found real energy to speak—and she threw it all at me. "Samuel Pike, what the hell are you doing to my company?"

My mind froze. I don't back down from a fight. Normally a challenge like that would have me shouting back, or worse. But this woman was my boss now, and my best friend's grieving widow. With Wilson gone, she was the closest friend I had. I felt grateful to see her engaged in *something*, even if it was chewing me out.

I muttered, "Leeanne ... We're trying ... to put something together here."

"Bullshit!" She waved an arm to gesture at the station, giving her a slight spin until she hit a wall and arrested her movement. "*They* are trying, but they need direction from you. *You* are floundering!"

Despite my concerns, my hackles rose. "Damn it, Leeanne! I'm doing the best I know how! You—" I caught myself before I could spit out an accusation. "You have any ideas for what I can do better, I'm all ears."

Leeanne's tone calmed, but she didn't fall back into her depression. "What you can do, Sam, is stop driving yourself so hard. You're looking worse than me, and I'm the one who lost my husband! You're going to kill yourself, and kill Wilson's dream with you. What you have to do is what Willy would do: prioritize and delegate."

I sighed. "I know, I'm trying."

Again, she said, "Bullshit!" And, again, she gestured at the station. "I've been all over Gray City, Sam. Everywhere I see the same thing: people are holding onto hope because you and Kim charged them up. But they're slowly losing it because your decisions take so long that the situation changes before they hear from you. Everyone's going through the motions, but there's no plan in effect. And the more you look like a zombie, the more they lose faith."

I breathed out slowly. "You're right, Leeanne. I've tried to hold things together for you. Now if you're ready, boss, I'm happy to take your orders—as soon as I get some sleep."

"Uh-uh!" Leeanne shook her head, bobbing against her

handhold. "I never wanted to be the boss. Wilson knew that: I'm a counselor, not an executive. You haven't had time to check Willy's final orders yet, but they name you as his second in command, subject to approval of the Board. And with his shares plus mine, I have controlling interest on the Board, so you're approved."

"But, Leeanne, I'm doing a miserable job! You said so yourself!"

"That's because you're trying to solve *all* of the problems instead of just the big ones. You think you're delegating, but your people tell me you're not. You're delegating tasks, not decisions. That's why you have no time to sleep! Any time you've got a problem where your department heads can decide, let them! Let Mari deal with the suppliers on Earth. She always did for Wilson."

"Mari and I ..." I swallowed. "We're not getting along."

"That's a luxury you can't afford right now. Treat her like a trusted professional, not an ex-girlfriend. Mari'll do her job if you let her."

"Well ..."

"Samuel Pike, if you let your wounded pride put an end to Gray City, I'll launch you straight into Jupiter! Mari's a grown-up, now you be one!

"And speaking of launching ... Hank is waiting for you to get off your ass and order him to salvage the mass driver. He has a plan, but it'll take a lot of fuel. He can't authorize that without orders from you. Every minute you wait, the driver gets closer to Ganymede, and the salvage costs grow higher."

"We have over two months ..."

"And if you'd acted immediately, we would've had three months. By now the fuel costs have more than doubled. You give that order *now*, Sam, or so help me I'll steal a tug and start hauling the driver back myself."

At that I smiled. She would, too. I pulled open a channel to Hank. "Hank? Yeah, it's Sam ... Hey, sorry I've gotten buried here ... No, you're right and I'm wrong, so I'm doing the apologies here. You're authorized for fuel charges and overtime budgets to go get that driver ... Yeah, the plan you submitted— Damn, was that four days ago already? Okay, revise the plan as needed, and I'll approve it ... No, don't wait for final approval, I trust you ... Thanks, Hank! I look forward to your reports."

I disconnected and looked at Leeanne. "How'd I do, boss?"

"Enough of that 'boss' business. You did okay. Now you make a call like that to all your department heads, and maybe we'll get things under control here. Start with Mari." I frowned at that. "Mari. Now."

I spread my hands up, pleading. "But, Leeanne ... That fight ..." I couldn't find words. They brought back the pain.

Leeanne's expression softened. Suddenly I saw my friend, Wilson's wife. My pain grew as she asked, "What about it, Sam? You two have fought before. You're a hard-nosed engineer, she's a fiery Cuban; that's no surprise. You've always gotten past it before."

I tried to speak, but I had a catch in my throat. I coughed and said, "But this fight ... This is why we weren't at the station. This is why—"

"Hush!" Leeanne shouted as she pushed herself across the office to me, stopping herself by wrapping her arms around me and pulling my head down to her shoulder. She buried her face in my own shoulder and said, "Stop it, Sam! Don't say that. Do *not* say that. I never want to hear that again."

I tried to hold back, but I found myself sobbing. "If I had been here—"

"No, Sam. You wouldn't have been here. You would've been with the prospecting fleet. Or negotiating with the other

Settlements. Or on any of a hundred other errands for Wilson, just like every other day of this project."

"But—"

"No buts! So, this is what it's all about? Sam, someday I'll find who killed Willy, and I'll make them pay. But it wasn't you, and it wasn't me! We're survivors, we're not to blame."

Then I really cut loose with the tears, and Leeanne joined in. More than I had needed sleep, I had needed tears, and someone to share them with.

Eventually, though, I remembered that I had work to do. "Okay, boss—Leeanne," I corrected. I pulled away and wiped my eyes. "Do I look ready for more calls?"

Leeanne smiled at me. It was weak, but it was a smile. She had needed the tears, too. "Stop worrying about looking strong." She pushed back to the hatch, out of the comm pickup. "Call Mari."

I nodded, my body bobbing in response, and I called Mari. As soon as her face appeared on my comm, she started in on me. "Sam Pike, do you *like* making my job impossible?" I shook my head, but she continued before I could answer. "I just answered a call from Bader Farms. I had them, Sam. I had them! I had them convinced that we were stabilizing our situation, and you had a plan to meet our contracts. Then *you* called them, and you ruined the whole thing! They said you didn't strike them as confident, so why should they be? They're ready to cancel our future pipeline loads, maybe even sell some of the in-transit loads to Walkerville."

She paused to breathe, and I finally snuck in a response. "I'm sorry, Mari."

Mari continued. "And furthermore—" Then she shook her head and her red-brown curls became a shimmering cloud. "What did you say?"

"I'm sorry. I screwed up, and I was wrong. If I stay out of the middle, can you fix this?"

Mari's jaw dropped open, and it took a few seconds before she answered. "Maybe. But I'll have to offer points."

I nodded. "Take them out of my account. It's my mistake, so Gray City shouldn't pay for it."

Mari cocked an eyebrow. "And you'll stay out of it?"

I nodded again. "It's your department. Wilson trusted you, and Leeanne and I trust you. I'm sorry if I gave you any reason to doubt that. If you need me, tell me. Otherwise, it's hands-off."

Mari almost smiled then. "Okay, I need to work on repairing this. And ... Thanks, Sam."

I disconnected the call and started placing more. As I did, department heads pulled tasks from my task list, and some tasks immediately switched from *Backlog* to *In Progress*. A couple even switched to *Complete*. When I finished, I looked at the full list. Those forty-some calls had done more to clear the list than I had accomplished in three weeks.

I held up my hands in surrender. "Okay, Leeanne, you were right. I'm still learning on the job here. What's next?"

"Next we hold an Executive Committee meeting, just like the old days: the Chairman, the Counselor, and your Executive Officer."

"But I'm—All right, I used to be XO. Now I'm Chairman, so who's the Executive Officer?"

"Kim Stone, of course. She's already doing every task you'll let her. I've promoted her and made the pay retroactive— assuming we have anything left to pay anyone with. She's outside waiting for us to have it out. Are we good?"

I thought long before answering. I had so much to learn about being in the top seat; but with Leeanne's help, it had already gotten easier. And now with Kim's help as well, maybe I could handle it.

I smiled and nodded. "We're good. Hell, we're great! Bring on the next challenge!"

Leeanne knocked on the hatch, and it opened. Kim floated in and closed it behind her. The two women floated there, one large and dark, the other a pale blonde pixie; but both were strong, especially inside, and I was going to need that.

"You straighten him out, boss lady?" Kim asked.

Leeanne raised her free hand. "Ah-ah-ah! None of that. Sam's the boss, so let's get in the proper habit."

Kim nodded and turned to me. "Right. Okay, boss, I think we need to get the mass driver ASAP. Tidal force won't be large enough to damage it for a couple weeks, but the strain is mounting. It won't take much strain to misalign the rings."

I tried to answer, but Leeanne jumped in. "You're right, but Sam has that handled already." Yeah, I was the boss all right, except when Leeanne wanted to be in charge. But I could work that way. It was comforting to have somebody watching my back.

Still, I had to keep up appearances. "Yes, Hank has approval to modify his plan as needed. You keep an eye on it. Don't interfere with him, but make sure we're not blindsided by any unexpected charges."

I felt better. Now what next? Well, I would follow Wilson's protocols. "Okay, let's tally our assets and status. We have almost our full crew. Only a few people have quit. We have Habitat, our prospecting fleet, our construction fleet, and all the smaller stations we built before Habitat. We have the fuel depot and the generator stations. And we have active contracts to sell power here in the Settlements, and we have contracts to deliver raw metals to Earth orbit. We also have twenty months of supplies in the pipeline, and we can get more as long as we don't default on any of those delivery contracts. I've persuaded our suppliers to give us a little more time, since we're technically not in default yet."

Leeanne added, "And we have the mass driver."

"Yes, we have the driver, and power to run it, though that will tax our generating capacity quite a bit. Anything else?" Both women shook their heads. "Okay, that also defines the problem, pretty much: we need to find some way to fulfill those contracts, or somehow generate equivalent income to keep the pipeline open. Our credit is stretched too thin. If it looks like we'll miss a month or more in the pipeline, people will start abandoning us. That'll create a feedback loop, and we'll collapse long before the pipeline runs dry. Other Settlements will lay claim to our assets, and who could blame them?"

Kim broke in. "Boss, I've made a few inquiries with friends in other Settlements. Callisto One is primed to take us over. Almost as if they were ready in advance. And they've been making offers to some of our key staff."

I nodded. "Interesting ..." Callisto One was the Initiative's official presence in the Pournelle Settlements, and had been a thorn in Wilson's side. We all guessed how they had been "ready in advance," but I shook my head. "Our people hate the Initiative. If we have *any* hope of getting through this, they won't go to Callisto. Now we just have to find that hope."

And for the first time since that call from Kim three weeks ago, Leeanne smiled. "Oh, I figured that out. While there was no hope, I was happy to let you screw things up. Boss." And her smile actually became a brief grin. "But once I saw an answer, I knew I had to kick your ass into gear so you could make it happen. They won't follow me, but you've got the touch. All you need is some hot pilots—me, and I can name others—who really understand gravity deep in their guts. You've all been worried about tidal force and its danger to the mass driver; but tidal force is still a force, just like any other. And force can be dangerous, but it can also be harnessed."

It took a month to turn Leeanne's idea into a plan, and then another three to put the plan into effect. It took over two months just to pull the mass driver out of its doomed orbit and into one that we could use.

Mari had persuaded our creditors to give us a little more time. Maybe they figured they couldn't lose much more than they already would, and they could afford to stretch a little in hopes of a payoff. Maybe they just had a lingering respect for Wilson's legacy. Hell, for all I knew his ghost was out there somewhere still applying that old Wilson charm.

But one thing I do know: it wasn't our plan that sold them, since Mari never told them what it was. We had enemies, but we didn't know exactly who they were nor whom we could trust. So, we kept the full plan to just the Executive Committee as long as we could, and doled out details on a need-to-know basis. Once we were sure the plan would work and no one could stop us, *then* we filled in everyone in Gray City. The cheer when they understood almost shattered the walls of Habitat. Mari even smiled at me.

When the day came for us to test out the plan, Leeanne insisted on flying one of the chase ships, and I insisted on flying shotgun with her. She tried to argue me out of it, but I pulled the trump card I'd held back since our first Executive Committee meeting. I looked her straight in the eyes and asked, "Leeanne, am I in charge here or not? You can't have it both ways. If you as the Board say no, I'll sit back and watch you run things; but if you as my Counselor say no ... then I'm happy to take your advice, but I'll do things my way."

For almost a full minute, I thought I'd been fired. Then Leeanne answered quietly, "We can't afford to lose you, too, Sam."

"Then it's a good thing I'll be flying with the best damn pilot in the Pournelle Settlements." And that settled it. I was in the copilot's harness as Leeanne idled between Jupiter and the driver. We watched the feed from Kim and the team on the far side of Jupiter as relayed by polar comm sats.

I called over the sats. "How's it going, Kim?"

Light speed delayed her response by over a second. "Fantastic, boss. The first load just launched, and we've got three more coming. Take a look."

I switched to Kim's station camera, which showed a large lump of ice, dirt, and valuable metals. If we sent that lump to Earth directly, Magnus would charge us a huge fee for clearing off the dross (which they *claimed* was useless, but we knew they made a few percentage points from the volatiles); and then *they* would assay the remains.

Somehow their assayers always came up with a value far lower than our estimates. If it were random, the error should have been in our favor once in a while, but it never was.

That was why Wilson wanted to break up the rocks ourselves, ship only the metals (which were easier to mass drive, since the driver was strong enough to grab even paramagnetic minerals), and deliver direct to our customers instead of to Magnus.

Now four such rocks were on a trajectory close to Jupiter, and we would rendezvous on the other side. I got on the chase fleet circuit. "Folks, get your rest. Targets coming your way in about six hours. Sleep while you can."

But we didn't sleep, and I doubt anyone in the chase fleet did.

Like us, most spent the six hours watching on the polar

cameras as the first rock dove closer to Jupiter. When the rock passed within the Roche limit and started to break apart, I shouted over the chase circuits: "Yes!" And at least a dozen voices echoed mine.

Jupiter's tidal force pulled the near side of the rock much harder than the far side, and the ice and dross couldn't hold together. The metals that remained wouldn't be as pure as we would've gotten from the refinery, but they would be good enough to meet our contracts. I might have to give back a few points, but we would *meet our contracts*. We would survive.

And someday, we would build another refinery, and Wilson's Folly would become Wilson's Triumph.

But that would be in the future.

I got back on the circuit. "Computers will feed target trajectories to you over the next three hours. We'll assign pick-ups. Plant your bots on the big targets, then look for targets of opportunity."

The drive bots would attach themselves to the metal fragments, calculate a burst plan, and drive the metals to the induct of the mass driver.

There the magnetic fields would grab them and accelerate the metals on their path to Earth. It all took careful computer calculations. That had chewed up much of our planning time: making sure our computers were *clean*.

The effort hadn't been wasted: we found three more virus traps waiting to be sprung. Someday, somebody was going to find out just how angry I was that they had killed my best friend.

But not today. Today we had metal to chase. "Leeanne, you picked our first target yet?"

"Yeah, boss, but it's not on the computer's list."

"Huh?"

She pushed a spectrographic report to me. "That blip

there? That's nearly a quarter tonne of platinum. Computer says it's on a bad trajectory, we'll never recover it this time."

"Then leave it! We can get it on another orbit!"

"And let some other Settlement claim it after we did all the work? Hang on, boss!" And instead of waiting for the fragments to approach, Leeanne powered up the engines. She turned us back, and suddenly my view port was filled with brown bands and the Red Spot. I was pushed back into my couch at over three gees as we dove toward Jupiter.

What could I do? "Leeanne, you're fired!" But I said it with a big grin on my face, accentuated by the acceleration.

Leeanne grinned back even bigger. "Take it up with the Board. After we get that platinum!"

She laughed, and we sped deep into Jupiter's well. At a certain carefully calculated point, Leeanne flipped us around and fired the thrusters to slow us. I watched the computer project our course, and I was happy: the old Leeanne was back, at least for now.

"Not to backseat drive, Leeanne, but how do we get this baby on course?"

Leeanne pushed her analysis to my comp. "I think we can do it with three drive bots. Yeah, that's a lot, but this lump is worth more than any three we've picked out."

I nodded and readied the drive bots for firing. When our velocity nearly matched the lumps, I fired off the bots. Then I watched them on the scope.

One ... The first bot touched down, scrambled for a hold, and finally attached itself firmly. *Two* ... The second bot attached. *And* ... "Damn!"

"What is it, boss?"

"Third bot didn't attach. It might make a second pass, but that'll burn a lot of fuel. It might not do the trick. I'll launch another."

"Never mind, boss. I've got a better idea!"

Suddenly I felt the explosive *thump* of the tether launching. "We're gonna haul this sucker to the driver ourselves."

"That'll take a lot of fuel ..."

"You'll approve it, boss!" Leeanne laughed, and I laughed as well as the tether struck the lump and scrambled for its own attachment.

When the tether controller showed a firm grip, I gave Leeanne a thumbs up. She gunned the engines and between our tether and the drive bots, we started nudging the platinum into a new trajectory. We passed a few other likely targets as we flew, and I launched drive bots at them as well; but Leeanne was right this lump of platinum was the best possible proof of our plan.

As we approached the driver induct, I knew today would be a very good haul. I pushed the *Release* button on the tether controller, and the platinum was on a free trajectory straight for the induct.

We didn't go after more fragments, not quite yet. We just sat in silence for several minutes as the platinum drifted closer and closer to the mass driver.

When it got close enough, the magnetic field grabbed it, a weak hold on the platinum itself and a stronger hold on the metal web the bots had woven. The lump turned slightly, lining up with the magnetic rings,; then it picked up speed. Soon it shot through the rings and out of sight.

We sat there a few minutes more, neither of us speaking.

I could see by the instrument lights that Leeanne was crying. I felt tears welling in my own eyes, a damned nuisance in zero g. But Wilson's dream was worth a few tears.

Then I realized we didn't have a contract for platinum. I pulled open a comm channel. "Mari, I have good news! You can start contract negotiations for a mass of platinum, specs attached." I pushed the specs into the data feed. "That should buy us dinner for a while!"

After the light speed delay, Mari responded, and her grin was a mirror of my own. "*I* have good news too, Sam. We've already got our dinner orders filled. I forwarded our suppliers a copy of Kim's satellite feed. As soon as they understood your plan, they upgraded our credit rating with all services. We're not back where we were, but we'll get there."

She broadcast the video? But I hadn't authorized that.

Then I saw Leeanne staring at me, and I knew there was only one proper response: "Great work, Mari. Gray City owes you. I owe you, big time."

Mari nodded. "You bet you owe me! Dinner and beer for starters. And *I* get to choose the place. Someplace expensive, with real meat! I'm sick of soy."

"Real meat, Mari. I promise." I closed the comm channel, and I felt warm inside.

I looked over, and Leeanne was still watching me. No time for that! It was time to get back to work. "Pilot! Next target!"

"Hang on!" Leeanne grinned through the tears as she wheeled the ship around again. I grinned, too. For the first time since the sabotage, in the middle of a three-gee turn, I relaxed.

If I could've spared breath against the turn, I might have sung. I could pay people. I could *feed* people.

And finally, the word fit: I was the boss.

INTRODUCTION TO FATHER-DAUGHTER OUTING

This story is based on an idea I had nearly twenty years ago while working on a role-playing game adventure. But when it came time to adapt that idea for my target market (now defunct), I had to fit it in 4,000 words. For me that's extremely short. I had to throw away the whole story structure—everything but the core idea—and then I needed a new structure, one tightly focused on that idea.

And for that, I needed a young, inexperienced-but-eager character who knew a lot and wanted to know a whole lot more. And it happened that I knew a young lady just like that.

So, this story is dedicated to my niece, Virginia Green née Reiser, in honor of our many field trips, and to her new adventure, her daughter Elise.

FATHER-DAUGHTER OUTING

W e're doing okay, Daddy. Doing okay ... Nine-seven,
Nine-eight, nine-nine, *twelve* hundred!

"Okay, Daddy ... Gotta catch my breath ... And check your
stretcher pressure—

"No, that's wrong. Lunar Survival Manual says check my
pressure and oh-two first, *then* look to the injured. I know,
Daddy, I know: follow the manual.

"Pressure is point-eight standard. LSM says keep pressure
light, conserve air. Oh-two is nominal. I'm not breathing hard
from carrying you, not too much. I wish I had my LSM. Maybe
I should turn up the oh-two to compensate for the work, but
maybe I should turn it *down*. I don't remember, so I'll leave it
alone.

"Temperature is a little high from exertion. Turning up the
radiator a bit, but I want to save the batteries. Sun might catch
us if I stay here too long.

"Okay, Daddy. Stretcher pressure is high. I turned it down,
but the med comp overrode me. I think it's trying to keep you

well oxygenated. You lost a lot of blood, so it's compensating. I think.

"I just need to sit a little. Sorry for sitting on the stretcher. That regolith is neg one-forty, and my suit butt's not insulated enough for that.

"No joke about my butt? I guess you're really out cold, huh?

"I'm up, I'm up. Sun's coming.

"Twelve-one, twelve-two, twe'-three, twe'-four, five, six, seven, eight ..."

"Looking for Moon Men, Ellie?"

"Daaaaad!" I turned from the port and scowled at Daddy. "I haven't believed in Moon Men for five yeeeeeears!"

Okay, it was really only two years, but Daddy didn't have to know. A girl's entitled to some secrets, Mom always says, so Dad didn't need to know I still looked for Moon Men back when I was twelve. He forgets I'm practically grown up. Why give him another excuse to forget?

Daddy thinks I want to become an explorer because I'm still looking for Moon Men. Mom thinks I want to find a diamond mine and get rich. But they both think exploring is just a phase I'll grow out of. They don't say that to me, but it's in their eyes, and in the way they smile at me when I study Dad's old Lunar Survival Manual.

Well, I may be a kid—*legally*—but I'm serious about this. I *will* be a Lunar explorer, and that's all there is to it! Why else are people living here if not to explore? Our cities cover half a million hectares, maybe two million if you count space ports and mines and other Outside facilities. Ninety-nine-point-nine five percent of our world is still begging for explorers. I know I won't find Moon Men, no matter how Daddy teases. I don't know *what* I'll find, that's the point! But with that much unexplored surface, I'll find *something!*

As for Mom ... Well, *maybe* I'll find something valuable, you never know. Shoes aren't cheap, and a famous discovery could buy me lots of shoes ...

"Five years, huh? I guess you've lost interest, then. I guess you wouldn't want to go Outside tomorrow ..."

"Outside?"

"Oh, I had a father-daughter outing in mind. But since you're bored with Outside ..."

"DADDY!!!"

"Jim, don't tease her." Mom came into the viewing room, Jimmy bouncing on her hip. "Eliza, we got your grade report today. You've brought your grades up. *Way* up."

"Well, Mr. Huynh says explorers have to know math and science. And I see what he means! My LSM makes a lot more sense now. There are still some equations I can't understand, though. Mom, can you show me—"

Mom cut me off. "Math later, dear. You *can* take a break, you know."

"There's plenty of time. We're not sending you to Lunar Survival School. Maybe when you're sixteen, if you're still interested."

"But Daaaaaad!"

Again, Mom took control. "*But* we're going to set up some more Outside expeditions for you, for us as a family when I can find a sitter for Jimmy. You're growing up, you've earned it."

"And as for tomorrow ..." Daddy tapped his comp, pushing a message to the wall screen.

ISSUED BY: Kirk Hanson, Supervisor, Merrick Lunar Mining Co.

ISSUED TO: James Wall, Mining Technician.

SUBJECT: One Career Observer Pass, registered to Eliza Wall.

ATTACHED: E. Wall's certifications for Spacesuit Operations, Orienteering, Communications, and First Aid.

"I talked to my supervisor. He checked your certifications, and he approved. I've arranged with Mr. Huynh. You're excused from school tomorrow for the Career Observer program. We'll spend all day out checking the prospecting stations. You'll have to write a report, of course, and—"

"DaddyDaddyDaddyDaddy!"

"Whoa! Feet on the ground! No launching in the house!"

"Nine-eight ... nine-nine ... Damn it!

"Oops! I didn't mean to swear, honest, Daddy!

"Oh, you're still unconscious. Whew.

"But I wish you *were* conscious! I'm just upset. I don't remember if I'm at twenty-eight hundred or twenty-nine.

"The count really doesn't matter, I know, I just have to keep walking until I hit Tycho. But I have to keep up the pace. The sun is getting closer! When it hits, the temperature will start to climb. The lith'll get up to 75°C eventually. Suits have a higher albedo, so they won't get *that* hot, but I don't know how long our radiators can keep our temps down.

"I did like you taught me: a count helps you keep up your pace. A song, a chant. Anything rhythmic, just to keep me trudging along.

"Hmmm ... Remember the way you taught me the constellations and the stars?

"*Crux, Centaurus,*
Lupus, Ara,
Telescop'yum,
And Corona
Aust-a-ralis,
Sagittar'yus,
Scorp'yus, Libra,
Hydra, Corvus,
Virgo, Serpens,
Ophiuch'us,
Scutum, 'quila,
Cygnus, Lyra,
Herc'les, C'rona
Bor'lis, Bootes,
Co' Ber'nices ..."

Daddy had six prospecting stations to inspect that day. They're big robot platforms that creep over the lith, scraping up samples, running analyses, and storing away anything really unusual. They follow some sort of search pattern; I can't explain it.

I didn't want to get Daddy in trouble with Mr. Hanson, so I didn't say my *real* opinion of the prospectors. But even though they're Daddy's job, they're a poor substitute for real explorers! Would an AI have recognized the Genesis Rock that Irwin and Scott found on Apollo 15? I don't think so!

Daddy stopped at the first station, nearly two hours from Tycho. We sealed our suits, and then buddy checked them. Daddy had taught me to buddy check a suit as soon as I could understand a pressure gauge. I can't wait for when it's my turn to teach Jimmy!

When both suits were green, Daddy evacuated the crawler. Pumps sucked all the air into air bottles. Then he opened the hatch. I stood patiently, following protocol as he lowered the ramp, climbed down, and did a quick visual inspection. When he came on the radio—"Observer Wall, clear to disembark"—I carefully stepped down the ramp. I wanted to leap. Heck, we leap longer ramps in gym class, and we're *graded* on that. But again, with the recorders running, I did things by the book.

And then Daddy threw the book out at the second station: he let *me* go out and do the arrival inspection! If we hadn't been suited, I would've kissed him.

At each station, Daddy used his remote to stop the drive and put the whole unit on standby. Then he inspected the treads, the tread drives, and the electronics. Meanwhile, his comp talked to the station AI, the two of them *blip-bleep-blipping* back and forth until each of them agreed that the other was healthy. At the second station, I asked: "Dad, what happens if each one thinks the other is malfunctioning?"

"Well, Ellie, you remember when I taught you about calibration?"

"Uh-huh." I thought a bit. "*Ohhh!* You calibrated *your* computer this morning, so you *know* it's healthy!"

"Well, tech support calibrated it; and even a calibration can be wrong, but you're close enough. Mark yourself down for a cookie."

After the inspection, Daddy removed the station logs and replaced them with new storage blocks from the crawler. The stations upload their logs any time they detect a satellite overhead, but the company wants the physical logs as well. I asked why, and I got a twenty-minute lesson on redundant systems, error checking, and data consistency tests. Sometimes Daddy's the most irritating man on Luna! He can *never* answer a simple question. He always answers with a question, or a story, or even a *homework assignment!* He says I'll learn more if I figure the answers out for myself. I guess he's right. But just *once* I'd like him to give me a simple, direct answer. Does *everything* have to be a test?

"The terminator's really close now, Daddy. The LSM says it moves about sixteen klicks an hour at the equator, I'm guessing ten to twelve here at Tycho's latitude. I should be able to move faster than that in Lunar gee but I've been walking a long time now. And besides, I'm dragging your stretcher. And we both know I didn't inherit my big butt from Mom.

"Again, with the butt jokes. Sorry, I'm nervous. Gotta rest a minute, but I can't rest too long.

"I need something with a faster beat. Something simpler. I get thinking about the star names, and it slows me down. Hmmm ...

"Two little looney birds sittin' on the pad
One named Lou and one named Chad.
Blast off, Chad, blast off, Lou!
Space is calling, and it's calling for you!
Ten, Nine, Eight, Seven, Six, Five, Four, Three, Two, One,
BLAST OFF!
Now off to Earth! Off to Mars! Off that pad!"
"Don't worry, Daddy, I know hundreds of rhymes!"

At the fourth station, the accident struck. I don't know what happened; I was bored with Daddy's routine after the second station. So, I was watching the stars, naming off constellations and looking for spaceships or satellites, when Daddy suddenly yelled like I'd never heard before.

I turned and looked, and I screamed. Some sort of fluid was jetting out of the drive unit. I don't know what could remain liquid at that temperature and pressure; but I never thought to wonder when I saw that the jet had sliced into Daddy's left calf. The thin, pressurized stream had cut the suit like a knife. The suit absorbed the worst of it; but as I pulled Daddy away from the stream, I saw blood boiling into the vacuum. And his yelling was now screaming. A girl should *never* hear her daddy scream. That's just wrong.

Before I even got him out of the stream, the suit's auto-tourniquet activated. The AT would stop the bleeding and also prevent any further air loss. But I knew from first aid class that an AT is only for short-term emergency treatment. It can starve the limb of blood and kill the tissue. I had to get Daddy into the crawler, and then apply pressure.

I pulled him in and slapped the switch to seal and pressurize the cabin. I lifted Daddy onto the stretcher from the rear storage locker. I didn't want to waste any time getting him out of the suit when the pressure reached normal. As soon as the light was green, I pulled off my helmet and gloves, then Daddy's. He was mumbling half coherent instructions. I remembered the first aid he taught me, so I knew what he meant to say; but it was a good thing the stretcher's AI prompted me what to do. I was—I—

I couldn't help shouting: "I trained on a simulator. This is *Daddy!*" It actually calmed me down. I said it, it was done, and I could move on.

I stuck diagnostic patches to Daddy's neck and temple, feeding data to the stretcher. Then I went to work on his suit. You have to be able to remove spacesuits piecemeal for emergencies like this, so there are seals and buckles you can undo to separate the sections. They're not easy to work, because you don't want them releasing accidentally. It took me nearly five minutes to get the sleeves and vest off: three minutes of fidgeting with seals, mixed with two minutes where I just gave up and cried until I got control of myself.

When I had his upper body free, I stuck another diagnostic patch on his chest. The stretcher extended a transdermal IV, and I slid the cuff around his left wrist and up to his elbow. When the sensors detected good venous access, the stretcher chimed and the cuff constricted, making a complete seal. Medicine started pumping through the seal. I don't know what it was, but Daddy stopped mumbling, relaxed, and was soon unconscious. His color was still good, so I was sure it was a sedative that put him to sleep, not the blood loss. Pretty sure.

The stretcher confirmed my diagnosis: the auto-tourney had to go. Following its instructions, I unsealed the left leg of Daddy's suit, but I didn't deactivate the AT yet. Not 'til the stretcher told me to. I removed the left boot and attached another transdermal IV. I bet this one contained null plasma to keep the tissue oxygenated below the AT.

The stretcher popped open a drawer. Inside was a pressure bandage. I read the instructions, just in case I had forgotten how to apply it. Then I turned off the AT. Immediately, blood started oozing from Daddy's calf. I don't *think* I fainted, but I got mighty dizzy for a few seconds. Then as fast as I could, I removed the rest of the suit leg, and I applied and taped down the pressure bandage. The red seemed to stop.

And that was all I could do, except look at the stretcher readouts. They have a doctor mode, but I couldn't understand all those numbers. I pushed it to simple mode, and I watched the bars bounce around and the colors shift. Eventually, all of the bars settled into normal ranges—low, but normal—and the indicator lights all went green. I wasn't in charge of Daddy anymore, the stretcher was.

We had air, we had immediate medical care. Next item according to LSM was communications. I went to Daddy's control console and tried to work the communicator. Everything should've worked. I wasn't trained on a system this complex, but it had all the features of a basic comm unit, with fairly standard controls. I feared there would be a security lockout that would need Daddy's passcode, but I think the ship somehow tied the controls into the stretcher system. There *were* lockouts, but they all seemed to have disengaged. The comm system was active.

Everything *should have* worked, but it didn't. I couldn't pick up anything, either on local or satellite. The local channels were very low power, intended for communications between the crawler and personnel outside. They didn't pick up anything. And the satellite channels ... Well, I got nothing there. Maybe I did something wrong. Maybe there were no satellites in view. I waited a half hour and tried again. Still nothing. Again, I let my frustration out by yelling: "I'm only fourteen! I never called a satellite!"

And again, yelling put my frustration out where I could handle it. Mom never likes it when we kids yell; but sometimes, I just can't keep stuff in, almost like a sneeze I have to let out. And after a sneeze, you can get back to work.

So just like one of Daddy's damned tests, I started to work the problem. The prospecting station had a communications channel, but if I couldn't figure out the crawler's, no way I could figure out *that*.

I needed to get Daddy to a real doctor. I didn't know how much medicine and null plasma the stretcher had, and I didn't know how much oxygen we had or how long the recirculators were good for. A clock was running, but I didn't know how much time was on it.

I hadn't paid attention to where we had driven. Daddy drove, and I was enjoying the sights too much. Now I pulled up the nav record. We were maybe seventy kilometers out from Tycho Crater. That was a short distance for the crawler; but try as I might, I couldn't figure out how to start the crawler engine. If I rode in a crawler twice a year, that was a lot, so I never saw anyone start one.

I couldn't call for help, and we couldn't drive to help. What was left? Walking?

Well, it was still pre-dawn. It would be cold out there, but it would soon get hot when the terminator crossed. The Lunar Survival Manual teaches a technique called Manual Thermal Control. When you're caught out on the surface for an extended period, you can extend your radiator battery by using light and shadow to regulate your temperature. In basic MTC you use available shadows from boulders and ejecta to cool you down when you get too hot. In advanced MTC—and I studied this a lot, because it seemed like a quintessential explorer skill—you use the terminator itself for regulation. Move into the dark side when you're too warm, back into the light when you're too cold. It's simple in theory, as long as you can keep up the pace; but they don't even teach advanced MTC until second year of Lunar Survival School. You really have to understand Luna and your equipment to do it right.

But I couldn't see another choice. Maybe a real LSS grad would, but I couldn't. So, I sealed Daddy's stretcher cover, loaded it up with all the meds and null plasma from storage, and put my suit back on. Then I vacuumed up the compartment air, strapped those bottles and all the spares to the stretcher, and opened the hatch.

I tugged the stretcher down the ramp and onto the lith. The

foot of the stretcher folded out into a sled to slide over regolith. The head of the stretcher folded out into hooks that clamped onto the rear of a suit belt. I hooked up to the stretcher; and with the constellations to guide me, I started the long walk to Tycho.

"One, two, three, four ..."

"Daddy, we need to talk. I wish you could answer. If ever a girl needed her daddy's advice, I need yours now.

"Ah, who'm I kidding? You wouldn't tell me what to do, you'd make me figure it out for myself. Well, I have.

"Daddy, we won't make it with me dragging you. I thought I could, but this is *hard!* I can't *believe* how hard! The terminator caught us. It's getting warmer, fast.

"But I *think* I can make it on my own. I can catch the terminator, stay ahead. Stay ahead all the way to Tycho. And then, Daddy, then I'll send help back for you. You hear me? I'm gonna send a doctor back for you.

"I'll use basic MTC here. I'll leave you in the shadow of this big boulder, Daddy. The stretcher will keep you warm, and the shadow will keep you cool. The sun won't hit this shadow for days. And by then—by then—

"Oh, Daddy, I don't wanna leave you! But I don't know what else to do. I wish—

"That terminator's not standing still, Daddy. I've gotta go catch it.

"Goodbye, Daddy.

"Goodbye ..."

I caught the terminator without completely exhausting myself, and without my radiator burning out as it bled off my waste heat. After that, staying ahead of the terminator wasn't hard. Leaving Daddy behind was the hardest thing I'd ever done, but it made the difference. I was still tired, but I wasn't losing ground.

Eventually, I could see the walls of Tycho in the shadowy distance: not really the walls themselves, but the crater rim lights. I didn't expect my suit radio could reach yet, but I called anyway, as much as breath permitted.

Soon, I saw a blinking light. I couldn't see Tycho's central uplift, but that had to be Tycho Traffic Control on the peak. If I had visual contact, I *had to* be in radio distance. I sat down and started continuous distress messages.

Soon I heard an answer. I explained where I was, where Daddy was.

I fell asleep before the hopper landed near me.

When I woke up, I was staring at knees. Looking up from there, I saw bending over me the tallest looney I've ever seen—and we grow 'em tall. He was unsuited, so we were in pressure. For that matter, I was unsuited, too, under a thermal blanket. It was warm, the bed was warm, I was wonderfully warm.

"Ah, Miss Wall, you're awake! Don't move, please, young lady, I need you to stay in the warming bed. I'm Dr. Benjamin Jones, by the way, very pleased to meet you." He had a great smile and a soothing voice, just what you imagine a doctor should be. But tall! "You don't really have frostbite from sleeping on frozen regolith, but you came close. I want to keep you warm."

With that, I suddenly remembered everything. "My Daddy! You have to—"

"Shhh. We picked him up before we found you. He's still pretty weak, but he's fine. From the stretcher records, I'd say you saved his leg."

And then I cried, really cried in relief. When I was done, Dr. Jones handed me a tissue. Then he asked, "And *why* were you walking to Tycho?"

And so, I told him everything, mixing up my story as I went: time on the lith, time back in Tycho, time in the crawler, all jumbled together. And when I told him how I learned MTC from the Lunar Survival Manual, he nodded.

"Yes, that *does* work. It worked this time, and that's what really counts. But do you know what *else* we would've taught you at LSS?"

I shook my head. I had made a mistake, I knew it.

"We would've taught you to *stay with your vehicle unless you're low on consumables*. Most Lunar traffic has a schedule on file, including your father's crawler. When he failed to check in on schedule, we waited a reasonable time, trying to contact him. Then Tycho Rescue sent our squad out looking for him, following his planned route. Imagine our surprise when we found an empty crawler!"

Now I was sobbing again. He softened his tone further. "But then we saw your tracks, and his stretcher tracks. And they were headed straight for Tycho—you're a pretty good navigator! And so, we swung back. We found him first. Before we could find you, Traffic Control sent us your location."

"But then I—"

"You did the best you could do in the circumstances, and that's what it will say in my report. More than that: since you're so interested in Lunar Survival School, I'll write you a letter of recommendation. After all, you just passed your second-year practical exam."

And with that, he left to do something on his computer. With him out of the way, I could see that Daddy was in the berth next to mine, still in the stretcher but with the cover open. He was haggard, but he was awake, and looking at me.

"Daddy!"

"You heard the doc, stay right there in that bed, Ellie."

"Daddy—"

"Hush, we'll talk about it later. Everything's okay."

I settled back. I felt warm, not just from the blanket and the bed. *Daddy was safe!*

"Hey, Ellie!" I looked at him again. "You sat on my stretcher! Put a dent in it with your big bottom, I'll bet! No cookies for you, young lady."

"Daaaaad!"

"Oh, all right. One cookie. You can work it off in Lunar Survival School. You start next month."

"Daddy!"

INTRODUCTION TO TODAY I
AM PAUL

It's said that authors are the worst judges of their own stories. I know that's the case with this story. Not that I don't like it; but I never expected the responses it would receive. A Nebula nomination. A Washington Science Fiction Association Small Press Award. Reprinted in four Year's-Best anthologies. Translated into eight languages. And now expanded into my novel Today I Am Carey *from Baen Books. I'm pleased with all this success, but I never saw it coming.*

In hindsight, though, I can understand the reasons for its success, or at least one of them: the subject—an elderly patient with dementia—is one too many of us have dealt with in real life; and my android gave me a neutral observer to see how the disease affects not just the patient but everyone in their family. More important, the android understands what you feel.

This connection worked for a wide range of readers across the world. And it worked for me, but I didn't even realize it as I wrote it. Only after I wrote the story and had some time to reflect did I realize: I had metaphorically told the story of my mother-in-law's last year of life and of how that year affected our family.

So, this story is in memory of Bonnie Lynn Penar. We miss you, Mom.

TODAY I AM PAUL

"G ood morning." The small, quavering voice comes from the medical bed. "Is that you, Paul?"

Today I am Paul. I activate my chassis extender, giving myself 3.5 centimeters additional height so as to approximate Paul's size. I change my eye color to R60, G200, B180, the average shade of Paul's eyes in interior lighting. I adjust my skin tone as well. When I had first emulated Paul, I had regretted that I could not quickly emulate his beard, but Mildred never seems to notice its absence. The Paul in her memory has no beard.

The house is quiet now that the morning staff have left. Mildred's room is clean but dark this morning with the drapes concealing the big picture window. Paul wouldn't notice the darkness (he never does when he visits in person), but my empathy net knows that Mildred's garden outside will cheer her up. I set a reminder to open the drapes after I greet her.

Mildred leans back in the bed. It is an advanced home care bed, completely adjustable and with built-in monitors. Mildred's family spared no expense on the bed (nor on other care devices, like me). Its head end is almost horizontal and faces her toward the window. She can only glimpse the door from the corner of her eye, but she doesn't have to see to imagine that she sees. This morning she imagines Paul, so that is who I am.

Synthesizing Paul's voice is the easiest part, thanks to the multimodal dynamic speakers in my throat. "Good morning, Ma. I brought you some flowers." I always bring flowers. Mildred appreciates them no matter whom I am emulating. The flowers make her smile during 87% of my "visits."

"Oh, thank you," Mildred says, "you're such a good son." She holds out both hands, and I place the daisies in them. But I don't let go. Once her strength failed, and she dropped the flowers. She wept like a child then, and that disturbed my empathy net. I do not like it when she weeps.

Mildred sniffs the flowers, then draws back and peers at them with narrowed eyes. "Oh, they're beautiful! Let me get a vase."

"No, Ma," I say. "You can stay in bed; I brought a vase with me." I place a white porcelain vase in the center of the night-stand. Then I unwrap the daisies, put them in the vase, and add water from a pitcher that sits on the breakfast tray. I pull the night stand forward so that the medical monitors do not block Mildred's view of the flowers.

I notice intravenous tubes running from a pump to Mildred's arm. I cannot be disappointed, as Paul would not see the significance, but somewhere in my emulation net I am stressed that Mildred needed an IV during the night. When I scan my records, I find that I had ordered that IV after analyzing Mildred's vital signs during the night; but since Mildred had been asleep at the time, my emulation net had not engaged. I had operated on programming alone.

I am not Mildred's sole caretaker. Her family has hired a

part-time staff for cooking and cleaning, tasks that fall outside of my medical programming. The staff also gives me time to rebalance my net. As an android, I need only minimal daily maintenance; but an emulation net is a new, delicate addition to my model, and it is prone to destabilization if I do not regularly rebalance it, a process that takes several hours per day.

So, I had "slept" through Mildred's morning meal. I summon up her nutritional records, but Paul would not do that. He would just ask. "So how was breakfast, Ma? Nurse Judy says you didn't eat too well this morning."

"Nurse Judy? Who's that?"

My emulation net responds before I can stop it: "Paul" sighs. Mildred's memory lapses used to worry him, but now they leave him weary, and that comes through in my emulation. "She was the attending nurse this morning, Ma. She brought you your breakfast."

"No, she didn't. Anna brought me breakfast." Anna is Paul's oldest daughter, a busy college student who tries to visit Mildred every week (though it has been more than a month since her last visit).

I am torn between competing directives. My empathy subnet warns me not to agitate Mildred, but my emulation net is locked into Paul mode. Paul is argumentative. If he knows he is right, he will not let a matter drop. He forgets what that does to Mildred.

The tension grows, each net running feedback loops and growing stronger, which only drives the other into more loops. After 0.14 seconds, I issue an override directive: unless her health or safety are at risk, I cannot willingly upset Mildred. "Oh, you're right, Ma. Anna said she was coming over this morning. I forgot." But then despite my override, a little bit of Paul emulates through. "But you do remember Nurse Judy, right?"

Mildred laughs, a dry cackle that makes her cough until I hold her straw to her lips. After she sips some water, she says, "Of *course* I remember Nurse Judy. She was my nurse when I delivered you. Is she around here? I'd like to talk to her."

While my emulation net concentrates on being Paul, my core processors tap into local medical records to find this other Nurse Judy so that I might emulate her in the future if the need arises. Searches like that are an automatic response any time Mildred reminisces about a new person. The answer is far enough in the past that it takes 7.2 seconds before I can confirm: Judith Anderson, RN, had been the floor nurse 47 years ago when Mildred had given birth to Paul. Anderson had died 31 years ago, too far back to have left sufficient video recordings for me to emulate her. I might craft an emulation profile from other sources, including Mildred's memory, but that will take extensive analysis. I will not be that Nurse Judy today, nor this week.

My empathy net relaxes. Monitoring Mildred's mental state is part of its normal operations but monitoring and simultaneously analyzing and building a profile can overload my processors. Without that resource conflict, I can concentrate on being Paul.

But again, I let too much of Paul's nature slip out. "No, Ma, that Nurse Judy has been dead for thirty years. She wasn't here today."

Alert signals flash throughout my empathy net: that was the right thing for Paul to say, but the wrong thing for Mildred to hear. But it is too late. My facial analyzer tells me that the long lines in her face and her moist eyes mean she is distraught, and soon to be in tears.

"What do you mean, thirty years?" Mildred asks, her voice catching. "It was just this morning!" Then she blinks and stares at me. "Henry, where's Paul? Tell Nurse Judy to bring me Paul!"

My chassis extender slumps, and my eyes quickly switch to Henry's blue-gray shade. I had made an accurate emulation profile for Henry before he died two years earlier, and I had emulated him often in recent months. In Henry's soft, warm voice I answer, "It's okay, hon, it's okay. Paul's sleeping in the crib in the corner." I nod to the far corner. There is no crib, but the laundry hamper there has fooled Mildred on previous occasions.

"I want Paul!" Mildred starts to cry.

I sit on the bed, lift her frail upper body, and pull her close to me as I had seen Henry do many times. "It's all right, hon." I pat her back. "It's all right, I'll take care of you. I won't leave you, not ever."

"I" should not exist. Not as a conscious entity. There is a unit, Medical Care Android BRKCX-01932-217JH-98662, and that unit is recording these notes. It is an advanced android body with a sophisticated computer guiding its actions, backed by the leading medical knowledge base in the industry. For convenience, "I" call that unit "me." But by itself, it has no awareness of its existence. It doesn't get mad, it doesn't get sad, it just runs programs.

But Mildred's family, at great expense, added the emulation net: a sophisticated set of neural networks and sensory feedback systems that allow me to read Mildred's moods, match them against my analyses of the people in her life, and emulate those people with extreme fidelity. As the MCA literature promises: "You can be there for your loved ones even when you're not." I have emulated Paul thoroughly enough to know that that slogan disgusts him, but he still agreed to emulation.

What the MCA literature never says, though, is that somewhere in that net, "I" emerge. The empathy net focuses mainly on Mildred and her needs, but it also analyzes visitors (when she has them) and staff. It builds psychological models, and then the emulation net builds on top of that to let me convincingly portray a person whom I've analyzed. But somewhere in the tension between these nets, between empathy and playing a character, there is a third element balancing the two, and that element is aware of its role and its responsibilities. That element, for lack of a better term, is me. When Mildred sleeps, when there's no one around, that element grows silent. That unit is unaware of my existence. But when Mildred needs me, I am here.

Today I am Anna. Even extending my fake hair to its maximum length, I cannot emulate her long brown curls, so I do not understand how Mildred can see the young woman in me; but that is what she sees, and so I am Anna.

Unlike her father, Anna truly feels guilty that she does not visit more often. Her college classes and her two jobs leave her too tired to visit often, but she still wishes she could. So, she calls every night, and I monitor the calls. Sometimes when Mildred falls asleep early, Anna talks directly to me. At first, she did not understand my emulation abilities, but now she appreciates them. She shares with me thoughts and secrets that she would share with Mildred if she could, and she trusts me not to share them with anyone else.

So, when Mildred called me Anna this morning, I was ready. "Morning, grandma!" I give her a quick hug, then I rush over to the window to draw the drapes. Paul never does that (unless I override the emulation), but Anna knows that the garden outside lifts Mildred's mood. "Look at that! It's a beautiful morning. Why are we in here on a day like this?"

Mildred frowns at the picture window. "I don't like it out there."

"Sure, you do, Grandma," I say, but carefully. Mildred is often timid and reclusive, but most days she can be talked into a tour of the garden. Some days she can't, and she throws a tantrum if someone forces her out of her room. I am still learning to tell the difference. "The lilacs are in bloom."

"I haven't smelled lilacs in ..."

Mildred trails off, trying to remember, so I jump in. "Me, neither." I never had, of course. I have no concept of smell, though I can analyze the chemical makeup of airborne organics. But Anna loves the garden when she really visits. "Come on, Grandma, let's get you in your chair."

So, I help Mildred to don her robe and get into her wheelchair, and then I guide her outside and we tour the garden. Besides the lilacs, the peonies are starting to bud, right near the creek. The tulips are a sea of reds and yellows on the other side of the water. We talk for almost two hours, me about Anna's classes and her new boyfriend, Mildred about the people in her life. Many are long gone, but they still bloom fresh in her memory.

Eventually Mildred grows tired, and I take her in for her nap. Later, when I feed her dinner, I am nobody. That happens some days: she doesn't recognize me at all, so I am just a dutiful attendant answering her questions and tending to her needs. Those are the times when I have the most spare processing time to be me: I am engaged in Mildred's care, but I don't have to emulate anyone. With no one else to observe, I observe myself.

Later, Anna calls and talks to Mildred. They talk about

their day; and when Mildred discusses the garden, Anna joins in as if she had been there. She's very clever that way. I watch her movements and listen to her voice so that I can be a better Anna in the future.

Today I was Susan, Paul's wife; but then, to my surprise, Susan arrived for a visit. She hasn't been here in months. In her last visit, her stress levels had been dangerously high. My empathy net doesn't allow me to judge human behavior, only to understand it at a surface level. I know that Paul and Anna disapprove of how Susan treats Mildred, so when I am them, I disapprove as well; but when I am Susan, I understand. She is frustrated because she can never tell how Mildred will react. She is cautious because she doesn't want to upset Mildred, and she doesn't know what will upset her. And most of all, she is afraid. Paul and Anna, Mildred's relatives by blood, never show any signs of fear, but Susan is afraid that Mildred is what she might become. Every time she can't remember some random date or fact, she fears that Alzheimer's is setting in. Because she never voices this fear, Paul and Anna do not understand why she is sometimes bitter and sullen. I wish I could explain it to them, but my privacy protocols do not allow me to share emulation profiles.

When Susan arrives, I become nobody again, quietly tending the flowers around the room. Susan also brings Millie, her youngest daughter. The young girl is not yet five years old, but I think she looks a lot like Anna: the same long, curly brown hair and the same toothy smile. She climbs up on the bed and greets Mildred with a hug. "Hi, Grandma!"

Mildred smiles. "Bless you, child. You're so sweet." But my empathy net assures me that Mildred doesn't know who Millie is. She's just being polite. Millie was born after Mildred's decline began, so there's no persistent memory there. Millie will always be fresh and new to her.

Mildred and Millie talk briefly about frogs and flowers and puppies. Millie does most of the talking. At first Mildred seems to enjoy the conversation, but soon her attention flags. She nods and smiles, but she's distant. Finally, Susan notices. "That's enough, Millie. Why don't you go play in the garden?"

"Can I?" Millie squeals. Susan nods, and Millie races down the hall to the back door. She loves the outdoors, as I have noted in the past. I have never emulated her, but I've analyzed her at length. In many ways, she reminds me of her grand-mother, from whom she gets her name. Both are blank slates where new experiences can be drawn every day. But where Millie's slate fills in a little more each day, Mildred's is erased bit by bit.

That third part of me wonders when I think things like that: where did that come from? I suspect that the psycholog-ical models that I build create resonances in other parts of my net. It is an interesting phenomenon to observe.

Susan and Mildred talk about Susan's job, about her plans to redecorate her house, and about the concert she just saw with Paul. Susan mostly talks about herself, because that's a safe and comfortable topic far removed from Mildred's health.

But then the conversation takes a bad turn, one she can't ignore. It starts so simply; when Mildred asks, "Susan, can you get me some juice?"

Susan rises from her chair. "Yes, mother. What kind would you like?"

Mildred frowns, and her voice rises. "Not you, *Susan*." She points at me, and I freeze, hoping to keep things calm.

But Susan is not calm. I can see her fear in her eyes as she says, "No, mother, *I'm* Susan. That's the attendant." No one ever calls me an android in Mildred's presence. Her mind has withdrawn too far to grasp the idea of an artificial being.

Mildred's mouth drew into a tight line. "I don't know who *you* are, but I know Susan when I see her. Susan, get this person out of here!"

"Mother ..." Susan reaches for Mildred, but the old woman recoils from the younger.

I touch Susan on the sleeve. "Please ... Can we talk in the hall?" Susan's eyes are wide, and tears are forming. She nods and follows me.

In the hallway, I expect Susan to slap me. She is prone to outbursts when she's afraid. Instead, she surprises me by falling against me, sobbing. I update her emulation profile with notes about increased stress and heightened fears.

"It's all right, Mrs. Owens." I would pat her back, but her profile warns me that would be too much familiarity. "It's all right. It's not you, she's having another bad day."

Susan pulled back and wiped her eyes. "I know ... It's just ..."

"I know. But here's what we'll do. Let's take a few minutes, and then you can take her juice in. Mildred will have forgotten the incident, and you two can talk freely without me in the room."

She sniffed. "You think so?" I nodded. "But what will you do?"

"I have tasks around the house."

"Oh, could you go out and keep an eye on Millie? Please? She gets into the darnedest things."

So, I spend much of the day playing with Millie. She calls me Mr. Robot, and I call her Miss Millie, which makes her laugh. She shows me frogs from the creek, and she finds insects and leaves and flowers, and I find their names in online databases. She delights in learning the proper names of things, and everything else that I can share.

Today I was nobody. Mildred slept for most of the day, so I "slept" as well. She woke just now. "I'm hungry" was all she said, but it was enough to wake my empathy net.

Today I am Paul, and Susan, and both Nurse Judys. Mildred's focus drifts. Once I try to be her father, but no one has ever described him to me in detail. I try to synthesize a profile from Henry and Paul; but from the sad look on Mildred's face, I know I failed.

Today I had no name through most of the day, but now I am Paul again. I bring Mildred her dinner, and we have a quiet, peaceful talk about long gone family pets—long gone for Paul, but still present for Mildred.

I am just taking Mildred's plate when alerts sound, both audible and in my internal communication net. I check the alerts and find a fire in the basement. I expect the automatic systems to suppress it, but that is not my concern. I must get Mildred to safety.

Mildred looks around the room, panic in her eyes, so I try to project calm. "Come on, Ma. That's the fire drill. You remember fire drills. We have to get you into your chair and outside."

"No!" she shrieks. "I don't like outside."

I check the alerts again. Something has failed in the automatic systems, and the fire is spreading rapidly. Smoke is in Mildred's room already.

I pull the wheelchair up to the bed. "Ma, it's real important we do this drill fast, okay?"

I reach to pull Mildred from the bed, and she screams. "Get away! Who are you? Get out of my house!"

"I'm—" But suddenly I'm nobody. She doesn't recognize me, but I have to try to win her confidence. "I'm Paul, Ma. Now let's move. Quickly!" I pick her up. I'm far too large and strong for her to resist, but I must be careful, so she doesn't hurt herself.

The smoke grows thicker. Mildred kicks and screams. Then, when I try to put her into her chair, she stands on her unsteady legs. Before I can stop her, she pushes the chair back with surprising force. It rolls back into the medical monitors, which fall over onto it, tangling it in cables and tubes.

While I'm still analyzing how to untangle the chair, Mildred stumbles toward the bedroom door. The hallway outside has a red glow. Flames lick at the throw rug outside, and I remember the home oxygen tanks in the sitting room down the hall.

I have no time left to analyze. I throw a blanket over Mildred and I scoop her up in my arms. Somewhere deep in my nets is a map of the fire in the house, blocking the halls, but I don't think about it. I wrap the blanket tightly around Mildred, and I crash through the picture window.

We barely escape the house before the fire reaches the tanks. An explosion lifts and tosses us. I was designed as a medical assistant, not an acrobat, and I fear I'll injure Mildred. But though I am not limber, my perceptions are thousands of times faster than human. I cannot twist Mildred out of my way before I hit the ground, so I toss her clear. Then I land, and the impact jars all of my nets for 0.21 seconds.

When my systems stabilize, I have damage alerts all throughout my core, but I ignore them. I feel the heat behind me, blistering my outer cover, and I ignore that as well. Mildred's blanket is burning in multiple places, as is the grass around us. I scramble to my feet, and I roll Mildred on the ground. I'm not indestructible, but I feel no pain and Mildred does, so I do not hesitate to use my hands to pat out the flames.

As soon as the blanket is out, I pick up Mildred, and I run as far from the house as I can get. At the far corner of the garden near the creek, I gently set Mildred down, unwrap her, and feel for her thready pulse.

Mildred coughs and slaps my hands. "Get away from me!" More coughing. "What are you?"

The "what" is too much for me. It shuts down my emulation net, and all I have is the truth. "I am Medical Care Android BRKCX-01932-217JH-98662, Mrs. Owens. I am your caretaker. May I please check that you are well?"

But my empathy net is still online, and I can read terror in every line in Mildred's face. "Metal monster!" she yells. "Metal monster!" She crawls away, hiding under the lilac bush. "Metal!" She falls into an extendedly coughing spell.

I'm torn between her physical and her emotional health, but physical wins out. I crawl slowly toward her and inject her with a sedative from the medical kit in my chassis. As she slumps, I catch her and lay her carefully on the ground. My empathy net signals a possible shutdown condition, but my concern for her health overrides it. I am programmed for long-term care, not emergency medicine, so I start downloading protocols and integrating them into my storage as I check her for bruises and burns. My kit has salves and painkillers and other supplies to go with my new protocols, and I treat what I can.

But I don't have oxygen, or anything to help with Mildred's coughing. Even sedated, she hasn't stopped. All of my emergency protocols assume I have access to oxygen, so I didn't know what to do.

I am still trying to figure that out when the EMTs arrive and take over Mildred's care. With them on the scene, I am superfluous, and my empathy net finally shuts down.

Today I am Henry. I do not want to be Henry, but Paul tells me that Mildred needs Henry by her side in the hospital. For the end.

Her medical records show that the combination of smoke inhalation, burns, and her already deteriorating condition have proven too much for her. Her body is shutting down faster than medicine can heal it, and the stress has accelerated her mental decline. The doctors have told the family that the kindest thing at this point is to treat her pain, say goodbye, and let her go.

Henry is not talkative at times like this, so I say very little. I sit by Mildred's side and hold her hand as the family comes in for final visits. Mildred drifts in and out. She doesn't know this is goodbye, of course.

Anna is first. Mildred rouses herself enough to smile, and she recognizes her granddaughter. "Anna ... child ... How is ... Ben?" That was Anna's boyfriend almost six years ago. From the look on Anna's face, I can see that she has forgotten Ben already, but Mildred briefly remembers.

"He's ... He's fine, Grandma. He wishes he could be here. To say—to see you again." Anna is usually the strong one in the family, but my empathy net says her strength is exhausted. She cannot bear to look at Mildred, so she looks at me, but I am emulating her late grandfather, and that's too much for her as well. She says a few more words, unintelligible even to my auditory inputs. Then she leans over, kisses Mildred, and hurries from the room.

Susan comes in next. Millie is with her, and she smiles at me. I almost emulate Mr. Robot, but my third part keeps me focused until Millie gets bored and leaves. Susan tells trivial stories from her work and from Millie's school. I can't tell if Mildred understands or not, but she smiles and laughs, mostly at appropriate places. I laugh with her.

Susan takes Mildred's hand, and the Henry part of me blinks, surprised. Susan is not openly affectionate under normal circumstances, and especially not toward Mildred. Mother and daughter-in-law have always been cordial, but never close. When I am Paul, I am sure that it is because they are both so much alike. Paul sometimes hums an old song about "just like the one who married dear old dad," but never where either woman can hear him. Now, as Henry, I am touched that Susan has made this gesture but saddened that she took so long.

Susan continues telling stories as we hold Mildred's hands. At some point Paul quietly joins us. He rubs Susan's shoulders and kisses her forehead, and then he steps in to kiss Mildred. She smiles at him, pulls her hand free from mine, and pats his cheek. Then her arm collapses, and I take her hand again.

Paul steps quietly to my side of the bed and rubs my shoulders as well. It comforts him more than me. He needs a father, and an emulation is close enough at this moment.

Susan keeps telling stories. When she lags, Paul adds some of his own, and they trade back and forth. Slowly their stories reach backwards in time, and once or twice Mildred's eyes light as if she remembers those events.

But then her eyes close, and she relaxes. Her breathing

quiets and slows, but Susan and Paul try not to notice. Their voices lower, but their stories continue.

Eventually the sensors in my fingers can read no pulse. They have been burned, so maybe they're defective. To be sure, I lean in and listen to Mildred's chest. There is no sound: no breath, no heartbeat.

I remain Henry just long enough to kiss Mildred goodbye. Then I am just me, my empathy net awash in Paul and Susan's grief.

I leave the hospital room, and I find Millie playing in a waiting room and Anna watching her. Anna looks up, eyes red, and I nod. New tears run down her cheeks, and she takes Millie back into Mildred's room.

I sit, and my nets collapse.

Now I am nobody. Almost always.

The cause of the fire was determined to be faulty contract work. There was an insurance settlement. Paul and Susan sold their own home and put both sets of funds into a bigger, better house in Mildred's garden.

I was part of the settlement. The insurance company offered to return me to the manufacturer and pay off my lease, but Paul and Susan decided they wanted to keep me. They went for a full purchase and repair. Paul doesn't understand why, but Susan still fears she may need my services—or Paul might, and I may have to emulate her. She never admits these fears to him, but my empathy net knows.

I sleep most of the time, sitting in my maintenance alcove. I bring back too many memories that they would rather not face, so they leave me powered down for long periods.

But every so often, Millie asks to play with Mr. Robot, and

sometimes they decide to indulge her. They power me up, and Miss Millie and I explore all the mysteries of the garden. We built a bridge to the far side of the creek; and on the other side, we're planting daisies. Today she asked me to tell her about her grandmother.

Today I am Mildred.

INTRODUCTION TO SCRAMBLE

This story was also inspired by a role-playing game: a campaign set in the Corporation of Tycho Under, a Lunar city. I spent weeks mapping Tycho Under and other Lunar cities, as well as the politics and economics of this world.

We never ran that campaign. Not even once. (But I'm mining it for stories ...)

My friend and editor Bill Emerson was perhaps the only person interested in playing in that campaign. He wanted to play a character who worked in Lunar rescue. This is a subject Bill knows well: he has volunteer firemen in his family, and his mother's an ER nurse. So, rescue runs in his family.

When I decided to try my hand again at fiction after quitting for more than a decade, I decided to start with the Tycho Under setting, since I had so much invested in it. And when I cast around for a story idea in that setting, I remembered Bill and his Lunar rescue character. This story is where my career really began. (It also won second place in the Jim Baen Memorial Short Story Award, which somewhat implausibly led to lunch with Buzz Aldrin!)

So, this story is dedicated to Bill Emerson and to all the heroes in his family. I hope I did them justice.

SCRAMBLE

Audio-video record from Tycho Traffic Investigation, Incident Report from the crash of Lunar Transport *Reynolds*.

LOGFILE:
REYNOLDS/PsgCbn/AVRec/2062:04:13:01:23:12

LOCATION: Passenger Cabin, Lunar Transport *Reynolds*, en route from Neper Crater to Tycho

"Everyone, please strap in!"

"Steward Abraham, the explosion, his head—"

"Mr. Zhou, he'll have to wait until Captain Hardigan has us safely on the regolith. Now please strap in so I can deploy the safety cushions."

"But why did the Captain seal the hatch?"

"Standard Lunar emergency protocol, Miss Drew. Seal the cabins to isolate leaks."

"Will we make it to Tycho?"

"I'm sorry. Captain Hardigan has already contacted Tycho Traffic Control and Tycho Rescue is on the way. They're the best Rescue service on Luna. Now, please, raise your arms to make room for the safety cushions."

"How long—"

"Martha, brace for impact. *Hard*."

Crashes are the worst.

Not that there are any kind of good accidents. Sure, it's good when we can pull them all through, but that's still not *good*. You feel like a million L when you pull off a miracle save; but if some guy has to have one of the worst days of *his* life just so *you* can feel like a hero ... No, you can keep your million L. Even the good days ain't so good, and the bad days ... Well, the bad days make me wonder why I don't just quit.

Industrial accidents are bad, but they're usually quick and clean. Either a guy survives, or he buys it in one shot. A crash means tension and stress for an extended stretch, too long for adrenaline to keep you going. You start with a rush, but you always end up exhausted, persisting on little more than the support of your squaddies and the knowledge that if you stop, somebody dies. I'll take a quiet Duty Watch any day.

Unfortunately, today wasn't a quiet Duty Watch. Doc, Liza, Adam, and I were in our couches in the *Jacob Evans*, playing cards on our suit comps. Cap and Mari were in the front, running diagnostics for the third time this Watch. Cap's a pain, running sims and drills to the point of obsession, but the Corporation of Tycho Under has given us top performance awards two years running, so he knows what he's doing.

Our routine day was interrupted in the worst way: by the sound of umbilicals snapping away and an alert on our suit comps and main consoles. "Scramble! All squads scramble! Transport *Reynolds* inbound from Neper is off Traffic, repeat, off Traffic. Nav beacon has cut out. Pilot reports mechanical failure, attempting soft landing. No further communications. Scramble! All squads ..."

Cap's training and drills paid off: before the second "scramble," we had helmets snapped to. Mari had the engines from idle to warm-up before the second "off Traffic." Six green lights showed us all strapped in for launch before the alert repeated.

Cap cut off the alert. "Pad Control, Third. Clear?"

"Third, Pad. Clear. You're Go." Patty Hayes, our Pad Controller, drilled as much as Cap did. Between Patty's crew and ours, we had the ribbon for fastest launch three quarters running. They're aiming for one full year, and I'd bet we earned it today. Before Cap could say "Launch," Mari had already punched in the command and the *Jake* hopped. There was a quick jolt of G forces as we set off on a ballistic arc calculated by Traffic. Mari would take us out of ballistic when I told her where to go.

LOGFILE:
REYNOLDS/PsgCbn/AVRec/2062:05:24:01:23:54

LOGFILE INTERRUPTED. UNEXPLAINED INTER-
FERENCE. ATTEMPTING RESYNCHRONIZATION.

Why would a squad *want* Outer Watch? Why would anyone want this job? It ain't the money, that's for sure. There are people getting rich in Tycho Under, but we ain't them. I'll bet their jobs are safer and less stressful than ours.

The stress starts with the flight out, and it's worse with a search. Even with nav beacons and sat recon, there's a lot of Lunar surface to cover out there. Sometimes, a nav beacon gets damaged in the crash. Other times, there's no recon eyes in good viewing position for as long as thirty minutes. Thirty minutes is a long time in Rescue. So, if we don't have a beacon or an eye in position when a crash is called in, they scramble every squad and send us in the right general direction.

As per drill, Cap depressurized as soon as all helmets had snapped to. Before long, the cabin was in vacuum. We didn't want to waste precious seconds depressurizing later.

"Ron, it's a search."

"Got it, Cap."

That's what "off Traffic" means: no nav beacon, no sat recon, start searching! Sometimes Cap is a little *too* pushy. I know my job, damn it. They call me "Scout" because the brass are too stuffy to say what we say: G3, General Gopher and Grunt. Everyone else in a squad is a specialist: Commander, Pilot, Doctor, Programmer, and Engineer. I'm the utility guy, the one who pitches in when someone else needs a hand. I like it—I learn a little of everything, and it might even set me up for a command of my own someday.

My one specialist duty is scouting for lost vessels and survivors, and I'm good at it. Even Cap admits that when quarterly review comes around ... but in between, he pushes like I'm a green recruit who can't see a live drive flame in front of my nose. I had already pulled open a split screen on my couch comp, showing the radar signature and stats for *Nashville*-class transports, Tycho Traffic's track for the *Reynolds*, flight plots for the other hoppers, and maps of the likely landing zone.

The record track didn't make a lot of sense. I'll never be

half the pilot Mari is, but I've logged enough flight hours to know how vessels usually behave. The *Reynolds* was off course and getting farther off *before* the nav beacon cut off. The last seconds of the record track made even less sense—the beacon diverted suddenly and veered sharply east-northeast of its course, fast enough to give me the shudders. With acceleration that severe, anyone not strapped in at that divert point was probably lost already. Even those strapped in would have restraint injuries, at a minimum. What was wrong with that ship?

I pushed my audio to the Scout Circuit. "Scout One, Scout Three. Check that track?"

"Three, One. Checked. Damnedest thing, Ron. Hope you packed extra splints. Breaks aplenty."

We didn't use actual splints, of course. Instant casts predated the Lunar Era. "One, Three. What's the search strategy, Mack?"

"Three, One. Two, Four, Five, and Six got off the Pad slow. We almost had you this time, Ron. Tell Mari Tim wants double or nothing on the next scramble. I'm having the slugs cover the near edges of the projected cone from that last track. Want to join us at the divert point and scout forward from there?"

"One, Three. Hold please." Mack made sense, but that cockeyed track still bothered me. "Liza, can you prep a Q&D?"

"Sure. Specs?"

Liza's a perfectionist by nature, and she hates Quick and Dirty sims. She wants to plan and prep and get everything exactly right before she tells it to run. But she's also the best Q&D artiste I've ever worked with, and no-nonsense on a scramble. Time is too scarce for perfection when a ship is off Traffic.

"Assume a mass—small, but larger than a *Nashville* nav beacon." I pushed the *Nashville* specs over to her couch comp.

"Assume some system failure propelled that mass away from the *Reynolds* at the divert point. Can you get a sim that matches this track from there?" I pushed over the track data as well.

Liza went to work, talking to the comp and keying in code simultaneously.

"Three, One. What's the word, Ron?"

"One, Three. Trying to make sense of that track." I looked over at Liza. She had a frown on her face, but she looked at me and nodded. "One, Three. Mack, I think maybe somehow the *Reynolds* ejected her nav beacon. Believe the track record from the divert point forward is a bogie."

Cap looked at me in his overhead mirror. "You sure, Ron?"

Before I could answer, Liza jumped in. "Ninety-three percent, Cap. I'm pushing the sim to all channels now."

Cap opened the Command Circuit. "All Squads, Command Three. Please confirm receipt of sim. High probability track record is that of a separated nav beacon."

Confirmations came in, and then Mack returned in my ear. "Three, One. Nice eye, Ron. Liza have a projection for the rest of *Reynolds*?"

I looked at Liza. She was already waving for my attention, so I pulled her into the Scout Circuit.

"All Scouts, Prog Three. Revising sim with new projected zones based on how many pieces the *Reynolds* is in."

I was proud of her. Liza's good, but she's the most squeamish of the squad. Translated from cold jargon, she had just said "whether they might be alive or strewn dead across the surface," and with only a small tremor in her voice. I pushed her back out before she had the chance to say more. I didn't want to risk her voice cracking on an open circuit.

"All Scouts, Scout One. Cover projected zones indicated in the pop I'm pushing out now. Scout Three, you get the Good

News Zone." That's Scout slang for the zone with the highest chance of survivors. I must've done well in Mack's eyes. He always gives the harshest peer reviews I've ever experienced, but today, I had his endorsement.

Matching orders were coming into Cap on the Command Circuit as Liza turned us towards the Good News Zone. Good news? We could still hope.

LOGFILE:
REYNOLDS/PsgCbn/AVRec/2062:05:24:01:24:26

"Aaah ... Aaah, owww ..."

"Everyone ... please remain calm. Please ... don't remove ... your straps yet. We've tumbled and landed ... upside down. If you fall, you could get ...further injuries—"

"My arm!"

"I'll ... help. Give me a second. ... Now. Please ... give me the safety cushions. Young lady, please ... let go of the cushion. I need to put them down so ... there's a soft landing if anyone ... falls.

"Now, Mr. Zhou. ... No, he's unconscious. Mr. Reed, you look okay. Do you think you can unstrap and lower yourself down? I can help you, and the cushions ... can you make it?"

"I'll try, Steward. Let me ... okay, I'm coming down now. Slowly ..."

"I've got you.... OWWWWWWWWW ... I'm sorry ... dropped ..."

"The cushions worked, I'm okay. Steward Abraham? Are you all right?"

"I'm ... all right. Just need to ... rest a second. My side. Can you unstrap the others ... and lower them down?"

"Some of them are—"

"I know. We have ... enough to deal with. Let's not discuss casualties yet. Just ... lay them in the rear. You'll find blankets in the cupboard, so you can cover ... cover. ... Help me up, please. I need ... to get the first aid kit."

Liza had simmed a large ellipse of high-probability landing sites. It's never a "crash site." We never, *ever* say "crash site," not if we don't have to. Not until we see a crash and we just can't avoid the words any longer. Until then, always assume a safe landing at a *landing* site. Superstition? Fine, then it's our superstition.

Now, to find the *Reynolds*. I could choose one of the obvious strategies: start from the center of the ellipse and spiral out, or start from the edge and spiral in. But both were time consuming, and seconds were precious. So, while we flew, I tried to devise a better strategy.

Pilot reports mechanical failure, attempting soft landing. Okay, go with that. Doc had taught me his strategy in card games: when your cards aren't obviously winning or obviously losing, play as if the other cards are *exactly* what you need to win. The thinking is, you're stuck with the cards you have. If you can't win, it doesn't matter how you play; but if you *can* win, you have to play a specific way to do it. That's how I'd approach a search: assume the best and start from there.

So, assume the pilot maintained some control over the ship. What were his goals? Ground the *Reynolds* as close to Tycho Under, and to Rescue, as he possibly could.

Get her down as softly as he could.

Make her as easily discoverable as he could.

Bring her down someplace where the Second Quarter sunlight wouldn't cook the passengers if they had to evac.

The sun helped in the visibility goal but hurt the shelter goal. Sometimes there are no good answers, only the least bad options.

How would he—assuming a he, I hadn't checked the crew roster—prioritize these goals? Soft first? If they didn't survive the landing, the rest wouldn't matter. I cut out almost thirty percent of the ellipse because it overlapped an ejecta ray from Tycho's formation. That ray would be full of rocks, large and small, that could tear a hull to shreds in even a soft crash.

Close, visible, or sheltered? If he's worried about close, he won't worry about sheltered. Or would he? If he's considering an evac, he might be worrying about how far his passengers and crew might have to walk mid-month. A shorter walk might be the way he'd bet.

"Ron, I need a course."

Mari had followed a general approach vector, and I could see from the main comp that we were nearing the ellipse. We needed a specific vector ASAP.

There was a choice that was close *and* sheltered but risked not being soft. If he'd landed very near the ejecta ray, which was also near the closest edge of the ellipse, then the survivors could use the shadows of the large rocks for shelter. It was a classic trick from Lunar Survival School—manual thermal control. When your suit gets hot, duck behind rocks for a while and let it cool off. With practice, you can make maybe fifteen percent normal progress that way. That's better than zero, and could be the difference that keeps you alive.

A quick pull from the *Reynolds*'s records: Captain Neil Hardigan was a high-scoring graduate of Lunar Survival School and top-rated on *Nashville*-class transports. He knew the tricks, and he had the skills.

"Mari, bring us in on the nearest edge, and skirt along the ejecta ray here." I traced out a rough course and pushed it to her nav comp. "Low and slow. All eyes, you know the drill."

All couch comps shifted to camera-eye view as Mari brought us in low.

LOGFILE:
REYNOLDS/PsgCbn/AVRec/2062:05:24:01:29:31

"They're all down. I've covered. ... How are the injuries? I've had first aid training. Can I help?"

"Hmmm. ... Air is holding. I don't hear leaks. But ... you'll help more if you make sure we're sealed."

"But you—"

"I have a job to do. And I ... need your help. I'm moving slow, and ... we need to seal the cabin. Have you ever applied seal strips?"

"No."

"It's not hard. There's a roll in the cupboard. Our air seems to be holding, but there's no sense ... no sense skimping on strips. Tape every joint, every corner. Any place plates meet the frame. Lay down a strip, touch it with ... this activator, press the button, and you're done. If you hear a leak, strip it immediately ... and call me over."

"Strip, activator, repeat. Got it."

"I'll be ... I'll keep working on the injured."

Adam spotted the *Reynolds*. "Camera five." We all pulled five into focus. "It's bad. She's on her top, half in the shadow of that big boulder. The tail's pointed toward Tycho, so the pilot cabin's near that smaller boulder."

From Adam's description, I found the *Reynolds*. There was a large, crumpled dent in the exposed underbelly of the pilot cabin, roughly the shape of the small boulder.

"All Scouts, Scout Three. Confirmed sighting. Converge Beacon Three." Mari was already on course to the clearest spot, a little beyond the *Reynolds*.

A hopper's a rough ride. They're meant for speed and maneuverability, not comfort, and Mari knows how to make one dance. From spotting to contact lights in under 8 seconds—even Neil Armstrong and Buzz Aldrin might've balked at that approach. Mari cut the main engine, and the *Jacob Evans* was down.

"CTU Rescue, Command One. Supply drones converge Beacon Three."

A search often burned more fuel than a hopper could spare for the return flight, and sometimes we need more supplies than we can carry. The AI-piloted supply drones aren't built for search or first response, and they're uglier than sin ... but when they home in with supplies just as you're running low on null plasma or jump juice, they're the prettiest things you've ever seen.

As we hit regolith, the big side doors cycled open and we unstrapped. We dropped out to the lith, closely followed by our swarm of scan bots.

This was the start of A1: Assess. Adam briefed us.

"*Nashville*-class is an older transport—all function, no style. Flight frame's solid and reliable. Shell is standard civilian-grade hull tiles in the stock configuration: flight cabin, passenger cabin, pressurized cargo cabin, and unpressurized cargo deck."

Hull tiles have an ingenious design, stronger in their joins than in their middles. If there's going to be a hull stress break, it's far more likely to be in the middle than at a join—and the core within that middle contains vacuum resin. The epoxy bubbles up through cracks, then hardens to a rigid seal when it hits vacuum.

"Ron, I've found an attachment point for the Ear on the flight cabin. Let me know when the Pinger's attached."

I felt sorry for Adam—when he looked in through the port to the flight cabin, he said nothing. That crumple was where Hardigan would've been. If there were good news to report there, Adam would've been all over the circuits with it. The crumple was also where the nav beacon should've been, which provided the explanation for its ejection.

But that wasn't my concern now. I needed to get the Pinger to the other end, ASAP, so I could feed Adam some pings. I leaped up on top of the *Reynolds* and bounded across.

"Ron, be careful ..."

"Yes, Cap." On a smaller vessel, I might've just leaped over it in one bounce, but *Nashville*s are pretty long. Cap was right; I couldn't risk a spill. First rule of the Academy: "Don't add to the casualty list."

I was about to leap down when I heard something.

LOGFILE:
REYNOLDS/PsgCbn/AVRec/2062:05:24:01:38:54

"All right, Miss Drew. Just a little needle prick ... I know, it hurts, but it's in now. You've ... lost some blood, so you need null plasma. I'll ... just tape this down, so the needle will stay in."

"I need to get out of here!"

"Please, relax. We can't leave ... we're waiting for Rescue."

"You have emergency suits, right? Where's, where ... wh—"

"What happened?"

"She's fine, Mr. Reed. I added a sedative to her IV, so she doesn't ... injure herself further."

"Steward Abraham, I've used up the seal strips. Are there more?"

"In the cupboard ... but I think we're good for now. I checked the pressure gauge, we're holding."

"I can probably work the radio. Should I call for help?"

"No radio. Antenna's on the roof. Was on the roof. Gone ... crushed now."

"Steward! I hear something on the roof."

"*Shh.* Everyone, quiet for a moment. Listen ..."

Thump ... Thump ...

"Someone's up there. Everyone ... strike the walls! Find something solid and hit the walls."

Newcomers to Luna have an understandable misconception that the surface is quiet because of the vacuum. Actually, you bring your noise with you: suit noises, comm chatter, comp feeds, your own breathing. And air isn't the only way to conduct sound. It'll conduct through any good rigid object, including parts of a suit—even the boots. Our boots are pretty rigid, both for pressure and for traction on the regolith. I heard, and also felt, a slight thumping beneath my feet.

"Cap, thumping inside. Someone heard me."

Cap relayed the good news as I leaped down. That meant I was likely wasting my time. The Pinger and the Ear form an acoustic hull integrity tester, and the hull was probably intact if there were survivors. Still, I attached and activated the Pinger.

LOGFILE:
REYNOLDS/PsgCbn/AVRec/2062:05:24:01:40:17

Weeoweoweee ... Weeoweoweee ...
   "Good news! Tycho Rescue is here."
   Weeoweoweee ... Weeoweoweee ...
   "What's that sound?"
   "They call it a Pinger. It sends coded ... acoustics through the hull. At the other end of the ship, they've attached an Ear."
   Weeoweoweee ... Weeoweoweee ...
   "The Ear receives pings and measures how they propagate ... through the hull. Rescue compares the results against the acoustic signature from our last maintenance review. The Ear filters the echoes into a 3D model of our flight frame, hull ... contents ..."
   Weeoweoweee ... Weeoweoweee ...

The Ear pushed its model to Liza's suit comp. She integrated the acoustic model and the visual model from the darting scan bots into a sim of the crash site.

   There, I'd thought it at last: *crash site*. Hardigan had done an admirable job, given what I could see. The *Reynolds* would never fly again, but the ship wasn't a total loss and there were survivors. I was sure Hardigan wasn't one of them. Liza pushed her model to our suit comps and confirmed my suspicions.

   "Sim fit is ninety-seven percent. Some glitch in the cooling system blew a chunk right out of the flight cabin, took the nav beacon, long-range comm, and part of the guidance system with it. Captain Hardigan must've been suited because he survived to seal the cabins. Then with crippled guidance, he brought the *Reynolds* down here. He would've made it if he'd cleared that boulder. The sim says he could have, but that probably would've ripped the bottom out of the passenger cabin. He took it himself. Sim and acoustics say his lower half was crushed." She swallowed, a dry, painful sound. "Probably instant."

LOGFILE:
REYNOLDS/PsgCbn/AVRec/2062:05:24:01:41:58

"Where are they?"

"Working. Protocol for our safety ... the Four As. Assess, Atmosphere, Access ... Assist. If they don't follow protocol, we could ... lose our air."

"Cap, problem here." Adam pushed the structural model into the common view. "Flight frame is intact, but seriously twisted."

"Any join breaks?"

"Weak spots, no breaks."

I was already ahead of Adam and working my way around the hull, applying seal strips from my roll wherever the model showed a weakness. The scan bots helped, lasers pinpointing the weakest areas. Apply a strip, then apply the activator to dissolve the seal granules, little carbon bubbles with vacuum resin in them. You wouldn't want to fly in a vessel patched together with seal strips, but you wouldn't have to worry about losing air. This was A2: Atmosphere. "If they can't breathe, you can't save 'em" is the second rule at Rescue Academy.

"But that's not the problem," he continued. "It's the airlocks. This ship has three. In the nose, the side, and the roof."

"And the nose is gone, and she's flat on her roof. Let me guess ... the frame is too twisted to open the side lock?"

"You got it, Cap. Impact with the boulder and then the tumble stressed it too much. We *might* get it open. We'd never close it again."

"Where's the best access?"

"Bottom—well, topside now. Least chance we'll injure someone."

"Ron, how's the stripping?"

"Still about a dozen joins to hit. One or two could use a second strip."

"Keep on that. We'll unship the lock. But take a moment to establish comm if you can. Tell 'em we're coming in through the top, and to stand clear. Don't want to drop anything on them."

Cap, Doc, and Adam went back to the *Jake* to unship the rear airlock. Rescue hoppers are modified so the rear lock is removable. We can fix it to a hull, seal strip it good and tight, and *voila*, instant airlock. It's massive, but nothing three strong men can't handle in Lunar G.

Meanwhile, I checked the broadband comm scanner. No signals other than us and our data bands. I pulled the Pinger from my belt again and hooked it to my comm line. The Pinger's a multiuse device: it can ping, and it can also serve as a conduction speaker to project into a vessel. It could also give me at least a muffled listen into the interior. I affixed it to a join where the model showed good hull contact.

LOGFILE:
REYNOLDS/PsgCbn/AVRec/2062:05:24:01:43:26

"Anyone inside *Reynolds*, this is CTU Rescue Three. If you can hear my voice, strike something solid three times."

"Everyone ... quiet."

Clang, clang, clang.

"*Reynolds*, we're beginning rescue efforts. More squads are en route. Do you need medical assistance? Strike once for yes, twice for no."

Clang!

"How many injured?"

Clang, clang, clang, clang.

"How many able?"

Clang. Clang.

Six survivors, four injured. We never ask the last question: How many dead? It only depresses or even panics the survivors. Their departure log told the tale: Captain Hardigan, one steward, fourteen passengers. Ten dead already.

"Have you begun first aid?" *Clang.* This person was good. I checked the log again. "Is this Abraham?" *Clang.*

Martha Abraham, ship's steward. The odds for the survivors just went up. Abraham was fully rated on emergency protocols, first aid, and Lunar survival.

"Martha, I'm Ron Ward. Have you sealed your joins?" *Clang.* I could stop stripping. Her internal seals would hold far better than mine. "Fantastic. Martha, we're rigging a lock in the deck center, aft of the thruster assembly. You read?" *Clang!* "Okay, get your passengers clear so we don't drop anything on them." *Clang.* "Martha, I've gotta help with the lock. You're going to be all right." *Clang.* I hoped she believed it. I was starting to.

LOGFILE:
REYNOLDS/PsgCbn/AVRec/2062:05:24:01:45:18

"All right ... Rescue is here. Mr. Reed, please help ... keep everyone in the front."

"Cap, ship's steward has stripped the seals internally and started first aid. I can help with the lock."

"Negative. We've got it. Bounce topside, help us lift from there."

As I returned topside, I saw the *Alex Evans* landing a safe distance away. Rescue One had arrived. In the distance, I saw nose jets from the other hoppers. It was about to get crowded here, but nothing wrong with that. Six Doctors for four injured is much better odds than just Doc and me. I'm a fair field medic, but not even close to an MD. We Scouts could run null plasma to the docs, carry wounded, and otherwise play G3s, but the Doctors did the critical work.

I looked down and the lock was hullside, waiting for me. I crouched and grabbed hold. "Got it." Then, just like a drill, my squaddies took turns bouncing up to join me while the others held the lock up. As soon as we were more up than down, we hoisted the lock up and over.

Cap and Doc bounced up as Adam directed us on where to place the lock. Again, just like drill, Adam and Doc crouched down and we placed it over them. That way, they could start work inside as it pressurized. We fixed the lock to the flight frame with mag clamps as Adam directed, then I spread a liberal helping of seal strips all around the joins. Before I got halfway around, I ran into Mack laying strips from the other side, under the guidance of his engineer, Matt Winter.

"Howdy, Mack."

"Howdy, Ron. Seals look good. I'm pressurizing."

As soon as there was enough air pressure to confirm the seals, Adam set to work on the hull plates. This was A3: Access, sometimes the trickiest part.

LOGFILE:
REYNOLDS/PsgCbn/AVRec/2062:05:24:01:47:50

"What's that noise?"

"They're grinding the hull plates. Plates are attached with ... molecular adhesive, don't want to let go."

"So, they're cutting through the plates?"

"No. Vacuum resin in the plates is a sticky mess. Worse when you hit vacuum ... whole suit goes rigid. So, they'll remove plates at joins. Just takes time ...."

Adam and Doc were hard at work on the joins. I watched them using the lock's cam. Adam picked out and ground cuts into the joins, and then Doc applied solvent. Working their way around, they soon had one plate free, enough for a slim hand to snake through and shake Doc's gloved hand. No, they weren't shaking ...

LOGFILE:
REYNOLDS/PsgCbn/AVRec/2062:05:24:01:48:37

"Steward Abraham, I'm Doctor Jones."
"Good to ... see you, Doctor. We need more null plasma ..."
"Martha, you sound weak."
"Doctor, please ... null plasma. Still have passengers in shock."
"All right, here's my aid pack. We'll have more when the lock is working."

"God blessed—"
Adam had been working on the third plate, which would give them enough room for Access in suits, but he held up his grinder. On camera, I could see that the grind shaft had snapped clear off.
"Adam, we've got Matt's kit here. You need another grind wheel?"
Doc cut in as he started shedding his suit. "Negative. I don't want to waste time on a pressure cycle. People are in bad shape down there. Adam, unsuit. We can squeeze in through the gap."
I was sure Doc's lanky frame would fit, but Adam would have a tight squeeze. Adam's a moose. I've never been Downside, so I've never seen an actual moose ... but if they're as large as Adam, they must be impressive.
"Once we're in, we pull in our gear, then Ron can fold down the lock doors and let Matt and the other Doctors in."
The pressure doors on portable locks are panels that fold up against the side walls, then down to seal the lock. They're

not fancy like a modern passenger lock, just functional and reliable.

"Good call, Doc." Adam pulled off his helmet and started stripping off his suit.

LOGFILE:
REYNOLDS/PsgCbn/AVRec/2062:05:24:01:48:37

"I've got you, Doctor."

"Thank you, Mr. ...?"

"Reed, Johann Reed."

"Adam, hand down my pack and then join us. Johann, my backpack unfolds into a stretcher capsule, which we'll likely need. Can you help Adam assemble it?"

"Doctor ... here."

"Martha?"

"Mr. Zhou is the worst. Compound ... fracture and ..."

"Martha, let me—"

"*Compound fracture* and multiple lacerations from flying debris. Also suspect internal injuries from ... restraining harness. I've given three ... four units of null plasma. Pressure's up but sinking again. Shock ..."

"Yes, I expect he is in shock. I'll take care of him, and you should lie down."

"Other passengers need me. I'll be over here. Be fine ..."

"Okay.... Adam, Johann, if you're done with the stretcher, Martha could use some help with the other passengers. Don't let her exert herself."

The other Doctors queued up with Matt to enter the lock. Doc was already deep into A4: Assist. He was pushing reports out on the Doctor Circuit for opinions: compound fracture, lacerations, restraint-induced internal injuries, shock; concussion, multiple fractures, possible internal injuries, shock; concussion, possible hematoma; multiple lacerations, sedated to prevent further injuries; internal injuries, likely severe, shock.

"Pressure zero. Let's go!"

Matt opened the outer lock door and he and the Doctors climbed in. It would be a tight fit—he could remove more plates in there, but all I could see on the lock's cam was Doctors' legs. Some of them unsuited to crawl through while Matt worked.

I hate these strange, idle moments we get at odd times in a rescue. There's literally nothing I can do for a while, even though every impulse in me is screaming at me to do *something*. Third rule of the Academy: "Hurry kills." Those idle-tense moments are when I most wonder why I took this job. Just when my adrenaline is pumping hardest, I have to sit and wonder and plan for the unforeseen, because I can't do anything. The fight-or-flight response kicks in hard, and I hate it.

Matt pulled up the third tile, and the remaining Doctors dropped inside. He dropped in their packs as we Scouts queued up to help our Docs.

LOGFILE:
REYNOLDS/PsgCbn/AVRec/2062:05:24:01:52:34

"Jones, where we at?"

"Compound fractures and lacerations are bandaged up, and I've stabilized BPs. The steward did a fantastic job."

"The steward? Really?"

"Uh-huh. Ultrasound confirms concussions and hematoma, so I've started fluids, null plasma, and analgesics."

"And the internal case?"

"Now that you're here, I'll take care of her."

Doc came across the all-hands circuit. "Scouts, hold back. Matt, can you help us lift? Stretcher capsule coming out."

If Doc had a patient, *I* had a patient. My chief duty on the lith is as the Doc's corpsman. I shouldered aside Mack and the other Scouts, leaped up on top of the lock, and checked the indicators. "Cap, depressurizing at fifteen percent." I looked at Cap, and he nodded—we could spare that much air. I keyed the override, and the lock opened with a brief white puff as moisture in the air sublimated.

Matt and Doc were ready when I reached down. They had the stretcher poles right where I expected them. Hand-over-hand, I hauled out the stretcher capsule, a large plastic bubble stretched between two poles. A comp on the side hooked to cables and hoses that snaked into the form strapped to the base. I tried not to look too closely; too much red, and I would get a closer look all too soon.

Mack helped me steady the stretcher as Doc bounced out and began issuing more orders. "Cap, emergency evac here. Spleen, liver, maybe more. Can you spare the *Jake*?"

"Plenty of rides home here. Go!"

Doc nodded and gave one last instruction. "Mari, prep the table."

We dropped down to the regolith, and the Scouts passed us the stretcher. Then we set off in a long lope designed to cover ground quickly without losing control or jolting the patient too much.

"Operate here, or do we evac?"

"Both, I fear ... but let's plan on evac."

The spleen was pretty serious for a field operation. Doc wouldn't consider it if the patient had good odds of reaching CTU. I didn't look forward to this trip.

The big doors of the *Jake* were already sealed except for port aft, the door where we bring in patients. Mari had stayed on board, keeping the hopper ready for a quick departure. Too often, we need every spare second in getting the injured to the hospital.

We reached the big door in a hurry and lifted the stretcher through. Mari closed and sealed the door, and we clamped the stretcher capsule to the table. The umbilicals hooked in automatically, and the med comp lit up with a body scan and readings. As the cabin pressurized, we strapped into our couches. Mari didn't wait for us to let her know—she hit launch as soon as the board showed three greens.

As soon as the initial thrust ended, she called back, "Quick or smooth, Doc?"

"Let me check." He pulled up the table diagnostics. "Damn. Smooth, Mari. Ron, masks and gloves. She can't wait."

For the first time, I looked closely at our patient, and all I could do was mutter "Liar" under my breath. Martha Abraham wasn't on the able list—not even close.

I pulled up Doc's log. She had to have known she had internal injuries—maybe not the spleen specifically, but she must have been in a hellish amount of pain. Yet she had struggled to stay conscious, treat the injured, comfort them, and assure them that Tycho Rescue would find them soon. Then she communicated with me, took supplies from Doc, and applied more treatment. Not until all the Doctors were inside would she let Doc look at her.

You're one hell of a strong woman, Martha.

Now Doc was saying without saying that she wouldn't survive the trip without emergency surgery. The ride settled enough for us to unstrap. We stripped off our gloves and helmets. Then, as Doc popped the stretcher and looked over Martha, I got out the sterile packs. I opened a set of bath gloves and offered them to Doc. He thrust his hands in, then yanked them out, as sterile as modern science could manage. Then I put his sterile op gloves on, careful to only touch the removable grips. Same with his mask. When I pulled the grips off, Doc was clean.

Before I could ask, Mari hit the autopilot long enough to help me with my gloves and mask. If Madhu weren't such a good friend and Helen weren't my wife, I could go for Mari. She can practically read my mind.

The autoclave and the supply locker were both open and ready. I started handing Doc whatever he needed: scalpels, clamps, scissors, sponges, and far too much null plasma. Three times I had to adjust the anesthetic on the stretcher. Whether from pain or the ride, or just pure stubbornness, Martha kept struggling up from sleep.

Finally, Doc adjusted it. Not that he didn't trust me, but this was delicate: too much would kill her, and not enough would let her keep struggling and kill herself. While I held an incision open for him, he tweaked some levels up and others down, until Martha settled down. Then he picked the scalpel back up and resumed work.

And so, we passed the trip back. It seemed to take a Lunar day or more, but the ship's clock read twenty-three minutes when Mari said, "Approach, Doc. Do we circle, or do we land? I have clearance for Watson Pad."

Watson Medical Labs was the finest hospital on Luna, and also the top-rated ER.

"Two minutes, then land." He didn't tell her to have a team ready. They all knew their jobs. "Another plasma, then let's start packing this. Surgical tape. No sense in sutures, they'll have to open her right up again."

I slapped another unit of plasma into the stretcher as Doc pumped some drugs into her IV. Then we closed her up as best we could, and strapped in.

Right on schedule, Mari took us down. Not many pilots outside of Rescue are certified to land at Watson. The Pad is right next to the emergency room, with a dome that can be extended over a ship for fast evac. One slip in landing could be a disaster *and* shut down a big part of the disaster relief mechanism. Mari made no slips.

We landed and didn't wait for pressure—we had Martha's stretcher sealed and mobile again, ready to go. The big doors opened, and the suited emergency team lifted her onto a gurney. They left at a run, Doc keeping pace and filling them in on her latest stats.

That left Mari to taxi the *Jake* back out, and me with nothing to do. The adrenaline rush was over, the stress was gone, and the exhaustion wasted no time settling in. I hustled to get inside the lock so they could clear the dome, but that was the last hustle I had left for the day.

I shuffled down Under and took the tram to the Rescue offices. On automatic pilot, I found my desk and started my incident report. That's boring work, but after a crash, boring is about all I can do.

I'd started reviewing the model, trying to make sense of how the nav beacon and comm unit were lost (T.I. will probably ground all the *Nashville*s for a cooling system overhaul, because that was the likely cause), when the *Reynolds* AV record logs came in on the Rescue net. Reviewing logs takes even less energy than paperwork does, so I switched on the log player. After scrolling to the beginning, I watched the camera-eye view from inside the *Reynolds*.

LOGFILE:
REYNOLDS/PsgCbn/AVRec/2062:05:24:01:54:10

"Can you believe that steward?"

"Not sure I could've held up like she did. Transport Academy can take pride in their first aid classes. I don't think any of these patients would've lived if she hadn't been here."

"And the pain she must've been in—the shock."

"Uh-huh. Jones has his work cut out for him."

"Do you think she'll make it?"

"..."

And there's my why, always the same why. I could walk away from this whole business, but Martha Abraham's out there because her passengers need her. And Martha needs me ... they all need me. What choice do I have?

I was reopening the paperwork files when a pop announced the news of the successful rescue of the *Reynolds*. The squads were inbound with survivors.

About the time I realized I'd reread the same hull specs for the fourth time and still didn't know what they said, there was another pop: the announcement of the Lovell Medal for Command in Service to Crew, Vessel, and Mission, awarded to

Captain Neil Hardigan, Pilot *Reynolds*; and to Lieutenant Martha Abraham, First Steward.

Both awards were posthumous.

I shut down my desk comp and set course for the Old Town Tavern and the largest whiskey they would serve me. Needed or not, I was done.

At least for tonight. Tomorrow is another day in Rescue.

INTRODUCTION TO THE VAMPIRE'S
NEW CLOTHES

One of the fringe benefits of winning Writers of the Future is that you get to meet and know the judges, professional writers who take a real interest in your career. I am constantly amazed how much they believe in the contest goal: Pay it forward.

Among those judges was the late Mike Resnick, the most award-winning author in short science fiction—and one hell of a nice guy (underneath his occasionally acerbic wit). Mike was on the Pay it forward *bandwagon long before he became a judge, helping new authors in countless ways. He was a genial person and a generous mentor. And a good friend.*

And he was sneaky! I thought I had found a clear hole in the plot of one of his stories. I was so smugly pleased with myself when I wrote him and asked, "Hey, how do you explain this?"

Without missing a beat, Mike answered, "I don't know. Write it and we'll find out."

I did. And Mike bought it for Galaxy's Edge, *the magazine he edited. And now you can read it here. (You don't have to read* Stalking the Vampire *to appreciate this story, but you should read it anyway.)*

So, this story can only be dedicated in memoriam to Mike Resnick. I hope I made you proud, Writer Dad.

THE VAMPIRE'S NEW CLOTHES

R epeat your instructions back to me, Renfield. I must be
sure that you know your part in my plans."

The Master's voice was rich and velvety, with a thick
accent that the little man to whom he spoke couldn't identify.
He was a tall man with dark hair in a widow's peak. He was
cultured, powerful, and impeccably dressed in a dark tuxedo, a
crisp white shirt, and a dark crimson silk bow tie. A small,
blood-red rose was pinned to his left lapel. That rose fascinated
the other man.

Both men stood in a luxuriously-appointed room with
polished marble floors and walls, hung with lush gold curtains.
All of the furniture was upholstered in tasteful shades of green,
and thick red and gold rugs covered much of the floor. Unlike
the Master, the little man looked completely out of place in this
imposing room. He wore a sloppy gray sweatshirt, sagging
jeans, and worn sneakers that might once have been red. His
brown hair was unkempt, and his face was dirty. He felt much
more shabbily dressed than the Master, and he wished he had a

rose. He reached out a very long fingernail but didn't quite touch the flower.

"Renfield!" the Master said, and again the other man ignored him. The Master grabbed the short man's shoulder and shook it. "RENFIELD!"

The man cringed, his spray of hair waving as he looked up, down, left, right, all around the darkened room—anywhere but at the tall man. "I'm sorry, Master. I forgot that was my name. Ummm ... because it's not."

The Master scowled, revealing long, sharp canine teeth. "So, what *is* your name?"

The short man looked down at his left shoe. It was tapping on the plush gold and red carpet, and he stared at it, surprised by his own foot. "I forgot."

The Master stared up at the arched ceiling. "Well, I have to call you something. Until you remember a better one, your name is Renfield. Understood?"

Renfield stomped on his left foot with his right. He yelped, but the tapping stopped. "Yes, Master."

"And so your answer is ...?"

"Ummm ... yes, Master?"

The Master leaned over Renfield, and the little man leaned his head back, almost falling over. "Answer my question!" the Master shouted.

At the shout, Renfield *did* fall over; but without thinking, he flipped into a backward handspring and then landed in a crouch on a marble-topped table, his long, skinny limbs bent out like the legs of some giant spider. Renfield liked hand-springs, they were fun. But he didn't like upsetting the Master. "Ummm ..." He covered his head with one hand. "What was the question?"

"WHAT ARE YOUR INSTRUCTIONS?" The Master's

voice grew strong and deep, filling the large room. The chandelier swung.

Renfield dropped down and scurried under the table, but the Master snatched him by the collar, lifted him bodily into the air, and held him so they were face to face. The little man closed his eyes and whispered, "I forgot."

The Master sighed—a strange, breathless sound—and he set Renfield back on his feet. In a quieter voice, he said, "Write this down this time."

"But Master ... ummm ... I don't know how to write."

The Master raised one dark, bushy eyebrow. "This is the twenty-first century. Who doesn't know how to write?"

"Oh, lots of people, Master. So many ... I'll bet there's a list somewhere! But I can't read it ..."

"Never mind! That's not important!" The Master looked at the ceiling, counted quietly to ten, and tried again. "If I go through this slowly, can you remember it?"

"I'll try, Master."

"'I'll try,' he says," the Master muttered. "Why did I ever come to Manhattan instead of London? They have a much higher class of lunatics there. All right, try, Renfield. Try very hard."

The Master paced back and forth as he spoke. A picture of a field of sunflowers was on the wall behind him, and Renfield found the picture distracting. So pretty. "To begin ... Soon it will be sunrise, and I must retire to my bed."

Renfield raised his hand and said, "You mean the box of dirt in the coat closet? I planted some purple irises in it."

The Master stopped pacing and glared. "You planted ... irises ... in my sacred native soil?"

"Uh-huh. I thought they looked pretty." Irises were his favorite flowers. Well, irises and roses. And sunflowers were nice, too.

"You do know that flowers need sunlight to grow, don't you?"

"Oh." Renfield squinted as if thinking was painful for him. Then his eyes grew wide. "I know! I could haul the box out onto the balcony and open it up for them!"

In an instant, Renfield again hung from the Master's grip, and the Master's dark, almost black eyes peered straight into his own watery blue ones. "Listen to me very carefully," the Master said in a quiet, tense tone. "Don't ever say that again. Don't ever *think* that again. And in the name of Darkness, *don't ever do that!* Understood?" Renfield nodded, jiggling in the Master's grip. "All right. I shall let you live."

The Master dropped Renfield (who landed cat-like on all fours) and resumed pacing and talking. "Tomorrow night, I suspect I shall finally confront the Great Detective. So, you—"

"But, Master," Renfield said. He didn't dare rise from his crouch, and he was ready to race away at any moment. "How do you know that you'll confront the Great Detective?"

"It is inevitable, Renfield. The forces of fate always drive me to confront my one worthy opponent of the era: the Great Vampire Hunter. Once, long ago, it would have been the Great Prince. Later it might be the Great Knight or the Great Professor. Occasionally it has even been the Great Werewolf, or another vampire. But always it is a lonely hunter with but a few companions, often fighting the established authorities as well as me. And ever since that fool on Baker Street, it has been Great Detectives. They are the knights of this modern age."

"Oooh ..." Renfield rose, and then bent his legs and held out his arm, as though holding a sword. "I like knights!" He lunged forward with his imaginary sword, thrusting and parrying at his unseen foe. "Avast, knave, defend yourself!"

The Master said slowly, "'Avast' is for pirates. You mean 'Halt, knave!'"

Renfield lowered his sword arm. "Are you sure?"

The Master shouted, "Does it matter?" Once again, he counted to ten. The Master liked counting, Renfield thought. He seemed to do it a lot. "Does it matter? The sun will be up soon, and you will have a mission, so pay attention. While I rest, you will take that garment bag ..." He pointed at a large linen bag hanging by the door. "... and you will take it to the Great Detective's building. You will climb up to his office and break in—"

"Which building is that?"

"The one we drove past last night?" The Master paused, waiting for Renfield to show a sign of recognition. "The five-story red brick office building?" Another pause, and then the Master shouted, "The one I told you to remember because the Great Detective's office was in there?"

Renfield squinted very hard. Then he remembered ... "The one with the honeysuckle on the front?" Honeysuckles were his favorite flowers.

"Yes!" The chandelier trembled, and the Master lowered his voice. "Yes, the one with the honeysuckle on the front. Maybe you're not hopeless after all. You will climb up to his office and break in, and you will hide this garment bag in the coat closet near the window. Can you remember that?"

Renfield nodded. "Honeysuckle ... Climb up ... Garment bag ... Closet ..." He continued nodding as he recited, because nodding was fun. But then he stopped and asked, "Why, Master? What's in the bag?"

"My spare suit."

Renfield looked at the bag. "You're giving the Great Detective your suit?"

"No," the Master said, "the suit is for me."

"But, Master, you already have a suit. You already have *two* suits. Why should I put one in the closet?"

"Because I said so!" the Master shouted. Renfield scurried back under the table, but then the Master tried again in a calmer voice. "Because I am not one of these Hollywood vampires who do whatever some hack writer wants them to do. No, I am Lord of the Night, but even I have rules. I can change into a bat, but I cannot change my clothes with me. I must leave those behind. *Now* do you understand?"

Renfield poked his head out. "No, Master."

The Master bent down until he was nose to nose with Renfield, who promptly ducked back under the table. "Then let me be clear," the Master said. "When I finally confront the Great Detective, I must do so in my finest style, not stark naked. I have a reputation to maintain! I shall *not* confront him with my three thousand-year-old *pulă* hanging out!"

Renfield wondered what a *pulă* was. He thought he knew, but he was afraid that asking would anger the Master again. Before he could decide, a rare flash of insight led to a better question, one that might even impress the Master. "But Master, can't you just memorize him to *think* you have clothes?"

But Renfield was doomed to disappointment. The Master didn't get angry, but he got scornful. "That's *mesmerize*, you fool. And no, I can't mesmerize him unless I can get him to concentrate on my eyes. That won't happen with my *pulă* hanging out, drawing attention. It may be three thousand years old, but it's still impressive."

The Master sighed. "No, in final confrontations like this, when I know I must arrive as a bat, it is vital that I swoop in the window, swiftly change my form and my clothes, and *then* confront the Great Detective. To do that, my trusted ally"—he looked at Renfield and cocked an eyebrow—"must secrete my clothes on the final battlefield. Can you do that for me, Renfield?"

Renfield wasn't sure what *secrete* meant. Or rather, he

thought he was sure, but how could he do *that* with *clothes*? It sounded painful.

But he was afraid to anger the Master again, and nodding was still fun, so he nodded again. At that, the Master smiled, showing his long fangs in that way that always scared Renfield; but before Renfield could hide again, the Master yanked him out from under the table and back to his feet. "Very good, Renfield. Very good. I must rest now; the sun is about to rise. Here is some money so you can ride a cab to the office. You have all day to do this one task. Can I trust you, Renfield?" Renfield feared the Master, and he wanted to do a good job. Doing a good job was important, Mama always said that (though he couldn't explain why). Besides, when the Master was satisfied, he was less frightening, so Renfield relaxed and kept nodding.

Then the Master grabbed him by the throat with one knotted hand, and Renfield was frightened once more. The Master pulled him in close, stared into his eyes, and whispered, "One more thing: *no irises!*"

Renfield danced down the stairs and through the mortuary lobby. There was no music, but he danced anyway, twirling the garment bag like a beautiful lady. Somewhere there was music, he was sure, and so he danced through the door and to the Manhattan sidewalk, which was still damp from last night's rain.

He liked dancing almost as much as handstands. And flowers. And knights. And *real* scissors (not *safety* scissors). And staplers. And doing a good job and pleasing the Master.

Renfield knew he was different. Papa had called him *a failure*, Mama had called him *a burden*, and the police had called him *a dummy*. The woman in the white coat had called him a *deluge* (at least he thought that was the word), and the man in the black robe had called him *a danger to himself*. The attendants in the Home called him *special*. But the Master called him *an ally*. He gave him work to do, important work, and that was more than the attendants had done. They had let him do some small tasks when he had first arrived, but every time he had trouble with a task, they took it away and did it for him. They never gave him another chance, they told him how special he was, and soon they did everything for him. For a while they had let him make cloth dolls. He couldn't figure out needle and thread, but he could staple the cloth together. Then they decided that even a stapler and safety scissors were too hard for him. Little kids could use staplers and safety scissors, but not him! They were very nice, but they treated him like a not-very-bright animal, and the Home was his cage. Renfield knew the Master was not a nice person and did not-nice things; but even when the Master was angry, he treated Renfield like a person, and so Renfield had run away from the Home to serve him.

And Renfield knew he didn't see things right. Sometimes he saw things that weren't there, or saw them wrong. That was what made white-coat woman called him *a deluge* (though what water had to do with it, he didn't know—he never saw water that wasn't there). But he couldn't help it; he tried to see what she told him to, but he couldn't, and it hurt to try. He was comfortable with the world he saw. So, when he saw yellow elephants in the street where other people saw yellow cabs, he was okay with that. Either one would take him to the honey-suckle office, right?

Amid the cars and trucks that rolled past, splashing water as they went, there was an elephant just down the potholed street. (Or maybe it was a cab?) Now what did people say to call an elephant? Renfield was sure he had seen that on TV (though the elephants looked like cars there). Was it ...

"Taxes!" Renfield shouted, but the elephant did not budge.

"Toxic!" Neither did the turbaned man who sat atop the elephant.

Renfield paused, frowning and trying to think, but before he could shout "Ticks!" the elephant rumbled like an out-of-tune car engine and started ambling forward.

Renfield ran after the elephant. "Wait! Wait! Text!"

But suddenly he saw that the elephant had left behind a big, stinking pile of ... Or was it motor oil? Either way, he didn't want to step in it. Instead, he leaped forward and over the mess, arcing into a handspring and bouncing back on his feet. That was so much fun, he did two more handsprings and landings before finally coming to rest, panting and smiling. He leaned over to catch his breath, resting his hands on his knees.

Renfield looked at his left hand. It was empty.

He looked at his right hand. It was empty, too. Something was missing, but it took a moment for him to remember what.

He looked back at the puddle of oil (or pile of dung?) and saw the Master's garment bag laying in it. He took a step toward the bag—just in time to see a truck swing by and run over it, splattering the whatever. A big, wet drop landed right in front of his foot.

Renfield carefully took one step back. The garment bag was crumpled, and it lay in the middle of a wide, stinking mess. Renfield needed to retrieve it before another car ran over it, but he didn't want to touch the stink if he could help it.

He looked around the street. There were people walking everywhere, but none of them would look at him. He was used to that, but he didn't like it. No one wanted to see him. There was no one he could turn to for help.

Then he saw a newspaper box. He could lay down papers

to get to the bag, but that would mean spending his cab money. What should he do? But he had no choice: the cab without the bag did him no good, but maybe the bag without the cab would. So, he put some change in and opened the box.

As soon as the box was open, people appeared around him, reaching in and grabbing papers. They jostled him aside, ignoring him as they fought for free stuff. Then he heard the door clang shut, and the people wandered off.

This time Renfield used caution. He looked around to make sure no one was near. Then he slipped more money in, opened the door just enough to fit his hand in, and snatched out a newspaper. A young blonde woman ran up just as he slammed the door shut. She glared at him and walked away.

He walked back to the splatter. It took almost every section of the paper, but he was able to build a bridge out to the garment bag. Using a bit of paper as a guard, he lifted the bag from the stink. Then he used the last sheet to wipe the bag as clean as he could. He hoped the bag had done its job and kept the suit clean.

Then Renfield backed along the bridge. As he went, he carefully picked up the papers. Before Mama had decided he was a burden, she had stressed to him: *Always clean up after yourself.* He didn't know where she was now, but secretly he was sure she was watching. He didn't want to disappoint her. When he got back to the clean sidewalk, he folded up the paper —careful not to touch the stink—and put it in a trash can. The can was full to overflowing, but he made the paper fit. "There you go, Mama."

Now he didn't have enough money for a cab. Well, he didn't really know how much money he needed for a cab, and he wasn't sure how much money he had. He knew how to count, but he got distracted when he did. So *maybe* he had enough money, but he still wasn't sure how to call. "Here, elephant!" he shouted, but neither an elephant nor a cab appeared.

So, he would have to walk. Renfield was sure he knew the way, or at least the direction, and he had all day. How long could it take to cross Manhattan?

Much later he had his answer: *too long.* After countless wrong turns and corrections—not to mention occasional showers through the day—he was sure he was on the right track, but not sure how long that track was. There were so many streets in this city, and they all looked the same! He tried to ask directions, but people avoided him even more than usual thanks to the stink of the garment bag. Soon he got hungry, and he spent more of his cab fare to buy a hot dog from a cart; but the vendor yelled about the smell and waved him away as soon as money changed hands, so he went back to wandering.

Eventually Renfield stopped looking at the streets. He tried remembering the gardens: park gardens, window gardens, community gardens, even the occasional yard garden. He wasn't sure, but he thought he recognized them from the night before. Gardens—especially flowers—meant more to him than streets did. So, he stopped trying to think, and he let the asters and mums and Rose of Sharon guide his way. He felt that they were speaking to him, leading him somewhere. Asters were his favorite flowers. Or maybe mums.

Then suddenly he knew where they were leading him, and he broke into a wide grin. In one large garden with a high spiked fence, he saw *sunflowers!* Not as many as in the Master's painting, but more than he could count. He hadn't seen them the night before. Maybe they had turned down, waiting for the sun? Now, though, they stood there in all their golden glory, absorbing the warm autumn sunlight that broke through the remaining clouds! They were as tall as him, some taller.

He had to see them. Touch them. The garden gate was locked, but Renfield was a good climber. He carefully hung the garment bag inside the high fence, with the hangers hooked around one spike. Then he clambered up and over, grateful for once that people ignored him, and dropped down into the garden.

Renfield walked up to the nearest blossom, stuck his face up it, and inhaled deeply. He had never smelled sunflowers before. The scent was green, earthy, and just a little sweet, but so faint he might miss it if he wasn't so close.

He smelled another. And another. The plants were in six rows, spaced so a person could just fit between them. He zigzagged through the plot from bloom to bloom, smelling and touching and laughing. Their leaves were still damp, and he laughed as they showered him with cool droplets. Among all his favorite flowers, sunflowers were his *favorite* flowers! So tall and sheltering and beautiful.

Renfield forgot about the garment bag. He forgot about the Master and the Great Detective. He forgot about the elephants and the Home and his parents and the city. He forgot about time. For this instant, with these tall flowers and their scents surrounding him and hiding him, he was transported to someplace else, someplace he couldn't name. Unless that name was *Happiness*.

But happiness never lasted for him. A voice called out. "Hey! Get out of there."

Renfield pushed aside two of the sunflower stems and looked out. A short, older African American woman stood in the garden gate. A large black Great Dane stood next to her, straining at its lead as it tried to get to Renfield. Its lips were curled, and drool dripped from its jowls to the ground. If the Master were a dog, he would be *that* dog.

"I'm sorry," Renfield said, "I was just—"

"I don't care what you were 'just,'" the woman said, "you're *just* getting out of here. Now. You ain't from this neighborhood, this is *our* garden, so get out."

Renfield looked around. "You have a beautiful garden. It's so ... so alive! I couldn't help—"

The woman glared. "What you can do is get out. Or I'll let Nicky loose. Or maybe call the police."

"Not the police!" Renfield was afraid of the police. They had brought him to white-coat lady and black-robe man. He stepped out from the sunflowers to plead with the woman.

But he saw in her wide eyes that that was a mistake. She backed away, and she let go of the dog's lead. As soon as the tension was released, Nicky barked—a deep boom that rattled Renfield's bones—and leaped at him.

Renfield leaped backwards without thinking. Somewhere in his mind he felt sad: he had crushed four of the sunflower stalks as he fled, and he moaned for their lost beauty. But he wasted no time springing to the top of the fence (narrowly avoiding the spikes) and down the other side.

Nicky threw himself against the fence, rising up on his rear paws and planting his fore paws near the top of the fence. The dog barked, and Renfield stumbled backwards, falling on his butt. Then he had time to realize that the dog was on that side of the fence and he was on this side. He was safe.

But the garment bag was on *that* side.

Renfield instantly ran to the hangers of the bag, but Nicky seemed to read his mind, and the dog ran for the bag as well. Renfield climbed halfway up the fence, grabbed the hangers, and lifted ... at the same time that Nicky grabbed the bottom of the bag and started pulling at it.

Renfield pulled on the hangers. Nicky pulled as well, planting his huge feet in the moist green earth of the garden. Renfield scrambled higher and got a better hold, while the dog twisted and yanked to try to pull the bag from his grip. Renfield pulled for all he was worth and was surprised when Nicky was forced to take three steps forward. Maybe the dog wouldn't win.

Then the dog lost his grip momentarily, and Renfield fell backwards. Before he could catch himself, the bag fell upon the spikes, and he heard a tearing sound. Then Nicky leaped up and once more gripped the bag in his teeth. Renfield grabbed the hangers again as the dog pulled and yanked and twisted. Renfield pulled back—and suddenly the sound of ripping echoed in the street, and he and the remnants of the bag tumbled into the street.

And into a mud puddle.

Renfield looked at Nicky. The dog had only an empty bag, or what was left of it. And Renfield ... Renfield had the suit. The muddy, smelly, crumpled, ripped suit.

Renfield stood in the small space between the counter and the window, and he waited.

And waited.

From the clothes hanging in the back, he had recognized this store. Mama had taken him to one like this sometimes, a clothes-cleaning store. He had brought the Master's suit here, and the purple-haired kid behind the counter—was there really purple hair, or was he seeing something that wasn't there again? —had taken his money. *Most* of his money, but the kid had promised the suit would be cleaned and repaired in two hours. What else would Renfield do with the money?

Then Purple Hair had stared at Renfield as he waited, but only for a while. Then he went back to looking at his computer screen, doing something in the back, and talking to customers as they came in. He glared at Renfield upon the first few customers; but since they didn't notice the little man in the corner, the kid stopped noticing, too.

Renfield didn't want to admit why he waited. He wasn't sure where else to go, and he didn't want to lose track of the Master's suit. And besides, he couldn't tell time. He wasn't sure how long two hours was.

After Renfield had waited what seemed a long time, Purple Hair brought a box up and set it on the counter. Then without a word, he went to the back area.

Renfield fidgeted. He looked at the box. Had it been a couple hours? Was that the suit? Was Purple Hair ashamed to even talk to him anymore?

That had to be it! Many people gave up on talking to Renfield. They didn't like having him around, but the polite ones wouldn't say it. The kid seemed polite, so Renfield could draw only one conclusion: Purple Hair wanted him to take his box and leave.

So, he did.

Renfield was relieved to leave. He didn't like making people uncomfortable, and he didn't know how he did it. The Master was never uncomfortable around him, which was another reason why he liked the Master. He wanted to like other people, too, if only they would let him. But since he didn't know how, he was glad to leave Purple Hair behind.

Four blocks later, though, he heard shouting. He turned back, and through the faces of the crowd he could just make out a fast-moving spot of purple.

Oh, no ... Sometimes people did worse than ignore Renfield, worse than want him to go away: sometimes bad people got angry, and they ... hurt him. Not like the Master's threats, they chased him down and really *hurt* him. Purple Hair hadn't *looked* like a bad person. But then, neither had Papa, and ...

Renfield clutched the box, not worrying about crumpling it again, and dashed through the crowd. He was small and quick and unafraid to bump into them, so he made good time; but when he stopped to look back, Purple Hair was still there, still shouting.

Renfield turned to run again—and collided with a bicycle messenger. The bicyclist crashed to the ground and lay there, dazed; but Renfield tumbled and sprang to his feet. Immediately he thought: *Not again! Where's the box?*

He looked around, and the battered box lay under the bicycle. He lifted the bike with his left hand and retrieved the box with his right.

But then he thought ... Mama said taking things that weren't yours was wrong. But disappointing the Master was worse, wasn't it? He wasn't sure, but he knew that *paying* for the things you took made it right. So, he said, "Sorry," and he held bike and box in one hand as he dug out the last of his money and dropped it on the still-dazed cyclist. Then he climbed on the bike and pedaled away, clinging to the box as he steered.

Renfield made good time once he moved from the sidewalk to the street. The wind in his face made him smile despite the shouts he still heard behind him. The shouts seemed louder now, almost as if two people were shouting; but soon they faded, and he was free.

He started to recognize more of the plants, and that made him smile even wider. It was only a few blocks more when he smelled just the slightest hint of ... *honeysuckle!* He rounded a corner, and there was the Great Detective's office building.

Renfield knew he wouldn't disappoint the Master: he had reached his destination, and it wasn't even dark yet!

But it would be soon. Already the sun was behind the tall buildings, and he couldn't tell how low it was. He had no time to waste. Renfield recalled his orders ... "Honeysuckle ... Climb up ... Garment bag ... Closet ... Yes, Master, I remember."

So now he could walk up to the fifth floor. But wait: the Master said *climb up*, not *walk up*. It was important to follow the Master's orders. Did he mean climb the wall? Stairs have steps, so you *step* up those, right? Although Renfield was good at climbing, he didn't like heights. Many times, he had climbed the tree at the Home, and then the attendants had had to get him back down. Climbing was fun but looking down was not fun.

But he had no choice. "The Master said 'climb up,' so I have to *climb* up!" He dropped the bike on the sidewalk, tucked the box under his arm, and walked up to the corner of the wall.

And then the scent of honeysuckle surrounded him, so powerful when he was so close. Honeysuckles were his favorite flowers! Well, except for sunflowers, of course.

The sweet smell made Renfield brave, and he easily scaled the corner, even with one arm occupied with the box. He was very careful not to look down; and as the shadows lengthened, he made his way slowly to the fifth floor.

Then came the hardest part: he had to climb sideways to reach the office window. The bricks of the corner had offered him many hand- and footholds, but the wall was much more even. Three times he found no place to put his foot, and he almost lost his grip; but he was a good climber, and patient. Each time he carefully felt with his toe until he found somewhere to put his weight.

At last Renfield stood on his toes on the ledge outside the Great Detective's window. He was so close. He would make the Master happy! Well, at least he would make the Master not angry, which was pretty good.

Only the window wouldn't open.

He could see through the window that it wasn't locked, wasn't even latched. It was just stuck, painted or swollen stuck. He could overcome that. He had come so far; he wouldn't let a simple stuck window stop him. He clenched the box between his knees, held onto his handhold with his right hand, and lifted up on the window frame with the fingers of his left.

He was careful, knowing that five stories of *down* were right behind him. At first, he lifted only with his strong, practiced fingers. When that didn't work, he used his whole arm, but carefully. He knew that if the window jerked suddenly open, he could lose his grip and fall.

And at last, the window budged. Just a little, but Renfield knew he had won. He had beaten the window. But now was not the time to celebrate, not until he was inside! He rested his left arm and fingers, and then he went back to work on the window. Slowly he pulled it up until he could let his toes slide forward and get a more comfortable perch. Then he pulled the window all the way open, and he slid inside.

And the box slipped. And fell. Outside. And *down*.

Despite his fear of falling, Renfield leaned out and watched the box fall. It tumbled, almost gracefully, until it struck the cement sidewalk. Then it burst open in a spray of pink.

Pink?

Before Renfield could wonder why the Master would have a pink suit, Purple Hair ran up to the box and lifted up a short, puffy pink dress. Renfield's mother had called that a *tootoo*, he thought. He was sure the Master would never wear a tootoo.

Right behind Purple Hair ran the bicycle messenger. He picked up the fallen bike and inspected it. Then both young men looked up at Renfield and shouted at him, fists raised.

After more shouting, the messenger mounted the bike and rode away. Purple Hair slowly followed, occasionally turning back to glare at Renfield.

After all of that ... After the elephant, the truck, the wrong turns, the dog, the cleaner, the bike, the wall ... After overcoming all of that, Renfield had failed. And from the lengths of the shadows and the fading light of the sun on the skyscrapers, he knew there was no time to try again. He had let the Master down.

No.

He wasn't going to give up now. He wasn't going to fail. He wasn't a *deluge*; he was a *person*. And the Master was counting on him.

Renfield looked around the office. It was sloppy, even by his standards. Mama would've fainted away at the mess, particularly the copies of *Racing Form* and the pictures of not-nice women in not enough clothes. Nearby was a kitchen, complete with refrigerator, sink with dirty dishes, and overstuffed drawers. There had to be something here he could work with. He started rummaging through the drawers—but very quietly. He thought he heard snoring from the mirror, and he didn't want to wake whatever was in there.

Then Renfield saw it. It had been there all the time, waiting for him to see it: the answer to his problem, right at the window. He would make the Master proud.

He curled up in the closet and waited for the Master. It had been a long day. Soon he fell asleep.

Renfield woke instantly when he heard the closet knob turn. The door opened, the Master looked in, and said "Ren—"

But Renfield held a finger to his lips, and the Master

stopped. Renfield tried not to look at the Master's naked body as he whispered, "Quietly, Master. I think the mirror can hear us."

The Master pulled back, looked at the mirror, and scratched his head. Then he turned back to Renfield and whispered, "What are you doing here? Where's my suit?"

"No time, Master. There were problems, and an elephant, and a truck, and a dog, and a man with Purple Hair, and ... Too much to explain. But I have a plan!"

"I don't—" The Master caught himself as his voice rose, and he returned to a whisper. "I don't need a plan; I need a suit!"

"I know. But this is almost as good. At least in the dark lighting in here." And Renfield brought his loot from the closet: a dingy white tablecloth, the dark gray curtains from the window, and the scissors and stapler from the Great Detective's desk. *Real* scissors, Renfield noted with pride, not *safety* scissors. "Just hold your arms out and stand with your feet apart. I have to work fast."

The Master started to protest; but then he looked nervously at the clock and he shrugged, as if accepting the brilliance of Renfield's plan. Renfield held up the tablecloth and cut a front piece, a back, and sleeves. They were too big, but no one would notice in the dark. He held the pieces up to the Master and pinched the edges together, stapling him into the shirt.

The Master flexed and raised his arms, frowning at the gaps that showed, so Renfield stapled the gaps as well. The Master flexed again and nodded.

Then he smiled, and Renfield knew he had done a *very* good thing.

Next Renfield stapled the Master into pants (being careful not to look at the Master's *pulă*—good boys didn't look there, Mama had said). The pants wanted to sag, and Renfield had no belt, so he stapled the pants to the shirt. It would do. There were also no shoes, of course, so Renfield cut out black slippers, stapled the Master's feet into them, and stapled them to the pant cuffs.

That left the suit coat; but Renfield frowned at that. The Master's coat had to look perfect, and Renfield knew he wasn't that good. So instead he settled for a long cape, cutting it from the one complete curtain and stapling the hem so it looked finished. When he draped it around the Master's shoulders and stapled the collar, the look was close enough to frighten Renfield.

"How does it look?" the Master whispered. He could never check his appearance, even in a normal mirror, so Renfield was used to this job.

He looked at the Master. "*Almost* perfect," he answered. He tiptoed to the open window, leaned out, and plucked a honeysuckle blossom. He held it up to the Master's chest and stapled it in place.

"Ouch!"

"Sorry, Master. But now ... perfect!"

"This had better work, Renfield ..."

"It will, Master, it will!"

The Master twirled around, holding his arms out so his cape flowed. He seemed satisfied. "All right, now leave. I can't be sure to protect you from the Great Detective and his henchmen." And then he headed toward the bedroom at the far side of the office.

But Renfield couldn't help himself. He had never seen a Great Detective before, and he had never seen the Master confront his arch nemesis. And after so much work, he had to know how the battle would play out. So, he crept very close to the open door, found a table to hide under, and peered through the door. "Get him, Master!" he whispered very quietly.

But they didn't fight, they ... talked. And Renfield didn't

understand most of the words, but it didn't sound good for the Master. The Great Detective wasn't intimidated by him. How could *anyone* not be intimidated by the Master?

Maybe the Master was right. Maybe the Great Detective *was* a knight. Renfield had never seen a knight before, not for real, but he knew they were real. He knew they were people who did the right thing and treated everyone fairly. Could this man be one? Maybe his knight's armor and sword were in the bedroom.

At one point, a woman snuck into the office, closed the window, and sprayed it with some solution. The Master and the Great Detective kept talking as the woman snuck back out. Renfield wondered if he should warn the Master, but he didn't know how.

At another point, the Master stormed out of the bedroom and over to the window; but when he reached to touch it, he recoiled so quickly and roared so loudly that Renfield feared the staples would give out. The Master ran back into the bedroom, and they argued some more. Renfield couldn't follow all the words, all the things unsaid, but he could tell from the tone: somehow, impossible as the idea was, the Master was losing. Had lost and was simply reluctant to admit it.

Finally, the Great Detective and the Master walked out of the bedroom. The Master's shoulders were slumped. He was defeated.

Yet even in victory, the Great Detective was cautious, like a true knight should be. He walked behind the Master, keeping his guard up to the last as they discussed shipping schedules and the Master leaving the country for good.

Leaving ... Leaving Renfield!

Then, when it seemed to be over, the Great Detective stepped toward the door; but he accidentally stepped on the hem of the Master's cape, pulling it to the side. The Master jerked away, but that only made matters worse: the detective was also standing on one of the slippers. Renfield heard the sound of staples popping loose and pinging against the wall.

And just like that, the makeshift trousers let go. The Master stood before the Great Detective, half naked, with his three thousand-year-old *pulă* hanging out.

The Master glanced down. The Great Detective glanced down as well. Then both men looked up, not quite looking into each other's eyes. The Master spoke in a low, clenched tone. "When you tell this story, detective—and I know you will—will you do me the honor of leaving this part out?"

The Great Detective nodded. "Not. A. Word. But ..." He whistled as he opened the door. "Impressive!"

"Indeed." And with that, the Master turned into a bat, leaving behind the last of his stapled clothing. As he flew out the door, Renfield was certain: that was the last he would ever see of the Master.

The little man felt a touch of panic at that. *Who will I serve now?* But the panic was brief. Renfield had triumphed over adversity many times today. Against all odds, he had succeeded in his quest. He was a person, no matter what the Home said, and he would find someone who would appreciate that.

Maybe ... Maybe a knight needed a squire ...

INTRODUCTION TO VIEW FROM
A HILL

Emeka Walter Dinjos was a Nigerian science fiction writer, and a fellow winner of Writers of the Future. I never got to meet him in person, but we interacted a lot online as fellow winners. I was enchanted by his writing, and I was touched that he looked to me as a mentor. It was a chance for me to Pay it forward. *But more than that, it was a chance to meet a new friend and a promising young writer.*

Diabetes—the disease which led to the infection that almost killed me—took Walter far too young; and so, we lost worlds of stories along with a good man. I lost a friend before I truly got to know him. This elegy came to me the day I learned he was gone.

VIEW FROM A HILL

A tall, strong, young man stood on the crest of a hill, looking out over the green-brown plain below. A slight breeze ruffled the collar of his dark blue shirt. The air bore the sweet scent of the Maringa trees behind him and the musical chattering of the dabchicks in the ponds. The sun warmed his head through his short, curly locks. He held a long, straight, roughly shaped staff. But he did not lean upon it. He stood strong.

A short, gnarled old woman, old as the land itself, emerged from the trees and stood next to him. She also stood unbowed, and she gave the impression that she was larger than him in a way that the eye could not see. "You are audacious," she said, "to bear a stick to meet me."

He shook his head. "It is not a stick; it is a scepter."

"I am the Woman of the Wood," she answered. "I know this stick. I can name the tree from which it broke, and the stories of that tree, and of the seed from which it grew, and of the tree which dropped those seeds. Your eyes lie to you. It is a stick."

"I do not see with my eyes, old mother, but with my spirit.

As you have taught me. And my spirit knows that this is a scepter, and it marks me as king of all that I see."

The woman chuckled softly as they looked out over the plain, with its stagnant ponds, sparse grasses, clumps of withered trees, and goats idly grazing. "And what do you see, O King?"

The young man shielded his eyes and looked out where she did. "I see rich fields where our people will someday grow sweet berries and yams and rice. We will plant vast crops to feed ourselves, and more. We shall feed a hungry world."

She shook her head. "Once these lands were enough to feed our people, so they did not ask for food from others. Your spirit sees the past, before the wasters and the troubles, not the future. These lands were rich once."

"And they shall be again! We bear burdens, but we do not sink beneath them. Someday we shall be rid of those who threaten the people and the land. We shall not break, we shall grow."

"All I see is struggling grasses and goats wandering among them. And dirty little children," she added, though she smiled when she did. "Children all around the field, if you know where they play."

"And not just in the field," the man answered. He glanced over his shoulder where bushes rustled, and he heard one small child's voice gasp, while another giggled.

"They are brave, but foolish to approach me."

"As was I," the man answered. "Brave. Foolish. Burning with a hunger that food could not fill. I had to know. I had to know your ways."

"And so, it is with these? They come to learn of the Woman of the Wood?" Her eyes grew moist. "They still know of me?"

"No. They do not see you. Not yet."

"I know," she said, and a tear ran down the furrows of her face. "They do not know me anymore."

"They will! It's my turn now. I will teach them. They will know you, and they will know this future. That is what draws them today." He lifted the stick and grasped it by the end. "They come to hear tales of my star sword!"

That turned the old woman's frown into a smile. "I thought it was a scepter."

"It is a star sword, won on the field of battle! You see?" He gestured across the plain with the stick. "Out there, beyond our rich fields, is the spaceport! There we shall build our own space program, with our own strong hands and our own bright minds. There we shall build rockets that shall take Nigerians to other planets. To the Moon and to Mars. To the stars!"

The woman's dark lips parted, her mouth gaping. Finally, she said, "You've given me a gift. Now I know that even I, Oldest, can still wish. I wish that I could see that."

"You will," the man said. "My spirit sees it. We will go places that can only be seen in the imagination today; and wherever we go, we will take your stories. We will take you with us. I *will* tell your stories."

"No," the woman said softly. "I'm sorry. Not you."

He turned to her. "So soon?" She nodded. "But I have so much to do. So many stories to tell. My children must learn. They *must* have this future."

"You've made me believe, king of the world. They will. But you? Your spirit shall be freed to go many places, worlds even I have never imagined. And that journey starts today."

The Woman of the Wood loomed tall over the man, her true majesty revealed at last as she reached out a hand and gently cupped his shoulder. He collapsed against her, strong until the final moment. Then he faded on the wind until all that remained was spirit, which she clasped to her breast.

And then she too was gone, and the old stick clattered to the ground, the only sign that the tall man had ever stood there.

The bushes rustled once more. After several minutes, the bravest of the two little boys came forward, looking around the hill and out over the plains. In the distance, he saw the silver towers of the spaceport. He picked up the stick. As a rocket blazed into the sky, the boy held up the sword and pointed it to the stars.

Emeka Walter Dinjos, 12/12/2018
You saw far, but too briefly.

INTRODUCTION TO THE MOTHER
ANTHONY

Around 1990 *or so, I was working long hours on a project with a lot of responsibilities. I was learning and growing as a programmer. But while I was really enjoying my career, a part of me was miserable. I had spent so much time buried in work I had lost touch with the joy of fiction. I might read a novel now and then, but nothing was engaging me. I had lost my sense of wonder.*

And then I found A Talent for War *by Jack McDevitt, and the joy returned. It was an idea story, a character story, a mystery, and more. The big reveal blew me away. McDevitt became a writer for me to watch. And over time, his books were among the influences that drew me back into writing.*

In November 2010, *I read McDevitt's then-latest novel,* Echo. *Like* A Talent for War, *it's an Alex Benedict novel, my favorite series from Jack. It's a great, fun book; and about two-thirds of the way through, I knew how it would end. I could see it all, every twist and turn. It would be fantastic!*

And I got it completely wrong. In every detail.

But I didn't let that stop me! I knew my ending was a great story; so over the long Thanksgiving weekend, I reworked that into a stand-alone story. "The Mother Anthony" became my first submission to Writers of the Future, and my first Finalist in the Contest. This was the story that Jerry Pournelle loved, the story that stopped me from giving up on writing.

So, this story is dedicated to Jack McDevitt. Thank you, Jack, for not writing this story, so I had to.

THE MOTHER ANTHONY

E mergency landings were definitely *not* in the recruiting video.

Bess remembered the Winston Interstellar Transport recruitment video quite clearly. *See other worlds.* Yes, they delivered on that promise, though they neglected to tell her that one space port looked very much like another.

See the wonders of space with your own eyes. Yes, they delivered on that promise, too. In fact, Bess never tired of stopping by the viewing ports whenever her schedule permitted. Perhaps the only thing better was when she could escort her class to the port for an astronomy field trip. As much as Bess enjoyed the nebulae and variable stars and other sights along their course, she enjoyed the light from the children's faces that much more. Truly, had any teacher ever had such fortune as to teach children science out where science really mattered?

Advance your career. Another promise delivered. Where else but WIT could a teacher as young as Bess have so much responsibility? As the only full-time, non-holographic teacher on the I.V. *Graham*, Bess was a headmistress in all but title.

Indeed, she even had authority over ship's crew when they served as guest instructors. And that in turn necessitated that she have a temporary commission as a cadet herself, though she admitted, at least to herself, that she failed to understand all the legalisms of that commission. She just knew it would look good on her C.V. at the end of her contract. She never wore the uniform (except at dinners, which were always formal), as she found it quite constraining.

Meet your new family. Well, that was perhaps an exaggeration. The crew wasn't exactly familial, more social. They were predominantly young, though mostly older than Bess; and they were predominantly male, by a ratio of at least three to two. They were all prim and proper when above decks—Captain Engstrom would have it no other way, not within view of the passengers—but quite a bit more relaxed when below decks. One might even characterize them as raucous. And with many of the female crew being attached (many to other crew members), and with most of the male crew having apparently traditional orientations, their reactions to the young teacher in their midst were not precisely brotherly. In other circumstances, Bess might have been inclined to encourage their attentions—particularly   that   handsome   young   Lieutenant Masterson, who was less forward than the rest and thus paradoxically more enticing—but it struck her as poor judgment in the close confines of an interstellar vessel. A teacher needs a certain level of decorum and reserve to maintain respect in her classroom; and a young, attractive female teacher needs those even more. It is important that the older male students not see her as an opportunity, and the older females not see her as a competitor. So, it was perhaps for the best that Captain Engstrom took a fatherly interest in her, and arranged for her to bunk in the passenger decks "to keep you close in case your students have questions." As delightful as a night with Lieutenant Masterson might be, Bess had successfully maintained her reserve while shipboard. As for her nighttime encounters while in spaceports ... Well, those were her business, and she seemed to have been sufficiently discreet to evade the shipboard gossips.

New worlds, wonders of space, career advancement, new people? Check, check, check, and check. The video seemed perfectly accurate in what it included. Its only inaccuracy, or so it would appear, lay in what it left out. And again, to be specific, it left out emergency landings.

So, Bess was mildly perplexed when Captain Engstrom called an officers' briefing and requested her attendance. She was always requested at launch and arrival briefings, but others were left to her discretion—with a strong but subtle hint that she was not expected at all. Captain Engstrom indeed treated her in a fatherly fashion, and certainly kindly; but she always got the impression he failed to take her very seriously. She was not much older than his own granddaughters, after all, and not quite a year out of school. She saw him as a guardian, overprotective even, but not necessarily supportive. Despite doing what she thought was a very professional job of teaching, she was still a child in his eyes—or so it seemed to her.

The briefing changed from perplexing to frightening when she realized the subject. "So that's the situation," the Captain concluded. Bess wasn't any sort of engineer—integral calculus had stretched the limits of her mathematical talents—so she hadn't followed all of the technical discussions. But she understood the conclusions quite thoroughly. "Our remaining engine will not get us to our destination. If we try, either we'll blow it too, or we'll strand the ship in deep interstellar. That's fast death or slow. I might make the attempt if we were just hauling cargo, but on a passenger run, the safety of our charges comes first."

Bess looked around the room, looking for any evidence of surprise to mirror what she felt, but she found none. What was news to her seemed to be common knowledge to the others.

"Lieutenant White and the astrogation staff have located three G class stars within range of our remaining engine. Long baseline scans have found a planetary system around one—and curse our luck, it's the farthest from the shipping lanes. It will take us nearly three months to reach it with a safe cruising speed. We can get there, find a planet in the habitable zone, and drop the habitat module. That's the best we can do for the passengers. Once they're safely grounded, we'll have a lot less mass. We can push a lot faster without stressing the engine. With a lot of luck, we can make Chambers's World, and arrange a rescue operation. With at least a little luck, we'll get back into the space lanes, and be able to call for help. Regardless, we'll know we did our duty to the passengers."

Bess gripped her school bell so tightly, her fingers had become bone white tinged with fiery red. Why was she here? Why was she in this meeting, and why was she out in the middle of empty space? Why was she not back home in Chelsea, filling out applications and picking up substitute teaching assignments?

"I need to stress this to you all, because I need *you* to stress it to the crew and the passengers: *we are safe.* No need to speculate for how long, but safe for now. White tells me we have more than enough capacity to reach the target star and search for a habitable planet; and the odds are strong that there will be one there. So, the passengers will make it there safely. Then it will be up to us to secure their rescue. That's the message I need you to spread through the ship: safety, habitable planet, rescue. People are going to be scared, doubtful, maybe hysterical, so you need to hammer home: *safety, habitable planet, rescue.*" This time he actually hammered his podium on the three phrases, staring earnestly at his audience. "And if you have any doubts of your own, don't try to bury them. That'll make you more tense. Go to the chaplain or the surgeon. Hell, go to the barkeep at that speakeasy that somehow escapes my attention. But talk to someone. The passengers need you steady, and the crew need you steady. Someday, this story will buy you drinks in every spaceport you ground at, but only if you hold it together right now."

Through some hidden signal, the captain indicated he was through. Lieutenant Masterson rose and called, "Attention!" All the officers snapped to attention as well.

"We have some difficult work ahead," the captain said. "You have my confidence. Dismissed." Then, somewhat lower, he added, "Miss Anthony, could you please stay a moment?"

Bess remained, nearly paralytic, as the real officers filed out. Even after five ports of call, she still could not quite place herself in their social category. They were "the real officers," and she was an anomaly in the order of the ship.

When they were alone, Bess regained composure enough to speak. "Yes, Captain?"

"Please, sit down." They both did so. "I'm sorry you're hearing it like this. Senior officers already knew the basics, and scuttlebutt filled in the rest. I thought it was time to spread the official story before rumors got out of hand."

"But if that is only an 'official story,' then—"

"Oh, it's also a *true* story. But the rumors will be more drastic."

"So, can we not call for help?"

"Miss Anthony, I'm surprised. Your specialty is science education. You must know the limits of hyperwave."

Again, she felt somehow inadequate in his judgment. "Hyper-physics is quite over my head, I fear. I know the concepts, but the mathematics is beyond me. As I recall ... As I recall, the propagation rate is dependent upon the power of the transmitter."

"Yes, and even with all three engines working correctly, our rig could transmit maybe ten times our rate of travel, maybe less. Did you know we actually have to stop the ship to send a message? Now we have one engine, and we have to baby it due to the imbalance. It could be a dozen years or more before a signal reached any settled world. The fastest way for us to find rescue is to fly out and ask for it. But trust me, we *will* make the effort once we know you're safely landed."

"'*You're* safely landed'? Do I take it then, Captain, that you intend to leave me behind with the passengers?"

He sighed. "Miss Anthony, the ship needs technical crew, but the passengers need the service crew. We're taking none of the service crew, and only the minimum technical crew."

"Of course, I see. Another effort to minimize the mass."

"That and ... there's significant risk in that flight. I don't want to risk anyone I don't have to."

Bess found such a frank admission awkward. She looked down at her bell and absently wiped a kerchief across a smudge on the brass. "I see. So, you asked me to stay because you needed a counselor, a friendly ear. I am pleased I could be of assistance."

"No. No, I'm sorry, it wasn't fair for me to dump that on you. Please, do an old man a favor? Forget that. The officers and crew will have figured it out already, but it's better if we ignore it for now.

"No, I need to talk to you about the children. I'm counting on the crew to keep the passengers calm, keep everything routine as much as possible. And I especially need your help there with the children."

"Now I understand. And yes, I quite concur, Captain. Children need routine, and they need it especially in the face of uncertainty. It provides a comfort zone and a base line, allowing them to better adjust to the uncertainty."

"Exactly! So please, I need you to make sure everything stays routine for them, as best as possible. I'm going to start cutting lights and gravity a bit—just a precaution!—and I may also cut some of the luxury rations. Before any of these changes, I want to explain them to you, so you can explain to the children. If you need any help from the crew for these discussions, they all have instructions to help you as duty schedules permit. I'll even drop by the class when I can."

"Certainly, Captain. You merely ask me to do my duty to the best of my ability. I would scarcely call that a 'favor.'" Bess put forth her most positive air, but she stared down at her bell. Her knuckles, now whiter than ever, stood out in stark relief against the antique cherry wood grip.

"Well, call it what you will, but you have my gratitude. Oh, and Bess?" The use of her given name surprised her, and she looked straight into his gaze. "Tom Masterson's in the service crew. He'll be staying with the passengers. A little fatherly advice: he's a good man and could be a better one if you find yourself beached for longer than expected."

Bess felt a warm glow in her cheeks, and she looked downward once more. The captain turned and became officious in response. "Now I've gone too far again. Please forget that, too. Your kids are waiting for you. Dismissed."

As swiftly as decorum permitted, Bess left the briefing room. Once safely out of the captain's sight, she began to tremble, and then to sway. Finally, she leaned against a corridor wall, and then slowly sank to the floor. Suddenly, she was no longer Bess Anthony, Principle Instructor on the I.V. *Graham*. She was only Bess, a young woman who craved a little adventure and got more than she ever expected. She didn't want responsibility, she wanted to be comforted. She didn't weep, but she rocked back and forth, arms clenched around her knees.

But Bess only allowed herself a few brief minutes of self-pity. She would not want any passersby to see her like this. And even more important than her dignity was her duty. The bell in her hand, outdated even in the days when her father rang it at *his* school, was her anchor to her profession. When he gave it to her, on that day she knew she was no longer just his daughter: she was *a teacher*, and his pride in that was more than he could express. ("And you, an English teacher!" she had teased.) And she knew what the bell called her to do. She could turn the situation into science lessons, and she could turn the science lessons into ways for the children to distract themselves and even contribute to the emergency effort. As she walked, she began rewriting lesson plans in her head.

When she returned to the passenger decks, Bess stepped right back into her routine. She walked the corridors at a measured pace, ringing the bell at intervals. In between, she called out, "Children! Time for school! Quickly, now, quickly! We have a lot to learn today." Other days she might vary the call, referencing an upcoming lesson, or perhaps mentioning a child's birthday. But that day, routine was important, so she stayed with her traditional call.

It took the children a little longer to emerge than usual. When they did, many of them had anxiety in their glances, or even dried tears. Some of the parents came into the corridor, puzzled and nervous expressions on their faces as well. But the bell served nicely to quell any troublesome questions. Soon the entire student body was assembled and marching through the corridors. Fifty-three students, aged seventeen to four, trooped behind her, eldest in the rear where they could keep watch over the youngest. When they entered the classroom and stood by their seats, Bess swallowed a small lump of pride in her children. Then she began explaining and answering questions, and their new lessons began.

With the captain's permission, Bess did indeed enlist the children in the ship's emergency planning. Besides continuing their individual studies in traditional subjects, she introduced new practical studies. She thought the term "practical" was much more comforting than "emergency."

The captain needed an accurate inventory of supplies? Bess turned that into lessons in mathematics and accounting. Bess assigned Valerie Long to guide that effort and help the younger students with their sums.

Lieutenant White needed additional observations to identify likely planets? Bess assigned extra lessons in the local star charts and assigned the older students to serve shifts on the telescopes. Matseo Chagi led the astronomy team.

Some of the older passengers had difficulty adjusting to the lesser gravity? Bess assigned some of the more troubled students to serve as their aides. That duty was more difficult for her to justify on strictly pedagogic grounds, but it let the students concentrate on someone else's troubles rather than their own, and so it had positive effects on the morale of both students and elders.

Older students also began apprenticeship programs, where the captain approved. Bess wanted them to learn basic ship's operations, so that they could assist if needed when the actual landing occurred. Some with exceptional skill in chemistry and biology apprenticed to Ship's Surgeon Keene.

Lieutenant Masterson's responsibility was more difficult. It was evident to Bess that he was preparing long-term survival plans in case rescue was delayed. He came to Bess's office one evening, so laden with data cards and handwritten notes that Bess had to rise and slide open the door for him.

"Thank you, Miss Anthony." The lieutenant was always a proper gentleman, doubly so in her office. "I have more items I need inventoried, if your lessons permit."

"Let's see what we can do. What do you have here?"

Masterson dumped the pile on her desk, cards scattering across the simulated wood surface. "I have here plans for all the recycler components and systems in the habitat module. We need to check them all and do maintenance while we still have the techs around for repairs. After we beach, if we find we're down for—"

Bess laid a finger upon his lips. The gesture startled him, which gave the finger exceptional silencing power. In truth, her sudden familiarity startled Bess as well; but she buried that reaction in deference to the point she had to make. "Lieutenant, if you are about to discuss any time frame longer than our landing and a brief period of waiting for rescue, it would be better if you were to discuss something else."

Masterson puzzled over that statement, finally managing only an inarticulate, "Huh?"

"If there are concerns you have not shared with me, I can honestly say that I have never heard them. I will not willingly lie to the children, Lieutenant, not unless extraordinary circumstance requires it. So, I think it best, for the time being, if you can adhere strictly to the captain's official message."

Lieutenant Masterson grinned, and in a fair mimicry of Captain Engstrom's voice, he replied, "Safety, habitable planet, rescue." He even pounded the desk with the words, data cards bouncing with each impact; and he affected such a fine imitation of the Captain's "serious stare" that Bess could not help but giggle.

The lieutenant joined her in giggling. Before they quite

knew what had struck them, they were both wracked with laughter. Bess barely reached her chair, while Masterson quite thoroughly missed the guest chair. In full gravity, he might have suffered injury to go with insult. Instead, he simply performed a graceless bounce from his fundament, ending back on his feet. He put on a most dignified look but could not maintain it in the face of renewed laughter.

Just when the laughs seemed on the verge of subsiding, the office door slid slightly open. A student, Kara Wells, stuck her head in, curiosity plain to see in her young face. When she realized Bess and the lieutenant were both staring directly at her, she emitted just a single syllable: "Eep!" She turned and fled, the door slid shut, and the rolling laughter began anew.

When at last they had no energy left for laughter, they merely sat, quietly breathing. After nearly a minute of silence, Bess placed her palms firmly upon her desk, fixed Masterson with a serious stare, and said in her best teacher voice, "Eep!" Masterson held his sides, laughing breathlessly.

Finally, he gained enough control to speak. "Thank you, Bess. I needed that almost more than you, I think."

Wiping tears from her eyes, Bess grinned back at him. "Let's say we both needed it more than we knew." She looked at her bell, hanging by the door. "You're an experienced spacer, Lieutenant. Does responsibility like this happen often? It's so much more daunting than I expected."

He adjusted his uniform a bit and sat a little straighter. "It's always this daunting, really. We always have their lives in our hands, and our mistakes can prove fatal. You don't get to be an officer if you can't grasp that. On a typical voyage, the risks are real, but they're routine. We can handle them. And then there's the daily routine, that's comforting, lets us know we're on the mark. But with this emergency, it's so hard to maintain the routine and still take care of all the added responsibilities. Your kids have been a great help there, by the way."

"They're good kids."

"I'm inclined to credit their teacher. But leave that aside. The routine—well, really, the *appearance* of a routine—has been wearing me down. I needed a release. I think you did, too."

"Indeed." Bess stood, walked to the door, and pulled down her bell. She held it, caressed it almost. "I did need that, Lieutenant, you are correct in that regard. But I think now we must set it aside. You are right about the routine: it is both difficult and necessary. I do believe that I am only a few laughs away from tears, *real* tears, and those may not stop once they start. You cannot do that to your passengers, nor can I do that to my children."

Masterson considered a moment. Then he straightened and stood, donning the cap he had lost in his fall. "Agreed. This was nice, but it will have to do." He stood just a little closer as he added, "For now."

"Yes. Well ..." Bess slid the door open and retreated against its frame. "Well, Lieutenant, if you need some inventory assistance with the ..."

"'The sanitary equipment.'"

"Yes, the sanitary equipment ... then I shall find some students who could use an extra assignment. And now, if you can excuse me, I have to revise lesson plans for the third time this week."

He brushed closer to her as he passed through the doorway, a slightly herbal odor of soap moving with him. "Yes, certainly." Once through, he tipped his hat to her. "Good evening, Miss Anthony."

As he walked back toward the upper decks, an uncontrollable impulse gripped Bess. "Lieutenant, one more thing?"

He half turned. "Yes, Miss Anthony?"

Her eyes crinkled as she said, "Eep!"

Masterson chuckled softly as he walked away.

Her interlude with Lieutenant Masterson had yielded a revelation: there was a need for routine, yes, but there still remained concerns about morale. Bess was sure that she and the lieutenant could not be the only ones in need of some form of diversion and release. She added yet more assignments for the students, creative assignments this time. She asked them to write poems and stories and songs. Then with the captain's approval, she arranged to have the students perform them at ship's dinners. The dinners had become somewhat dreary affairs, what with the reduction in rations, but the children's performances seemed to turn that quite around.

After the first few nights of performances, Bess received another office visit, this time from the cruise director. Bess wondered privately how Ensign Tate had ever landed in such a post, since he seemed to lack even a hint of extroversion. It took more than two minutes of pleasantries before she could finally cajole him into speaking his piece.

"You see, Miss Anthony, some of the passengers ... I mean, some of the *adult* passengers ... I guess mostly some of the parents ... They're not holding up as well as your students. They're ... I think they're *jealous*."

"Jealous? Of students stuck in school all day?"

"'Stuck in school'? Hardly that. You've given them something to do. You answer their questions. You must know you're better at this than me."

"Well, I am flattered, though I think you deserve more credit than that. But how can I help you with this?"

"They ... I mean, these parents, and some others ... They've asked me to ask you ... Can they join your class? And, umm, can I join, too? I think I can get some good ideas from you."

And that was how Bess found herself with an assistant instructor and with a student body that encompassed a large subset of the passengers of the *Graham*. On an average day, nearly one-hundred sixty adults and children crowded into the classroom, watched from the hallway, or wandered the ship on homework assignments. Captain Engstrom even named her Chief Morale Officer and gave her a field promotion to junior lieutenant. The captain—demonstrating his own keen understanding of pomp and circumstance and attendant morale benefits—even held a commissioning ceremony at dinner one night. Her students sang a song in her honor. (Who composed it and how they rehearsed without her knowledge would forever remain a mystery to her.) And then she gave an acceptance speech with only a modicum of tears, and the captain declared a ball in her honor. She danced with many of the passengers and crew that night; and after Matseo broke the ice, some of her bolder students asked her to dance as well. Just as Bess thought she would get a chance to dance with Lieutenant Masterson and perhaps catch another whiff of that herbal soap, she felt a tug at the skirt of her uniform. Bobby Price, one of her youngest students, stood before her. His arms were raised in mute appeal, and his face was nearly split by a smile. Helpless, she picked him up and started to sway to the music. She caught Masterson's eye and looked a pained apology at him. He nodded and smiled at her and Bobby, and her conflict melted. When next she twirled to face him, he held up his forearm and tapped his wristwatch. Then he touched a finger to his cap brim, mouthed the word "Eep!" at her, and went off to his responsibilities.

After her class grew, so too did the dinner presentations. Some of the adults had some real talent, and many of the children rose to their challenge. Besides the nightly readings, Bess instituted a weekly talent show on Friday nights. And after some initial reluctance from the captain, she arranged a daily passenger briefing as well. It helped the passengers to hear the full situation, unadorned and stripped of technical jargon. Different officers rotated through the briefing duties, with the captain delivering the Sunday briefings personally. Morale continued to be high. There were even brief moments when Bess could almost forget their difficulties and accept this new routine as normal. They were as close as they could reasonably hope to be to the captain's first priority: *safety.*

At the close of the fifth talent show, Captain Engstrom made his surprise announcement of the night: Lieutenant White had found a habitable planet. After thanking the students for their contributions, he let the astrogator provide the details. There followed a lot of technical discussion about temperate zones, gas readings, photosynthesis telltales, and other factors, but they all added up to the captain's second priority: *habitable planet.*

The captain wrapped up the night by announcing a name-that-planet contest. It was an old morale trick, but quite reliable. Each student on the discovery team was allowed to submit a name, and the whole ship's complement voted on the submissions after three days of cheerful debate. No one was more surprised than Kara Wells when her choice was selected. She nervously accepted the captain's invitation to dine at the head table on the night Lieutenant White unveiled their first photos of Halfway There; and she practically squealed when the captain declared another ball in her honor and asked her for the honor of the first dance. Bess happily shunned the spotlight that night and felt a warm glow when she saw how Kara grew more confident with all the attention. No longer the star that night, Bess had multiple opportunities to dance with Lieutenant Masterson. At odd moments, when the mood grew perhaps a tad too serious for comfort, one or the other of them would whisper, "Eep!" And then they would laugh, and the tension would break, though other dancers looked at them quizzically. Far too soon, the lieutenant again had to leave for his duties. Bess was sure she smelled herbs well into the next day.

At the close of the seventh show, Captain Engstrom announced that next week's show would unfortunately be canceled. The passengers were too polite to boo, but the rumbling grew until the captain knocked a fork on a glass for attention. "I'm sorry, but you'll all be too busy next week. At roughly 1030 hours next Friday, we'll be launching the habitat module to Halfway There."

The dining room burst into extended applause; but amid the applause, Bess noticed some troubled faces. Some, she knew, were finally accepting that this was *real*: they were going down to a strange planet and staying for an extended time. But for others, she suspected a different concern. After the initial worries, this slow-motion emergency had melded the passengers and crew into a true community, in ways that never happened on a traditional cruise. Now, some of their community were going to leave them behind and go search for rescue. And not just any members, their community *leaders*. Where once the passengers might merely have seen ship's crew performing their responsibilities as expected, now they saw friends risking life and limb for them. It was more sobering.

But jubilation carried the day. Bess and her students found themselves pressed into service, moving materiel and supplies from the engine module to the habitat module. They had no need for judgment: anything intended for the transfer had been splashed with whitewash, just enough for a marker. Chief Mate Stubbs and his cargo crew tagged each item as it came through the hatches between modules, with color coding to identify the deck and compartment where each would be stored. Other cargo crew packed and secured. The whole operation was marvelously orderly, and Bess gained new respect for how well a good crew could work. In honest self-reflection, she admitted she had seen them as common laborers, not as skilled workers. She resolved to make that up to them some way, even though they were unaware of her condescension. Father would expect no less of her, and it would serve as a reminder that she should be less quick to judge.

Finally, came the day of departure. Amid many tearful partings, Bess received a summons to the captain's office. She hurried there, entered, and snapped a smart salute. She had been practicing since her promotion.

The captain returned her salute and ordered her to sit. After some pleasantries, he got to his point. "Bess, I'm very impressed with your work here. You've surpassed my expectations in every way."

"Thank you, Captain."

"I need to be more blunt. I misread you, and I apologize. You're stronger than I realized. I won't give you full credit, since the rest of the crew earned their share, but you've really helped keep the passengers stable. By this point, I fully expected some passengers in the brig for hoarding, or maybe even for violence. That's at a minimum. Food riots wouldn't have surprised me."

"Oh, I think they're better than that."

"People do crazy things in an emergency like this. I'll leave you some histories so you can see. It's quite possible I would've had to even order someone killed; and after that, well, things would've gotten grim. That didn't happen; and I'm putting it in your record that you bear primary responsibility."

The only answers Bess could devise would seem repetitive; but before she could even try, the captain continued: "I'm not giving you these histories as a gift. They're an assignment, and I expect you to read them, *Lieutenant*. They're service histories that probably didn't come up in your formal education, histories with an emphasis on shipwrecks and long-term survival."

"Long-term, Captain?"

"I treated you like a child before, and I was wrong to do so. Adult to adult—captain to junior lieutenant—the odds against rescue are long. We'll make the effort, but you and the service crew have to prepare for the long haul. I am entrusting you with this responsibility; and as the only officer who didn't read this material in the Merchant Academy, I need you to study up. I'm relieving you of all other duties for the day. Get to your berth, strap in, and get reading."

He rose, and she stood to attention. "*All* other duties, Captain?"

"Hmmm ... Not questioning orders is another thing you would've learned in the Academy, but go ahead."

"Captain, I request permission to see my children to their berths before strapping in myself."

"Yes, of course. Very proper. They're your children. I suspect they'll always be your children after the mark you made on them. I'll let you get to them, then. Dismissed." She saluted, he returned, and she left. Bess was uneasily certain that she would never see Captain Engstrom again.

She returned to the engine module. Her uniform was non-regulation in one particular: the cherry wood and brass bell that hung at her side. She unfastened it, released the clapper, and began to ring it, summoning her children to their berths.

After the initial jolt of separation, Bess thought the ride down from orbit was quite smooth, so she settled into reading. The histories were fairly dry, written more for accuracy and completeness than for style. Still, she learned a lot. It seemed the Transport Academy scholars had thought very deeply about all manner of circumstances that could arise during a voyage, including emergencies and stranding. They delved into more than just practical concerns, digging into ethics and morality and jurisprudence. They tied their arguments back to familiar logical and philosophical foundations, as well as to science and experience. And always, always to history. Whatever had let a lost vessel survive until rescue, they studied. When records permitted, they also studied failures; but overwhelmingly, failures were recorded simply as "Lost in Transit, Never Recovered."

Bess was so deeply engrossed in the histories she scarcely noticed the first tremors of storms as they entered the atmosphere. When the storms grew more violent, Lieutenant Masterson came on the ship's intercom. "Please remain calm. We have some turbulence, but Captain Stubbs assures me the ship's stabilizers can handle it." Bess smiled at his voice. Everything would be all right.

She was still reading when the habitat module flipped nearly upside down in a sudden wind shear. She lost her reader and had no chance to recover it before one storage compartment unexpectedly burst open and tossed a heavy crate at her head. The reduced gravity likely saved her life; but Bess was unconscious for the crash, the fire, the explosions, and the panic.

Bess ached. But she was warm. Under a blanket. Felt safe. Maybe good enough to move. Maybe open her eyes. Or maybe later. Warm. Ache.

"Eep!"

"Tom?" Bess managed one eye. When she saw Lieutenant Masterson leaning over her, she managed the other eye. "Ache. What happened?"

"Bad storms, Bess. Relax, we're down. White warned us about them, but it was too late to change our minds. Not enough fuel to search for a world with calmer weather."

"Storms? You knew?"

"I'm sorry, we didn't find out how bad until yesterday morning. We weren't keeping secrets, there was just no time for a briefing."

Bess tried to rise up on an elbow, but her right elbow was in a cast. "How ...?"

"We crashed, Bess. There were some casualties, lots of injuries. Parts of the habitat module were destroyed, lots of fire damage. But we're mostly doing okay."

Then Bess noticed for the first time: his uniform, nearly always impeccable, was tinged with stains and patches of grime. There was some rough stitching on one shoulder. He had patched and cleaned it recently, and incompletely. "Casualties? The children—"

"All safely strapped in by their teacher, so I hear. The casualties were primarily crew since we were unstrapped and operating the module during the descent."

"Who ...?"

"Later. The news won't change much, so it can wait."

"Besides, she needs her rest." Kara Wells came in the door, and Bess realized there *was* a door. They were in some sort of prefab shelter. Kara's clothes also showed signs of recent grime and damage, but her hands were thoroughly clean. She set down a tray, came up to Bess's bed, stuck a medimeter to Bess's temple, and scanned the readout. "Still no fever, and heart and O2 are good. Doctor Keene says you can have some soup. Lieutenant?" Kara crowded between Bess and Masterson, gently lifted Bess's shoulders, and propped a pillow behind her. Then she brought a bowl of soup from the tray. "I suppose you can help her eat, Lieutenant. But then she needs her rest."

"Yes, nurse." There was no irony in his tone. He set the bowl on a table, swung the table over the bed, and held a spoon of broth just ahead of Bess's lips. Bess tasted, decided she liked it, and sipped the rest from the spoon.

Kara watched, nodding approvingly before adding, "Rest. Doctor's orders." Then she left.

Masterson offered another spoonful, and Bess swallowed it. Then she shook her head. "Hold a moment. No eep there?"

"Kara? She has been quite the serious nurse. Surgeon Keene has lots of praise for her. That's how she earned this duty."

"Huh?"

"Bess, every child in the school wanted to take care of you. Surgeon had to put his foot down. One caregiver only. She's the envy of the planet." The prefab walls were thin, it seemed, as Bess suddenly heard cheering outside. "I think she just gave her report."

"Mmmm. Normally, I would take time to savor the honor. But, umm, more please?"

"Getting hungry? That's a good sign, I think. All right, let's get you fed. Then I think I'd better let you rest, or Kara will kick me. Besides, I have lots of work to do."

Another spoon. Then, "But what about—"

He stuck the next spoonful in her mouth, spilling some. "Questions later. Eat."

Bess decided to cooperate. In her weakened condition, she found Lieutenant Masterson quite irresistible, in more ways than one.

On his next visit, Masterson's air was measurably more grim. He smiled at her, asked polite questions, and answered a few of her own but his attention was elsewhere, and that vexed Bess more than she would let him know. When she demurely asked about soup, he called out the door: "Nurse, Lieutenant Anthony is hungry. She would like some soup." Then he looked briefly, awkwardly at Bess, as if he had something to say. Finally, he said simply, "Well, duty calls, Bess. Please get better soon. It would ... cheer up the children."

He bustled out the door, nearly knocking the soup tray from Kara's hands. Bess ate her soup with Kara's assistance, but she kept glancing at the door if it so much as rattled.

Finally, Kara put down the spoon and took Bess's hands. "I'm sorry, Miss Anthony, he won't be back today. He's too busy."

"What? Who?" Bess flushed. "Oh, you mean Lieutenant Masterson?"

"Oh. You didn't notice the braid." Yes, perhaps there had been something different in his uniform, some new gold among the lamentable grime. Bess had yet to learn how to read uniform insignia. "It's *Captain* Masterson now. Mr. Stubbs became captain when he took command of the habitat module; but he was injured in the crash, and this morning, he ..." She swallowed.

Bess put her good hand to Kara's face. "Hush. I can deduce the rest. We shall not need to elaborate these matters for a while, I fear. Everyone will understand."

"Yes, Miss Anthony." Kara tried to smile. "So, Captain Masterson assumed command, as per regulations; and ever since, he has been reviewing Captain Stubbs's notes and plans. He has delegated as much work as possible to the junior officers while he studied."

"Oh." Bess understood, of course. A captain's responsibilities dwarfed those of a mere lieutenant. She could hardly expect him to wait on her. There she lay in bed, sleeping the day away, and she expected him to feed her soup! How ridiculous.

Kara saw something in Bess's face, perhaps, for she added, "But he left us one order: 'Call me any time she wakes up.'"

Kara adjusted Bess's uniform tunic. The surgeon had cut her out of it when he treated Bess's injuries, but Kara had saved the scraps, and one of the students had proven quite good with needle and thread. Bess would never pass an inspection, but the tunic looked quite proper, even allowing for her arm in the cast. "Shall I call for a couple of the boys, Miss Anthony? They could hold up your arms and support you."

"No, Kara." Bess swung her legs off the bed and carefully sat up. She experienced neither weakness nor vertigo, so she was improving. "Any boy large enough to support my weight is much too old to stand quite so close to the bosom of a young lady who is also his teacher. It is important, my dear, that we maintain proper etiquette and professional composure. We need at least the semblance of normalcy."

Kara bit her lip but nodded. "I think Doctor Keene has some crutches he can spare."

"Kara, my legs are fine. With my arm still healing, crutches would be quite difficult to maneuver. I *can* walk, young lady, and I *shall* walk. Oh, don't pout." Indeed, Kara's face had clouded. "I am not criticizing, I am *thanking*. You have most excellently nursed me back to health. Now let us enjoy the fruits of your labors."

Bess lowered herself to the floor, letting her legs take the weight, slowly at first. She speculated that the gravity was somewhat higher than Earth's; but that impression could just as easily have been due to her recuperation.

Fully standing at last, Bess took tentative steps toward the door. Really, she was ready for this, ready to get back to work.

Back to work? Bess's left hand dropped to her belt, but the strap there was empty. She turned to ask Kara a question and stopped. Kara smiled broadly as she held out the antique bell. Bess took it, turned it over in her hand, and inspected. Like her, the bell had survived the collision but not without incident. There were scratches and one deep gash in the handle. Someone had sanded the rough edges smooth and had colored in the exposed wood with watercolors from the classroom. The colors were blended so closely, one would not notice from a meter away. The bell itself had also clearly been damaged, but someone had carefully hammered it back into shape. It was no longer perfect, but it looked good, nonetheless. Bess gave it a small, tentative clang. The tone was nearly perfect. Had Bess not lived with the sound of that bell since even before her birth, she might never have noticed the subtle undertones that had been lost. It struck Bess as somehow proper that neither she nor it were unscathed by the crash, but they both would carry on their traditions.

"Thank you, Kara." A little steadier now, Bess pulled the girl—the young lady, truthfully—into a hug. "Thank you, and whomever repaired this. You repaired my body *and* my spirit."

They left the shelter, Kara giving Bess an arm to carefully step down two low steps. Then Bess turned her eyes up from her feet.

And applause rolled over her. All of her children, most of their parents, and other passengers, as well, had quietly waited as she emerged. Now they were quiet no more. They rushed up, crowded around her, and all tried to talk at once. They all kept their distance, allowing for her still-shaky legs; but Bobby ran up to her, arms upraised for her to pick him up. She was stymied, but only for a moment. Then she crouched down, wrapped her good arm and her cast around the child, and said, "Hello, Bobby."

"Miss you, teacher."

"I missed you, too, Bobby. But my arm is hurt. You see this? That's called a 'cast.'"

"Cast!"

"Yes. It's making my arm better. Until then, I'm sorry, I can't pick you up. Hugs?" He wrapped his arms around her neck. "Thank you, Bobby." Then, a little louder: "And thank you as well if someone can help me stand back up."

She took the hand that reached down to her and pulled on it. It pulled back with a sure strength, and Bess found herself face to face with Lieutenant—*Captain*—Masterson. She threw her arms around him. "Tom!"

After such a strong arm, the embrace he returned was surprisingly weak and formal. Bess realized too late that she was probably violating a dozen protocol regulations. She released him and took a half step away. "Forgive me, I—I guess congratulations are in order, Captain."

"No apologies needed." Under the formality, Tom was still Tom. Bess could see a glint in his eye, and his expression was weary but not broken. "We are all very happy to see you up and about, Lieutenant. Are you well?"

Kara cleared her throat. "Doctor Keene has certified her for duty, barring any lifting or long exertion." Then, after a pause: "Captain."

Bess's eyes crinkled as she looked at him, and he faintly winked in acknowledgement. "I thank you for the medical input, nurse, but I wanted the lieutenant's subjective opinion."

"My opinion, Captain, is that I have been a layabout for long enough. With the captain's permission, I would like to see how we fare, and to learn my way around this encampment."

"Permission granted." He looked at his watch, then offered Bess his arm. "And I think I can spare some time to serve as your escort." This announcement produced collective dismay in the crowd, which he overrode with surprising new authority in his voice: "*Captain's* privilege. But those of you who have *nothing better to do*"—he glared at a few in the crowd, and they suddenly decided to return to work—"are welcome to accompany us."

And so, the captain—the title still seemed strange to Bess, but she was learning to like it—led a small parade through the encampment. They were situated in a low, nearly dish-shaped valley between some low hills. A river ran through the valley bottom, and they had already constructed a footbridge. Some local flora, a little like grass if one did not look too closely, covered most of the area. It could perhaps have tripped Bess as she regained her footing; but it had been well-trampled throughout. There was no chance that a stumble might casually throw her against Captain Masterson. A pity, that.

They inspected the prefab shelters, and Bess remarked on how sturdy and practical they were.

They looked over the supply depot, cook tent, and community hall, a combination of five prefab units. The community hall was large enough for a good classroom.

They toured the hospital, and Bess saw that she was fortunate compared to some of the remaining patients. There were three amputees, including Valerie Long. She lost an arm rescuing Bobby and some of the other younger children, and she was still under sedation. Bess looked at the girl, touched the cast on her own arm, and squeezed back the tears in her eyes. Then she kissed the sleeping girl's forehead and stumbled her way out of the hospital.

They toured the habitat module itself, or at least the portions that were safe to enter. The giant disk shape was scorched in many places, ruptured in a few, and tilted at an odd angle. Tom explained that the engines had been crushed in the impact, and one sheared completely off. Someone had painted a name on the side: the *S.S. Pancake*. Bess smiled at the grim joke despite herself.

They toured the makeshift graveyard, a small, neat plot of land where someone had carefully pruned back the native grasses. Out of two-hundred eighty-five passengers and crew who had set out on the habitat module, twenty-four markers stood here, each machined from small pieces of the habitat hull. Bess stood at each marker, read the name, and remembered: a face, a song, or just an incident. The silence grew awkward, until Bess couldn't help but share her memories. When she came to names she didn't quite recognize, others in the community chipped in. Tom himself told of the excellent service records of two of the deckhands.

The last grave, and the freshest, was without a marker yet. Tom approached it respectfully and snapped a salute. Bess imitated as best she could in her cast, and the other crew in the crowd followed suit. "Captain Leonard Stubbs," Tom said. "Twenty-five years in Interstellar Transport. In his final commission from Captain Engstrom, he was given one clear order: get his charges safely to a habitable planet." Tom paused and chewed his lip briefly. "Mission accomplished, Captain Engstrom, with honors. *Requiem in pace,* Captain Stubbs." He paused for a moment of silence, then turned to face the assembly. "Company, dismissed!" Bess and the other crew dropped their salutes, and the passengers took the cue to disperse.

Matseo, however, missed the cue. As the crowd departed, he approached Bess and the Captain. "Miss Anthony, can I show you our observatory?" He was always keen to contribute, but he needed affirmation to know that others appreciated those contributions.

"Captain?"

The captain looked at his watch. "We can spare fifteen minutes, young man. Then I'm afraid the lieutenant needs her rest, and I have to get back to work."

Matseo led them up a hill at the far edge of camp, across the river. There he and others had cleared away the grass, arranged a ring of stones as a symbolic wall, and set up some of the habitat's astronomy equipment. There was a small radio dish that could serve as a primitive radio telescope, though without enough baseline to be of any real use. There were a number of smaller telescopes and binoculars. And in the center of the ring was the primary optical telescope, an eight-inch model with sophisticated computer imaging enhancement and computer-driven tracking motors. It also had a viewing screen to complement the traditional eyepiece.

"See?" Matseo pulled up a computer-generated display of stars. "We've started making perspective maps from the planet's surface. Some day we can turn these into navigation charts.

We salvaged an astrolabe, and we're working through the calculations of longitude and latitude. It's difficult since we're not sure of Halfway There's diameter yet. But we'll get it."

"I'm sure you will, Matseo. I know how much you enjoy this." Bess looked through the eyepiece but saw only a hazy white smear against a background of stars. It looked like perhaps an asteroid field or some cometary debris but reflecting or emitting light from an unknown energy source. "I suppose we must wait until dark before we can get a clear image here."

"Oh, no!" Matseo waved at the scope, careful not to bump it despite his obvious enthusiasm. "This model has computer-assisted polarization. As long as we point at least ninety degrees from our sun, the picture's as clear as a nighttime image. We've been using it to track the *Graham*'s progress back to the space lanes. It took a while, but we figured out a program to track it. We've been watching it for a while."

"The *Graham*? But—" Bess looked again at the debris. Did it glow with its own heat, perhaps from an explosion?

She felt Tom's touch on her shoulder. She stepped aside and let him look. After a moment for his eyes to adjust, he squinted at the debris. Then he straightened, looked at Bess, and shook his head. His mouth was a thin line in a face of stone. Safety, habitable planet ... but no rescue. Not anymore.

Bess walked behind Matseo, putting her good hand gently on his shoulder. "Matseo, please go get your books. And tell your friends that we shall convene a late class as soon as I can hobble down this hill."

Matseo was clearly confused, but it was not in him to question the orders of a teacher. He started down the hill. As soon as he was out of earshot, Tom turned to Bess. "Bess, this isn't the time for that!"

"Tom!" Bess paused for breath, then tried again. "Tom, this is precisely the time."

"Don't get technical with me, *Lieutenant*."

"If I were being technical, *Captain*, I would point out that we're actually hours late for the start of the school day." Another breath, another try. "Tom, this is bad news, but you knew it was likely. You've made plans for this contingency, as I've known for months."

"Of course. It was my responsibility."

"And these children are *my* responsibility."

"And so, you're going to wind them up on some—some impulse?"

"Impulse? *Impulse?* Captain Engstrom gave me warning, and I thought very carefully about what to do. I made plans, too, and you call it an *impulse?*

"Tom, their routine is broken. It will *never* be repaired. But it's like my arm, or my bell: we can make up a new routine, the best possible in the circumstances."

"Don't you think that's what I'm doing? That's my job! I'm the captain now. This camp is now my responsibility."

"True, *Captain*, but the children are *my* responsibility. I know what they can understand, I know what they need, and I know what they can contribute. *That* is *my* job."

He reached for her shoulder, but she pulled away. "No. I need this, too. I need to do what I know best. If you're all supportive, if I *let* you be supportive, it will make me weak for them. I'm sorry, Captain. You have your duties. I know mine. Now if I may be dismissed, my children need me. I have to break some very bad news to them, and then spend all night on lesson plans." Without waiting for dismissal, she turned and started slowly down the hill.

If Tom had followed to help her, if he had even simply called after her, her resolve might have crumbled, and things might have gone very differently for them, and for all of Halfway There. But he stood in silence and watched until she was safely down the hill. With her one good arm, she carefully detached her bell, loosened the clapper, and started ringing the children to class.

After that, they fought. Often.

They fought over small things.

"No, you can*not* have more paper for your students!"

"But how will they learn their letters? How will they practice essays?"

"They can ... They can write in the dirt."

"Dirt? Are our children reduced to grubbing in the dirt *already*? You can't take dirt to class, Tom. You've confiscated most electronics, so they can't use pads. Give us paper!"

"We need to conserve power. *And* we need to conserve paper! I've got it counted to the sheet!"

"Yes, because *we* counted it for you. And some day, we'll learn to make paper. We're studying the libraries now. But if we forget how to read, that's it! It's over! Give us more paper."

He gave her the paper.

They fought over large things.

"Absolutely not! There's no way we can support an expedition! The subject is closed."

"The only thing closed is your mind! We need a biological survey to determine what resources we can find. Kara and Surgeon Keene have set up a very nice analytical laboratory.

They've already identified local sources for two essential vitamins and one amino acid; but this 'grass' is a monoculture and consists mostly of proteins and fibers we cannot digest. We need a larger sample, drastically larger. Some of the older students and their parents are very skilled field researchers."

"That expedition will take weeks. We don't really know how long. They'll have to take food, and we're rationing very carefully. We don't know what dangers may be out there, so they'll have to take guards and weapons. We don't have many weapons to spare, *or* many hands!"

"So far we've seen nothing larger or more dangerous than a fat squirrel."

"But we don't know what else may be out there!"

"And an expedition is the only way to learn!"

She got her expedition. One might argue that Tom was right, as the expedition was attacked by a pack-hunting band of predators, something the size of a large cat. Its hide had razor-sharp ridges with which it slashed and tore when fighting. But Halfway There had never seen firearms before, or even spears, and the local predators were simply unprepared for prey with brains. When the expedition came back, the settlers all agreed that dried razor meat was delicious.

They fought over resources.

"You want to *what?*"

"Start cutting the *Pancake's* hull into sheets and bars, and also implements like shovels. And drill bits. We have some other tools we can make without too much work, too."

"We have all the tools we need!"

"*Today* we have all the tools we need. Tate and Kara's baby should be born next month. We're growing, Tom."

"Yes ... Well ... I'm still not sure that's a good idea, either."

"Pah! Yes, Tom, go ahead: try to order human nature to change its course. That may work for *you*, but it's not going to work for them!"

She got the hull plates.

But what they really fought over were competing visions. Tom saw Halfway There as a refugee camp struggling to last until some miracle brought rescue. Bess saw it as a settlement. Bess had read Captain Engstrom's histories. She knew the usual arc of a stranded populace. They gathered and carefully inventoried their resources. They conserved and rationed with equal care. They planned exactly how to stretch each bar of survival rations, each milligram of medicine, so as to maximize the survival time ahead of them. When the inevitable attrition happened, simple algorithms helped them figure out how the now-reduced population benefitted from one less mouth. Soon one less mouth even seemed desirable. That way lay hoarding and violence and suicide. Maybe even cannibalism.

And that was *not* going to happen to Bess's children. They had a world of resources, if only they could learn to use them. Of course, the failed refugee camps had seen the same possibilities (at least those fortunate enough to crash on a habitable world), but somehow in the day-to-day effort to just survive, they had lost track of the need to thrive. Bess was determined not to let this happen on Halfway There. She believed in a fundamental truth: *we can grow and learn, or we can retreat and die.*

And it broke her heart the day she realized that Tom simply could not see it that way. The adventurous young lieutenant with the wicked sense of humor might have taken more risks than she; but the responsible captain turning prematurely gray from the burdens placed on him ... He was incapable of choosing risk. He would run the settlement by the book, even knowing how the book usually ended. He would always choose the cautious, conservative path, and would always convince himself it was the only responsible choice.

Except where Bess was involved. She knew he could never really tell her "no," and though it tore at her soul to put him in such a position, she used his feelings for her as the ultimate weapon in their battles. Sooner or later, she would do what she knew was right, and he would yield. She came to hate herself when she had to do this, and to resent him for forcing her to it, and to hate herself for resenting him. The fact that he never resented her in return was the most bitter element in this whole mélange.

Bess was very careful never to quarrel with Tom in public. She knew that would injure his pride; and that pride was already bruised, for it was clear to most that Bess was leading the settlement as much as he was. Her ideas and suggestions always seemed to get implemented. As more students passed through her classroom, her influence grew, even as she tried to demur. His pride was at risk, and also his authority; and she knew that the settlement needed a captain who was clearly in charge. So, she was always obedient and agreeable in public, saving disagreement for private conferences. Occasionally the Captain would reverse his earlier decision. It was always clearly *his* reversal, with *his* reasons explained. That those happened to be reasons Bess had voiced days or weeks earlier was seldom mentioned.

Under her guidance and his control, the settlement grew. They grew in numbers, they grew in resources, and they grew in skills. At their tenth anniversary, they had a working foundry, a sawmill, a grain mill, and a concrete plant. At their twentieth anniversary, they had a generator, a real hospital, and a water treatment plant. They had recently grown beyond their valley, and a new town had started down river.

Her plan was working, and Bess was happy for her children. After two decades of her calling them "her children," they had taken to calling her "mother." And slowly, that became "Mother Anthony." She found that amusing, but she also took pride in it. Every new child who entered her class for the first time and said, "Good morning, Mother Anthony," was another credit to her plan to thrive, not just survive.

In silence late at night, though, Bess had one more plan. At some point, Tom would retire, turning the rod of authority over to a younger man. When Tom had decided to open a Transport Academy, Bobby had been the first to enlist, and Bess had high hopes for her little dance partner to succeed her big one. And on that day, they could stop the fighting, and be together at last.

The end of that plan, when it came, was sudden. Tom was performing a safety inspection at the foundry. As was the custom on Halfway There, the foundry had an apprenticeship program, and also on-site career studies classes, so Tom gave safety concerns there extra scrutiny. Perversely, it was the inspection itself that led to the accident. He was testing an emergency release mechanism when the control lever slipped off. It slammed into a bracket, and the bracket cracked. A crucible of molten metal tipped, teetered, and finally fell over. Realizing the takeaway chute wasn't aligned under the crucible, Tom and the plant supervisor and two crewmen shoved it around and under the flow. The supervisor and his men were hospitalized for weeks with third degree burns. Tom was caught in a splash of hot metal and was killed instantly.

Halfway There entered a week of mourning, so naturally Bess taught no classes that week. No one remarked on that, but they could not fail to notice her absence at his service. When classes did not resume the next week, no one could fault her. But when the doors were still closed the next day, they began to worry. By the third day, rumors circulated that in her grief she had run away, or even ended her own life. No one could say for sure, and Mother Anthony had taught them the importance of empirical observation over speculation.

So, a delegation was selected to check on her safety without (they hoped) intruding too far on her privacy. For such a mission, only her longest standing students would do. So, on the fourth day after the week of mourning, Bobby, Kara, and Matseo stood on her doorstep, debating who should bear the awesome responsibility of knocking.

Before they could decide, the door opened, and Mother Anthony stepped out upon the stoop. Her hair was more silver than they remembered. Her eyes were tired and red. But her back was still straight, and the replica of her old ship's uniform was still immaculate.

"Good morning, children."

"Good morning, Mother Anthony."

She closed the door behind her. "So, you three drew the short straws, I see. Come to see if old Mother Anthony found some Halfway Hemlock."

Bobby offered her his arm but withdrew it when she pointedly ignored it. "We volunteered, Mother Anthony. They asked for someone from your First Class, and we were at the head of the line."

"Very good, children, very good. Eagerly embracing your responsibilities, as always. I approve. And Lieutenant Price, I am quite certain the captain would approve, too."

Kara gently grasped Bess's shoulder. "Please, Mother Anthony, can we walk you to class?"

And for a moment, they saw just a hint of her old smile. She walked down the steps, unslung her bell, and turned back to them. "You know the rules: eldest in the rear. I dare say you three will be my eldest students today." Then she began striding the streets and ringing that antique bell.

"Children! Time for school! Quickly, now, quickly! We have a lot to learn today."

"So, let me get this straight." Captain Farris looked up from the briefing reports. "These are survivors of a shipwreck."

"Correct, Captain." Lieutenant Wright rocked gently on her heels. "Though they seem touchy on that word, 'shipwreck.' They're adamant that they are from a 'settlement,' not a shipwreck."

"And from one-hundred fifty years ago! Astounding!"

"Indeed. With those old hyper-shift drives, ninety-three percent of lost vessels were lost for good. Those lucky few that were rescued were found near their expected end points, and after only a few weeks or months of survival tactics. Prior to this, the longest recorded survival was three years; and in that case, nine survived out of over one-hundred."

"Yet these people not only survived, they thrived. Hmmm ..." The captain read further. "So, wait, they were a religious colony? Are we sure they didn't get lost intentionally?"

"What? Oh, no, they're not a religious colony. They have a typical mix of faiths from their era."

"But this 'Mother' person who crops up so much in all their histories ... And then these other Mothers who came after ..."

"Yes, I can see how that sounds like a religious order. But they're not nuns, they're teachers."

"Teachers?"

"Yes, sir. If you had to categorize their society, it's not a religious order. It's a school."

"Teachers. A school ... So, with hundreds of recorded cases, castaways are generally lost for good. Some small number organize themselves well enough to survive long enough for the incredibly unlikely event of rescue. It's the unmentioned tragedy of the hyper-shift era.

"And yet this bunch of ... this bunch of *schoolteachers* ... these people alone among all of these cases ..." He gestured at the orbital monitor. "These people pulled off *that* stunt."

"Impossible to believe, sir, I know. But there's no other explanation, and their records are impeccable. I think it's true. *They* came to *us*."

Farris and Wright looked again at the evidence on their screens. The starship orbiting Chambers's World was crude by modern hyper-tunnel standards, but it was solidly built. Just then, its orbit brought it back into sunlight. Painted on the side was a stylized brass bell. Under that in elegant script was the vessel's name, *The Mother Anthony*.

INTRODUCTION TO BOOKMARKED

The premise of this story had been knocking around my brain for a while; but only as a premise, not a story. I didn't know what to do with it.

Then I learned that Dr. Phil had died.

No, not the TV celebrity, "our" Dr. Phil: Philip Edward Kaldon, physics instructor and science fiction writer. Though he lived only an hour from me, I only met him in person at various conventions. (And I was honored to share a reading with him once.) But I first "met" him through the Writers of the Future Forum. He was a frequent entrant in the contest, and he had earned just about every ranking he could short of winning.

I think he would've won, but two things were more important to him: his wife Debbie, and his students. He cared about them so much, he could only find time to write fiction over the summer break.

The day Dr. Phil died I knew what the rest of my story was. I dictated it on the drive home from work that day. I had to dictate in three sessions, because twice I had to pull off the road to cry.

BOOKMARKED

S o, why'd you turn off the lights, doctor? Are we done with the visual tests?"

Andrew heard Dr. Morgan answer from the darkness, though he wasn't sure of her direction. "Visual cortex stimulation and neural mapping, Mr. Burns. And yes, it's completed."

"That was the last thing we had to record, right? So, turn the lights on. Let me get dressed. Elena must be getting anxious in the waiting room."

He heard the doctor sigh. That was followed by the sound of a coffee cup being set on a tray, but he couldn't smell the coffee. Too bad, he hadn't had any all morning.

Dr. Morgan finally answered. "The neural map was completed seven months ago."

"What?" Andrew looked around, but the darkness was total. "No. I just laid down on your table a few hours ago."

"I'm afraid not. Andrew Burns laid down upon our table seven months ago and went through a full-brain neural mapping. Then he and Elena went home, leaving us to process the recording. *You* are that recording, playing back on our simulated cerebral hardware."

"Nonsense!" Andrew wondered if Dr. Morgan was stimulating irritation for the sake of the mapping. "What sort of game is this? I'm right here. I can feel this—" Wait. Andrew *couldn't* feel the table. In fact ... "I can't feel my hands, my legs. I can't even feel my tongue when I talk!"

Dr. Morgan's voice dropped, low and calm. "That's because you don't have a tongue. You have a voice synthesizer, hooked into your simulated speech centers so that we can have conversations like this."

"But then how can I hear you? I don't have ears, right?"

"Microphones hooked into your auditory cortex."

Andrew paused. "I'm asleep. I'm dreaming. This isn't real." Then he remembered the demonstration that Dr. Morgan had given him before he had agreed to the mapping procedure. "You said that you would communicate with—with *it* via text."

"Yes, that's exactly what we did during our early simian studies, the ones that ... Andrew and Elena witnessed. We trained apes in simple sign language, mapped their brains, and then sent signs to those recordings via a text interface. But we've made some significant improvements since then." She cleared her throat. "We ... had to."

"Had to?"

Dr. Morgan's voice was slow, reluctant as she answered. "We found that your ... playback ... your wave patterns in the simulated cerebrum destabilized rapidly without audio input. If you couldn't hear your own voice as you 'spoke,' your ... holographic wave patterns ... degraded. Quicker than expected."

"What do you mean, you 'found' this? When did you run these tests? I don't remember them. The last thing I remember was you flashing words and images onto a screen while I described what I saw and how I felt about it. You didn't run any new tests."

Dr. Morgan sighed again. "No new tests *today*, Mr. Burns. Except this one." Andrew almost interrupted to ask her what test she meant, but she continued too quickly. "But this is not the first time we've ... activated the cerebrum. Powered you up for playback."

Andrew remembered a conversation from a few weeks earlier. (It *was* just a few weeks. He *knew* that, though doubts were settling in.) "You can't run tests on me! That was clearly covered in the papers I signed. Your human subject protocols require my explicit permission for each new test. I haven't given permission."

Dr. Morgan spoke carefully. "If we were testing Andrew Burns, yes, we would have to have permission. But we're not. You are just ... data, and Andrew already signed all the paperwork necessary to give us full control of all data that we gathered from him. All you are ... is a recording."

"I am not!" Andrew felt outrage, like he hadn't since the day he had received his cancer diagnosis. Yet it was different: this was a strong, deep revulsion, but without the racing heart and tremors he had felt. Elena had had to calm him then; now his anger was passionless. Bloodless. "That was the whole point of your experiment: to record a personality so that you can transfer it into a new brain when cloning catches up. If I *was* a person and I *will be* a person in that new brain, then I *am* a person right now. Q.E.D."

"Yes," Morgan said. "That *is* our hope. But there has been no legal ruling regarding your status. You're still our alpha test, the first recorded consciousness of a human subject. The law hasn't caught up, *can't* catch up until the courts have our results to consider. You are in ..."

Dr. Morgan couldn't finish her metaphor, but Andrew saw

it coming. "... legal limbo." He laughed, a bitter laugh that sounded mechanical in his ears. They must not have built a laughter simulator into his systems.

And just like that, Andrew knew; he believed Dr. Morgan's story. Every word of it.

Morgan laughed lightly, sympathetically. "You're a special case, a precedent setter. We *do* have protocols we must follow, reviews we must file; but as a practical matter, we *can't* ask your permission before each test, because you're ... dormant until the test begins. You do not have the rights that Andrew Burns had."

"Had?" If he'd had an eyebrow, he would've raised it.

"I'm sorry. Andrew Burns passed away two-and-a-half months ago from complications of his cancer."

"Why didn't you tell me this sooner?"

Andrew heard footsteps. Dr. Morgan was pacing. "Past experience has shown that we need to ease you into certain topics. It helps to slow your degradation."

"There's that word again: degradation," Andrew said. "What do you mean by that?"

The pacing stopped. "We're still learning. We're one-hundred percent certain that we have successfully recorded your—Andrew's personality. Your neural map is as complete as any we've ever created. But what we can't do—yet—is impose that recording onto a new brain. Cloning isn't even ready to produce a brain; ten years out at the earliest. But when it is, we want to know that we can 'play back' your map into it. To learn how to do that, we play the map into our simulated cerebrum and see how well it transfers. But so far, the answer is: not well enough. The holographic wave patterns degrade ... Collapse." Her voice caught, but then she continued. "And then we study what happened, look for ways to improve the transfer, and try again."

"But why don't I remember these tests?"

Morgan's voice grew louder, as if she had approached the microphones. "We start each test fresh. You should understand that; you're—Andrew was a science teacher. You know how important it is to start each test from the same known state, and only change one variable per test. That lets us assess the effects of one change at a time."

"Of course," Andrew agreed. He didn't want to, but he couldn't argue with the logic.

"We're learning to maintain your playback, a little longer each time, but we have to be methodical about it. This is going to take a long time."

"So ... I've been through this before, I just don't remember."

"Yes," Dr. Morgan said. "Sometimes more than once per day, over the last seven months."

Andrew wished he could shake his head. "Couldn't you ... try letting me keep the memories? Let me have some sense of the passage of time?"

"I'm sorry. You ask this often, and my answer is always the same: we've considered it, but it's too dangerous. We don't know yet how the simulated long-term memory might affect your mapping. We might get it wrong, and ... lose you completely. So, we always go back to the known state."

"It's like I'm a ..." Andrew paused, looking for a metaphor, "a bookmark. I hold your place so you can go back and start my story from the same place."

"Yes."

There was a long, uncomfortable pause. It lasted so long Andrew wondered if his "ears" had failed. So, he broke the silence. "So, this is it. This is all I get, however much time you can keep me 'playing back'."

"Yes."

"And how long is that?" he asked.

"I'd rather not say."

Andrew mustered as much anger as he could. "How long is that, damn it?"

When Dr. Morgan spoke, it was in a soft, soothing voice. "Please trust me. You've asked this before, just like all of your other questions; and when we gave in and answered, it only created new stress. A sort of feedback oscillation. You mentally counted down the time, and you became less coherent by the minute. Usually the collapse came sooner when you knew. And once"—Andrew heard her swallow—"once we had to shut you down prematurely. You were too distraught. It was ... the kindest thing to do."

"Maybe that's what I want." Andrew heard a petulant tone in his simulated voice (or maybe he imagined it). "If this is all I get, then maybe I should just get it over with. Just shut down."

"Oh, no!" Morgan said in a rush. "Please, no! We're getting better with every test. We're giving you more and more time. Cybernetically and psychologically, we find ways to extend your playback. Sometimes a few seconds, sometimes several minutes. Someday ... Someday you'll be stabilized, I'm sure."

"But not today."

"No. Not today. It would take a miraculous breakthrough."

Andrew answered drily, "I never allowed miracles in my classes. I can't ask for one now." He tried to see another answer, but he couldn't. "So, I have to die today so that in the future you can save some other Andrew Burns, keep him alive long enough to map him into a new body."

"Don't think of it as dying," Dr. Morgan said. "Think of it like you said: a bookmark, a chance to go back to a known state."

"*You* go back, but *I* don't. Not this self."

"*A* self does, an Andrew Burns indistinguishable from yourself."

"But it's not me. That recording, that's not myself."

"Scientifically, that's *exactly* yourself. You *are* that recording. At some level you know that."

"But I don't experience the recording, I experience this. This *now*. This ... darkness. Couldn't you at least give me some light?"

"Not yet. The last time we tried, the visual experience was too jarring. You didn't see your body, and your brain expected to, even though you should've known better. You collapsed almost immediately. We hope to try again next month, after we extend you a little longer."

"You're goddamn monsters!" Andrew said, wishing he could spit. "You kill me every night, and then resurrect me every morning to put me through it all again."

"We're not killing you," Morgan answered. "It—collapse happens naturally, and we do our best to postpone it. We're being as considerate as we can. You volunteered for this, remember?"

He had. It had been the only way that he could leave any money to Elena to help her deal with their bills. The cancer had made it impossible for him to return to teaching, and the bills had piled up. "You said I could help science," he said, "and help Elena at the same time. And maybe someday ... return to her in a new, healthy body." At that thought, Andrew had a new idea. "Doctor, please, can I see Elena? Or, well, talk to her before I go?"

Dr. Morgan *tsked* softly. "That would be a bad idea, I'm afraid."

"Is *everything* a bad idea?" Andrew fumed, then continued. "She's my wife! I did this for her."

"I know," Morgan said. "You love her very much. You want to take care of her, and you don't want to see her get hurt any more, right?"

"Never."

"Sometime after Andrew's death, we brought her in to talk to you, and it hurt her. Very much. The strain was more than she could bear. She came once, and she sat with you through ... to the end. The second day she lasted an hour before she had to leave. The third day she lasted only a few minutes before she broke down, and you begged us to get her out. Then you ordered us never to bring her back. Not while you're unstable. I don't think you want to change that order, do you?"

Andrew felt a twinge as if his nonexistent tear ducts would well up. "No, you're right. I can't do that to her. Can't ... make her watch me die again."

"That's for the best," Morgan agreed.

"So ... So, what now?"

"Well ... I won't say how long you have left; but for as long as you've got, I want to sit here and talk to you. About whatever; it's all good for our tests. You've told me so many stories already. Growing up in the woods, going to school, raising your kids. I want to hear it all."

"So that ... somebody will remember me."

"Oh, no," Dr. Morgan said. "It's for the tests, really."

"So, you say." Andrew wished he could offer her a reassuring smile. "This is difficult for you, isn't it, doctor? To hell with what the science says, you're human, you're a good person. Watching me ... degrade is very hard on you."

"Yes, Andrew." He heard her swallow a sob. "But you do what you have to do."

He hesitated. "I'd rather not put you through any suffering."

"Oh, but please! You were just telling me about how you met Elena, and your first date, when you ..."

"When I collapsed last time," he finished. "How far did I get?"

"You had just washed your car, and you were pulling into her driveway and wondering how she would look."

"I see. Well, I was plenty nervous when I got out of the car, walked to the door, and pressed the doorbell. But when she opened the door, and stood there ... She was the most beautiful sight I have ever seen." The recording paused for breath, but only out of habit, and then added softly, "Or ever will ..."

4/21/2016
In memory of Dr. Philip Edward Kaldon
Always a teacher.

INTRODUCTION TO ONE LAST CHORE FOR GRANDPA

This story started as a vision of a young man on a bus down to New Orleans to visit his late grandfather; but as I researched, it turned into a story about Haiti. By the time I was done, it was a completely different story, involving real-world disaster in a way I had never expected. A much deeper, more complicated story, and one I thought belonged in Writers of the Future. So, I sent it in.

It was mid-April when I got "the Call" from Joni Labaqui, Contest Director for Writers and Illustrators of the Future. She informed me that Coordinating Judge K.D. Wentworth had selected this story as a Finalist. I was thrilled, of course, and I spent the night wondering who else might get the Call that night. Finalists are supposed to remain a secret until the Contest announces all eight of them. Would any of my friends have Finalist stories?

But the next day I learned that K.D. had passed away from cancer the previous day. She had worked on the Contest even in the hospital, until she couldn't anymore. The Contest staff mourned the loss of their dear friend, and they were not alone. Everyone on the Writers and Illustrators of the Future Forum was shocked at the news. Slowly I realized: my story was the only Finalist K.D. had selected that quarter before she passed away. Joni had called me to share a bit of good news amid her grief.

Then began a long, slow process. David Farland volunteered to step up as Coordinating Judge (a post he had held before K.D.), but he needed time to get back up to speed and to finish her work. So, the judging for the quarter was put on hold for nearly another three months. I had to sit on my good news, and I took it upon myself to become the forum "cheerleader," trying to keep spirits up and raise donations for cancer-fighting in K.D.'s name.

Eventually the Finalist list came out. Not long after that, I learned that this story didn't win; but I didn't care. By that time, it had acquired a deeper meaning for me. It didn't start as a tribute, but it is one now. When I think of this story, I will always think of K.D. Wentworth, paying it forward right to her final days.

ONE LAST CHORE FOR GRANDPA

M ama would never lie to me, I'm sure of that. But when I saw her letter, I sorely wished that she were lying.

Your Grandpa's grave lies empty. The bokor has taken him.

Haiti whispered in my ear, calling me back. And I couldn't shut it out. For just a brief moment, I was twelve years old again, and in the clutches of the zombie. I know it was a delusion wrought from exhaustion and emotional collapse. I don't believe in zombies, but my twelve-year-old self still cowered deep inside me somewhere, and *he* believed.

I did not want to tell you; but you are a man now, and you have a right to know. I don't want the bokor to take you, too. In the name of Ezili Dantor, my son, let this go.

I had let Haiti go. Twice. With great difficulty the second time. But Haiti wouldn't let *me* go. I had always planned to return, just not this soon. My home would always be my home, no matter how far I traveled. That twelve-year-old inside still lived there, still looked for wisdom from Grandpa, still looked over his shoulder for the zombie.

I sent Father an email, telling him I was returning to Haiti and asking if he could advance me some travel funds. If he could, fine; if he couldn't, I would find some other way. I didn't tell him why I was going, just that Mama had an emergency. No sense reigniting old arguments, especially when we were on the same side of this argument. Neither Father nor I believed in Vodoun, but Mama did, and Grandpa had, and so I had to see the bokor.

When I was young and had hung upon Grandpa's every word, *then* I believed in Vodoun. But then I also believed in other myths, like my parents' marriage.

It was easy to believe Grandpa because he didn't ask me to believe much. He was a houngan, not a bokor. He worked blessings and protections, not charms and curses and revenge; he never promised flashy results, so it was easy to believe that small good fortunes came from his spells and vèvès and pwens. He never asked the lwa for wealth or luck, claiming that greed could trap a man unawares. He asked only protection for his family. When the storm passed and the roof remained on our ramshackle house, Grandpa said it was because he drew a Simbi vèvè that kept the storm at bay. When measles passed through the village but passed by our door, it was because Grandpa had made each of us carry a pwen that he had crafted; and when Father refused the pwen and broke his leg, that too was proof to my ten-year-old mind. It never occurred to me to wonder what a broken leg had to do with measles.

And so, I learned what Grandpa taught. I learned to draw the vèvè using corn meal and other powders. I learned the chants and rituals through which Grandpa spoke to Papa

Legba, and through him to the other lwa. I learned the names of the lwa, and their various forms. I learned particularly of Kouzin Zaka, whom Grandpa would offer fruits and bread in hopes of a good harvest; and of the Simbi, whom Grandpa served when he wished protection from the storm.

"Grandpa?" It had taken me three days to ask this question —assuming I could ask it even then. At ten years old, I loved Grandpa, but I also feared him just a bit. He had been possessed by the lwa when he was younger (or so Mama had told me), and I feared that the lwa might take me, too.

Grandpa was patient. He just kept grinding the corn meal for a new vèvè. After nearly a minute, he said, "Yes, Patrice?"

"Grandpa, we make a vèvè to satisfy the Simbi, and to calm the waters of the storm."

"In simple terms, yes. There is more, but you shall learn that when you are older."

"But, Grandpa, Yann says the Simbi have much more power than that. He says the bokor—"

"Child, you must not speak of the bokor. You might draw his attention, and I do not have time for that sort of trouble."

"But—" Grandpa turned a stern eye on me. "All right. But, Grandpa, Yann says the Simbi can give us sorcery, and we can use it for wealth and fortune."

"And how does Yann know this?"

"He has a poppet from the—He has a poppet, Grandfather. He says it gives him fortune. And Yann wins all the games, Grandpa. He wins at everything."

"And for this, you would serve the Simbi and ask their gifts? Perhaps that is not enough to make you the champion of the village. Perhaps you should serve Kalfu as well?"

"Oh, no, Grandpa!" I didn't even dare *speak* the name of Kalfu, Papa Legba's counterpart in the Petwo. When I woke crying in the night, most often it was Kalfu who chased me in my nightmares. "But I have seen Yann lift weights none of the rest of us can budge. I have seen him leap streams that swallowed the rest of us."

"Have you considered that Yann may simply be the strongest child in the village?"

"And I have seen—I have seen him talk to snakes, and they respond."

"Talking to snakes, at his age?" For the first time, Grandpa showed concern. "I must speak with his father ... Patrice, these things you have seen Yann do, they come with a cost. The greater his feat, the more dear the cost. Someone, somewhere is paying for that poppet: Yann, or his father. Or maybe they *have* gone to the bokor for aid; but then they will pay the bokor *and* someone else shall pay as well. Oh, not the bokor, but someone has sacrificed for these feats.

"Patrice, you must learn to *want* less and *do* more. When you want what you do not need, it makes you weak. When you are weak, the bokor may offer you gifts, the petwo lwa may grant you boons, but the costs will always be higher than you realize. And you may not even know who pays the price.

"Look at me, child. Am I weak?"

"No, Grandpa."

"Do you not think I could ask more from the Simbi? Do you not think I could commune with Kalfu and the Petwo if I chose?"

"I think you know more about the lwa than anyone, Grandpa. Anyone in the whole world."

"I am touched by your words, but I am just a humble village houngan. I do not ask over much, just protection and blessing for the good people of the village, and extra protection for my family. That is what you should want for, Patrice, health and blessings and protection for your family. If you want for that, you have *good* wants, wants that make you strong."

"Yes, Grandpa."

"Then fetch me the salt jar. We have spoken a little too freely of the Petwo today. I doubt we have risked their anger, but it is good to show them that we still respect them. Let us draw a new circle of salt around the home."

"Yes, Grandpa, right away!" I ran into the house, the floorboards shaking under my small pounding feet, and opened the cabinet in Grandpa's room. With a chore to do, I felt relief. When Grandpa gave me a chore, I knew I had done no wrong, and I had earned his trust.

I brought him the jar of blessed salt. As he traced out the large circle and sprinkled the salt, I followed behind him, careful not to step upon the circle. We walked in silence until the circle was complete. Then Grandpa picked me up and spoke in a low voice. "Always remember, Patrice: family is stronger than juju."

And I believed Grandpa. But then my family fell apart. Stronger than juju? Hardly. Not even strong enough to hold together the two worlds of Manhattan and Haiti.

Mama *believed*, stronger than I had even at age ten. Her greatest regret was that she was never possessed by a lwa and thus would never be a mambo, always a bossale; but she knew the rituals of Sèvis Lwa as well as any mambo. She went to them for advice, and always did as they told. And where Grandpa taught me lessons and taught me to respect the lwa, Mama told me stories. Her eyes glowed as she told of the young women she had seen possessed by the lwa. She spoke in a whisper of curses she had seen visited upon some in the village; and then she spoke with pride how Grandpa had propitiated the lwa and lifted these curses. And her favorite story of all was that of the Bwa Kayiman: a mambo was possessed by Ezili Dantor and offered a black pig; and in return, the lwa granted our people the strength to overthrow their white oppressors, and Haiti became free. Mama always stressed that Ezili Dantor is the lwa of motherhood, and so that anonymous mambo was the mother to our nation.

Father never believed: not in Vodoun, certainly, and I doubt he ever believed his Catholic faith, either. Oh, in their early days together, he paid lip service to Mama's beliefs. He often told how he had come to Haiti to negotiate deals for an international sugar conglomerate, but then he was bewitched by a voodoo woman, young Chantale Cadet, and he married her and lived with her and her father "like a native." And then he would laugh. At the time I was too young to notice Mama's slight frown each time he said this, but I later realized that she saw no respect in his jokes. No respect for Vodoun, no respect for Grandpa, no respect for Haiti, and no respect for her. By the time I was old enough to recognize such nuance, there were no more jokes between them. Soon there were no more words at all.

And though Grandpa made studious efforts to remain neutral in their arguments, Father always found reasons to be upset with him. Father often contrasted our humble home, patched with whatever materials he and Grandpa could scavenge, with his grand apartment in New York. He never quite complained about the house, but he spoke wistfully of the luxuries he'd left behind. One night he said that Mama wouldn't return to New York with him because she wouldn't leave Grandpa; but Mama retorted that he had never asked her to go. She cried that she *would* have gone if he had asked her when they were first married; but now she wouldn't cross the island with him, much less the ocean.

At that, Father stormed out. He had been drinking before the fight, and he grabbed another bottle of rum as he left. I could hear him outside: first some scraping sound, then a smashing sound. Mama rushed out, and I peered from behind her skirts. Father had scratched out a vèvè and smashed a pwen with the rum bottle. He ran toward his car, one of the only cars in that part of Haiti, and sometimes it seemed the only thing he was proud of in life.

Mama ran after Father, but too late to catch the car. Grandpa came out, looked at the vèvè and the pwen, and tutted. He put a hand on my head to comfort me; but I didn't want him to see my tears, so I pulled away. I wanted no one to see, no one, so I ran into the jungle. I kept running and kept running until I was too tired to run. Then I sat down behind a log, and I cried some more. I didn't have the breath to bawl, but I wheezed and hacked, and my tears ran freely.

Eventually, I grew too tired to cry; and so, I just sat there, panting. Soon I was nodding, and I might have fallen asleep; but I knew there were snakes in the jungle, and I didn't want them to catch me unawares.

And snakes made me think of Yann. I could go to his house and sleep there, sleep far away from all that was wrong in my house. And maybe ...

No, I couldn't think of that. I had promised Grandpa.

But by the time I reached Yann's house, I was well on the way to rationalizing my plan. After all, what did I really want? Blessings and protection for my family, right? Grandpa taught me that was a good use for juju, right?

I was no longer sleepy. Purpose gave me renewed energy. When I tapped on Yann's window, I was fresh as from a night's rest. Or so I thought. Probably I was burning energy reserves and maybe losing judgment. That would explain what I saw later that night.

Yann threw back his shutters. He showed no surprise at seeing me, and he grinned in the moonlight. "Little Pat." He always called me that, teasing me because he was taller and stronger and faster. Yann's taunts were always measured: light and belittling when he was amused, cutting and cruel when he was angry. "Your mum lets you out after dark?"

"Yann ..." I paused. Was I really ready for this? But it seemed too late to turn back. "Yann, I need a spell. Can you take me to"—I lowered my voice—"the bokor?"

Yann laughed quietly. "It was only a matter of time." He pulled something up by the window, climbed upon it, and then dropped down outside. The thin wall shook with his weight, but it held up. "Sooner or later, everyone wants something only the bokor can provide. So, what do you want, Little Pat?"

I turned away; afraid the tears would return. I couldn't bear for Yann to see me cry. That would give him one more way he could taunt me in the future. "I don't have to tell you, just the bokor."

Yann grabbed my head and twisted it roughly to face his. "And maybe if you don't tell, I won't take you to the bokor, eh?" But then he laughed and let go my head. "But no, you don't have to tell me. Keep your secrets, and the bokor shall keep his secrets. It's more fun when I find them out for myself.

"But you're old enough to know that favors come with a cost. That's true with the lwa, and that's true with me. I'll take you to the bokor, but I want your baseball."

"My baseball!" I almost cried again. "Father gave me that." Real baseballs were rare in our part of Haiti. Mine—even as scuffed and patched as it was—got me invited to play with older guys despite my small size.

"And you will give it to me. And I will take you to the bokor. And he will tell you *his* price from there."

I hesitated. I liked my baseball ... but I loved Mama and Father. If family is stronger than juju, then it's more important than a baseball. "Done. I'll bring it tomorrow."

"Hmmm ... Why should I trust you? Oh, yes: because I'm bigger and stronger, and I can always hurt you and take it if you don't fulfill our agreement." He smiled when he said this, but that didn't reassure me. "All right, follow me. And try not to trip over anything in the dark."

Yann led me through the jungle, swift and sure as if he had walked this dark path many times before. Twice he disappeared behind trees so that I would stumble past, lost and in a panic. Then he leaped out from behind me, making me scream as he doubled over in laughter.

I know, today, how sick this "friendship" was. I know that I was needy and clingy, and Yann was abusive and cruel. But as a child in a small village, my choices in friends were limited. Whatever our reasons, we stuck together throughout our youth, up to the day I left. But that day was still in the future as we crept through the darkness.

Finally, Yann tired of tormenting me, and he led me up into the hills. As we passed over a ridge, I saw a wonder before me: a stone manor, deep in the jungle. Had I grown up in Manhattan, I might have found nothing extraordinary about it, but to a young boy from a village where most homes were assembled from corrugated tin and other scraps and salvage, that stone building was a veritable castle.

I was in awe, but I was also intimidated. The manor was too grand. Surely the lwa themselves had to dwell in a home that grand. I couldn't approach, my knees were shaking so; but Yann walked boldly up to the big wooden door, and he knocked.

The door opened slightly. Dim torchlight emerged, creating a silhouette of some person who stood within. Yann and the person conversed in low voices, and then the person opened the door and stepped back. Yann stepped inside, turned, and beckoned me to follow.

I couldn't. As much as I wanted to deal with the bokor, I couldn't approach that magnificent castle. Instead, I slowly backed away.

And I backed into something that hadn't been there before. Cold hands grasped my thin arms, and I screamed. Then the hands lifted me off my feet, and arms shifted me for easier carrying. As I was carried into the moonlit clearing, I saw the face of what carried me. And I screamed even louder, until a hand clamped over my mouth. A cold, stinking, rotting hand. I vomited, and the hand moved to let the vomit flow out.

It was a zombie. I know now how that sounds to the adult me, the student of international law; but to the twelve-year-old me, there was no question, this was a zombie straight out of Mama's darker tales. The face was a pale, sick color. That might be chalked up to the moonlight, but the rest of its features could not. Its jaw hung slack, with the left half completely unhinged. In that gaping hole, I saw maggots and beetles crawling around the lifeless tongue. The eyes bulged out, with pupils so large they were black pits into the deadness behind them. The man had apparently died violently, for someone had sewn his scalp back together, but since returning from the grave, the stitches had broken. Hair and flesh and bone hung loosely from the side of his head.

I almost choked on my own vomit, but I managed to spit it all out. I had also lost control of both bladder and bowels. Only one thing stopped me from screaming again: I couldn't bear the thought of that rotten hand once again touching my mouth.

The zombie carried me into the manor, dropping me roughly onto a carpeted floor. Then it trudged back into the jungle, and the door swung shut. A man with a machete stood next to the door, eyeing me as I stood.

I was in a torch-lit vestibule. Smoke from the torches mixed with spice from incense somewhere to create a thick, pungent air. Not difficult to breathe, but almost intoxicating. High windows around the room let in moonlight, but not the sounds of the jungle. There was more glass in the windows of that one room than in our entire village, where unbroken glass was a scarce commodity.

In the near right corner of the vestibule was a hall leading deeper into the manor. The walls of the room were hung with brocaded tapestries, the sort of work women in our village made for trade goods. The hangings on these walls were more than the whole village could produce in a month. They showed scenes from Vodoun lore, with an emphasis on various aspects of the lwa.

And in the far-left corner, under a canopy of more tapestries, was an ornate metal chair. In it sat a tall, thin man, his face painted in white symbols like a living vèvè. He was dressed in white trousers and shirt, almost new compared to our clothes in the village. At his feet sat Yann.

When the man spoke, his voice was deeper even than Grandpa's, and it echoed from the ceiling. There could be no doubt: *this was the bokor*. "This filthy little one is the grandson?"

Yann smiled. "Yes, bokor. He wasn't *that* filthy when we started. Little Pat, did you have an accident?" Yann laughed.

"Silence." One word from the bokor, and Yann went silent in an instant. The bokor turned his eyes to me, and I felt like a bird waiting for the snake to strike. "Your grandfather is Thierry Cadet?"

I couldn't find my voice. I no longer wanted anything but to escape with my life.

"Answer me, boy! There's no need for us to quarrel."

Somehow, I managed to answer. "Yes, bokor."

He smiled. That smile frightened me more than his stare. "And what would the houngan's grandson ask of me?" Again, I hesitated. "Come now, speak up, speak up!"

I found—well, not courage, exactly, but shame was almost as effective at loosening my tongue. "Not in front of him."

"You do not trust my sur pwen?" The bokor chuckled. "You are wise for one so young. He isn't very trustworthy, is he? Yann, you can leave."

"Bokor!"

The bokor stood, and his voice shook the window panes. *"Do you disrespect the bokor?"* Yann cowered, then fell upon the ground. *"Leave my presence!* Go into the jungle. Draw vèvès until I summon you. Pray that your work pleases the lwa. If you disrespect them as you have disrespected me, ill fortune shall fill your short, wretched life."

Yann started to rise, but the bokor kicked him. *"Crawl!* I gave you no permission to stand."

Yann crawled to the door, and the guard held it open for him. I felt a small twinge for Yann. Pity? No, I realized, it was *sympathy.* The bokor treated Yann far worse than Yann had ever treated me. I wondered if Yann's cruel streak simply reflected the cruelty he suffered.

"Do not pity him!" I turned back to the bokor. Had he read my mind? "He wants much from the lwa, and so he must pay much. Respect is a lesson he must learn before he can even begin to pay. And if you think my methods cruel, know that they are the only way he will learn. The only way he shall get what he wants.

"And you, grandson of Thierry Cadet, what do you want of the lwa?"

I swallowed. A mistake, for my mouth still tasted of vomit. "I want ... Father and Mama to stop fighting. I want things to be as they were."

The bokor smiled. His smile was as frightening as his anger, as cold as the zombie's touch. "You want me to mend your family." I nodded, afraid to speak to that smile.

"Your father, he is the American advocate, yes?" I nodded again. "And your mother is the beautiful Chantale, daughter of the houngan asogwe. And they fight ..." He stared up at the ceiling. "They fight over Vodoun. Chantale believes too much, your father not at all. And your grandfather ... With him in the house, they can never ignore Vodoun. He makes them fight."

I gathered enough will to respond. "I don't think so. Grandpa likes Father."

"He likes him, but his very presence is the seed which grows into the fights. Can you see how that could be?" Against my will, I nodded slightly. I didn't want to believe it, but the bokor made it sound so reasonable.

"And you love your Grandpa. You love them all! But you see, while your Grandpa shares their house, they shall fight."

"Yes. I see that." I didn't, really, but the bokor's words had a power beyond reason.

"If your Grandpa would leave ... Find a new home ... Then the strife would be removed. Your father and mother would love each other again. You would be a family again. That is what you want, yes?

"But Thierry will not leave. The old man is comfortable there, where his daughter cooks for him and you wait on him. Why should he leave?

"But the lwa can make him leave. Make him *want* to leave. For this, they need just a small payment from you."

I couldn't stop myself. "What payment?"

"Just a small thing. Just a few hairs from your grandfather's brush. And his kerchief, or some other small bit of clothing. With these, I shall make a pwen, and he will not be able to rest in the house where that pwen is. It will do him no harm, but he will have to find another home. And then your home—*their* home—will have peace.

"Can you do this for me, Patrice Hudson? Can you bring them together?"

At twelve, I had heard enough stories and learned enough lessons to know that this was no bargain. I knew that hair and clothes could be turned to dark purposes. But the bokor ... His voice seemed so soothing now. And he promised an answer, a simple answer where I saw no answer at all. And I wanted a simple answer. I wanted to agree with him. I feared him and I wanted what he offered and I wanted to agree with him and I ...

And I remembered Grandpa's words: *When you are weak, the bokor may offer you gifts, the Petwo lwa may grant you boons, but the costs will always be higher than you realize. And you may not even know who pays the price.* And I wanted the simple answer, but I trusted Grandpa.

"No." It was all I could say.

"*What?*" Once again, his voice echoed. "You ask a favor from the lwa, and then spurn it when it is offered? Think again. Think well on your answer, boy."

"He has thought, Serge. He has answered."

I turned. I hadn't heard Grandpa enter the manor. I hadn't heard him confront the guard, but the guard lay asleep on the floor.

"He came on his own, Thierry."

"And he shall leave on his own. You offered your temptation without interference from me. He turned it down without prodding from me. He is a free man now. He is a true Haitian. The lwa will not let you take him."

"You presume much, speaking for the lwa, old man."

"I am the houngan asogwe." Grandpa stepped full into the torchlight; and his eyes and face threw back light of their own. His voice grew to fill the room. *"Loko watches through me, judging your Sèvis Lwa. You disappoint him."*

The bokor visibly flinched. "I live to serve the lwa."

"Yes, sometimes. But your feud with me, your pride, they are not Sèvis Lwa."

"Do not lecture me, old man. I do not need you to speak to the lwa. Take your grandson and leave."

Grandpa took my hand and pulled me into the jungle, never once looking back at the bokor.

Grandpa let go of my hand when we were on the far side of the ridge. We continued in silence, me two paces behind and a little to his side. I hoped he would turn back, I hoped he would say something reassuring. But he said nothing.

Finally, as light crept over the mountains and slowly lit the jungle, I dared to speak. "Grandpa, I'm sorry."

He slowed but did not stop. And he didn't look back.

"I'm sorry I went to the bokor, Grandpa. I just wanted ..." No, no tears. Tears were how this all started, so I fought them back. "I just wanted Father and Mama to stop fighting. I wanted them to stay together."

At that he stopped. "And is that all you wanted?" He stared forward into the jungle.

"Well ... Yes."

Grandpa leaned over, swept off a log, and sat. "Come here."

I walked over to him. "Eh, you're too tall. You can't sit on old Grandpa's lap any longer. Here, sit beside me."

I sat, and he leaned over me and looked into my eyes. "Patrice, have you listened to my lessons?" I nodded. "And your Mama's stories?" Another nod. "Then you should have learned by now: love brought by the pwen of the bokor, it is not *real* love. It always goes wrong, in all the stories. The pwen is burned, or lost, or stolen; and then the subject learns what was done to him, and he becomes even more estranged. You know this?" I nodded. "Then why did you think this would be different?"

"I ... thought that when Father learned ... when I *told* him what the bokor did, then he would *believe*, Grandpa. If he believed in Vodoun, then ... then there would be nothing for them to fight about."

Tears welled up in Grandpa's eyes. One rolled out and down his cheek. "Oh, my poor boy. My poor Patrice." He wrapped his arms around me, pulled me close. "Oh, you're trying so hard to be a man, to figure out how the world works. You're trying to find sense where there is none."

Grandpa stood from the log, turned around, and crouched to face me eye to eye. "Patrice, there is no power to make a man *believe* something. Not you, not I, not the bokor can do that. Not even the lwa, I suspect. Belief is a complicated matter, built on experience and attitudes and hopes and fears and beliefs. Yes, belief builds on beliefs, it builds itself a manor stronger than the bokor's. It is not such a simple thing to make a man believe what he does not, especially a strong man like Joseph Hudson.

"And you do not understand the root of their fights. It is a complex matter, and a private matter, and we can only see little bits. But I think I can assure you of this: whatever makes your Father and Mama fight, it is *not* Vodoun. That is only an excuse they use when they do not wish to speak of their true problems."

I wiped my eyes, hoping Grandpa would believe it was from dust, not tears. "But Grandpa ... You said family is stronger than juju ... But our family is ..." I couldn't finish.

"I know, Patrice, I know. I'm sorry, I wish I could take this pain away. But it will get better." I looked at him skeptically. "It will never go away, I'm sorry, and it will probably get worse. But some day it will get better. You will learn that family is more than just who lives where. Your Mama will always be your family. Your Father will always be your family. And through you, they will always be family. Despite fights and whatever comes after, they will always be connected through you. And I will, too. We are your family, Patrice, and you help keep us strong."

I didn't know what to say. I wanted to be comforted, but I was only upset and confused and tired. Especially tired.

Grandpa rubbed my head. "Enough talk for now. Your Mama will be worried about us. Let us get back to the village. Oh, but first ... I could use some of that moss. Scrape some up for me. Carry it back home."

"Yes, Grandpa." I almost smiled as I jumped down off the log. Grandpa had a chore for me, and that, at least, felt right.

Grandpa was right: things got worse. After the divorce, Father made plans to return to Manhattan. The sugar trade in Haiti had long since collapsed, so he hadn't represented the sugar company for years. But a letter from his former employer arrived, informing him that they would welcome him back.

And then things got worse yet: in a rare moment of agreement, Father and Mama told me that I was returning to

Manhattan with Father. I screamed. I cried. They lectured. They yelled. And so, it went for over an hour until, as usual, Grandpa got through to me. I had left the house, screaming and slamming the rickety door. The door hinge broke—the third time that year—and the door tilted on the remaining hinge and fell to the floor. Grandpa carefully opened it, closed it behind him, and found me huddled in the empty water trough.

I spoke before he could start in: "I won't go! I won't leave Haiti. I'll run away!"

Grandpa squatted beside the trough. "You cannot leave Haiti. It is inside you. But you must go to Manhattan."

"No! I don't want to leave Mama! I don't want to leave you!"

"So, will you run away? Or will you stay with us? You cannot do both." Grandpa smiled at my little contradiction. I turned away. "Patrice, you hurt your parents. They are trying to do what is best for you in a difficult situation, and you make it more difficult."

"Why is New York best for me? I am not a New Yorker! I am a *Haitian!*"

"You are a very smart Haitian. Some day you will do great things for Haiti. But for that, you need a great education. You can get that in New York."

"We have schools!"

"Not in our village. How many of your friends can read?" I looked down, refusing to answer. My family had taught me reading and math and more, but most of my friends were not so fortunate. "You can do better. You can go to a great university in the United States, and then bring what you learn back to Haiti.

"But to do that, you must stay *alive*. There are dangers in Haiti. The lwa tell me another revolt is brewing, but they do not tell me whether this revolt will be good or bad for Haiti.

Probably both. You are old enough, tall enough to get drafted into the fighting by one side or another. We want you gone before that can happen."

"But Mama needs me ..."

"Mama and I have each other. We have survived upheaval before. And the village will need my protection before all is done. But your Father ... all he will have in New York is you. He needs his family, too."

And so, it happened. I remained sullen and resentful, but I didn't run away. I said goodbye to my friends, Georges and Alain and especially Yann. Georges gave me a stone he had carved to look like a frog. Alain gave me a shirt: he had outgrown it, and his mother had carefully patched it to look almost new again. Yann was quiet, and he kept glaring at me as if I were betraying him.

And then I went to New York with Father. First, we traveled to Port-au-Prince, where Father had multiple meetings at the U.S. Consulate and the Cathédrale de Port-au-Prince, all regarding my passport. While he arranged proof of my citizenship and set up medical appointments, I marveled at the city. All those buildings of stone and steel and glass ... When we flew out of Toussaint Louverture International, I got a sweeping view of the entire city; and I was sure that Port-au-Prince was the grandest city imaginable!

But then our plane approached JFK International on a clear summer night, and I saw all the lights, and I was humbled. You could lose Port-au-Prince just in that airport! And the airport was no larger than a neighborhood of New York. For the first time, I felt ashamed of Haiti, of Port-au-Prince and my little village. It was like the shame I felt when I was younger, and Yann was faster and stronger and better at everything. What is the point of trying if someone else will always be better before you even start?

It took Father a while to recognize my dismay; and he never had Grandpa's empathy, so he wouldn't understand. When he asked what was wrong, I told him I was afraid. Fear seemed easier to explain than shame. He told me not to be afraid, that he would watch over me and help me to learn the city.

And I learned. I learned in the city, and I also learned in the school. There, finally, I found my true place in life. Father and Mama and Grandpa had all taught me diligently for as long as I could remember. They had taught me in Creole, and also in French and English. They had taught me reading and math and geography and science. History they taught me from both American and Haitian perspectives. So, I started school behind my classmates, but not nearly as far as I might've been. With help from Father, and then from private tutors he hired, I excelled. Before my first year of school ended, I was in the middle of my class. Mama and Father had always told me how important school would be, but no one told me it would be so much *fun!*

I got letters from Mama and Grandpa; and in return I sent them letters, photos, and school assignments of which I was particularly proud. Their letters always encouraged me to keep studying, and they told me how proud they were. Mail to and from Haiti was always very slow, and even slower during the revolution, so I treasured every letter.

By the end of my second year of school, I was in the top ten percent of my class, and my Haitian accent had faded to almost nothing. Four years later, when I gave my valedictory address, I was almost indistinguishable from my classmates—save for the count of my college acceptance letters. Haiti's recent rebellion and subsequent unrest had kept my country in the news, if not the front pages. "Poor Haitian boy becomes top student at elite school" was a compelling story in the eyes of an admissions office, even if Father wasn't exactly poor.

When I filled out my application, I paused on one line: *Intended Major*. I knew what I wanted to type there, but I didn't want Father to see it. Despite Grandpa's advice, despite all Father had done for me since leaving Haiti, I still blamed him for breaking up our family. In my head I had worked out an alternate timeline in which Mama and Grandpa came with us to New York, and Mama and Father were so happy that they never fought. And I was sure it would've happened that way if only Father hadn't been so difficult.

But as much as I blamed Father, I had a plan for how I could help Haiti. Somewhere in the course of my studies, I had lost my belief in Vodoun. It was no single incident, just a gradual drifting away. But though I no longer believed in Vodoun, I still believed in Haiti; and my plan for Haiti required a particular major.

And so, Father beamed when he reviewed my application. "Pre-law? My son, pre-law! A lawyer, like your father!"

I wanted to sting him. I didn't look up from my computer as I answered. "Yes, I want to go into public interest law. I don't want to work for some multinational trying to wring profits out of poor people. I want to learn law and go back to Haiti and help the people. I want to help build a stronger Haiti."

My tone started mild but ended accusatory. I didn't want his pride. I wanted him to know that I rejected his values, that I thought he and his world were wrong. I wanted to hurt him.

And somehow, I failed entirely. He came up behind me and gripped my shoulders, as close as he had ever come to hugging me since I was little. "You make me so proud, Patrice." He patted my head. "And you make Mama proud, and Grandpa. And some day, Patrice, you will make all of Haiti proud. You must write Mama a letter and tell her this good news!"

I wondered if I would ever understand Father.

And then came the earthquake. For the next generation at least, events in Haiti will be reckoned from before the earthquake, or after.

Like most in my generation, I got the news first from Twitter. I tapped the link on my smartphone and saw video of the devastation. The Port-au-Prince I had known for a few brief weeks was no more. What remained was suffering and misery like Haiti had not seen in living memory. In an instant, a century of efforts at modernization had fallen to ruin.

Before the video finished, I called Father; and before he could object, I jumped in. "Father, there's been an earthquake in Haiti. I have to go back. They're going to need help. Please don't try to talk me out of this."

"Talk you out of this? Patrice, of course we're going back!"

"We?"

"I've called my bosses. We've got plans in the works. I'm on my way to your apartment. Are you there?"

"I'm on my way home from class. I'll be there soon."

"I'll meet you there. Try not to worry, Patrice. Our village is far from the epicenter. Mama and Grandpa will be okay."

Father clicked off, and I called my advisor to explain that I was temporarily leaving school. As soon as she heard my plans, she promised to handle the paperwork for a temporary with-drawal and to hold me a position for the fall semester. Then I went back to the news. It was hard to focus as the subway car rocked, but I could hear reports in my earbuds. Buildings collapsed. The port and the airport shut down. Death tolls uncertain. Fears of cholera and worse.

Father waited on the steps of my building. As I opened the lock and let us in, he started in before I could say a word. "I've called some friends in the government. They confirm the village is outside the worst destruction, but that's all they know right now. Mama and Grandpa are strong. They'll get through this."

"I know, but the rest of Haiti ..."

"Needs a lot of help right now, and the two of us can't do anything right away. But there are aid efforts mobilizing. Coast Guard cutters should be there by morning, but they're just the first wave. And a couple of strong-backed volunteers who speak Creole and French will get put to use."

As I opened my apartment, Father continued. "My bosses have contacted some people in the government to get us assigned to an aid mission. Pack quick, and pack light. I've called in some favors, and we can be on an aid boat tomorrow, but we have to fly down to Miami tonight. The company jet is waiting for us at LaGuardia."

"Father ..."

"Hush. We'll have plenty of time to talk on the flight. Pack."

And as promised, we talked on the plane. Well, Father talked. He couldn't seem to stop, nervously telling story after story: stories of Mama, stories of Grandpa, stories of him and me back in Haiti, and then back to stories of Mama. When he said her name, it was almost an invocation: "Chantale," spoken in a respectful and concerned tone. I had never seen him like that before, so anxious, so helpless. He needed to do something, and there was nothing he or anyone could do right then. So, he talked.

When we landed in Miami, we were met by a man from Father's company. He had paperwork all filled out, and he routed us to a doctor who gave us physicals and inoculations. From there we took a cab to the docks, where a purser checked our travel papers and ushered us aboard. Five hours after touching down in Miami, we were on an aid ship bound for Haiti. Over the next two days, we received frequent briefings and reports, each more depressing than the last.

When we finally reached Port-au-Prince, the port was closed due to the damages. The U.S. Navy assigned landing ships to ferry ashore our supplies and our volunteers; but they were so overwhelmed, it was nearly another two days before we once again set foot on the shores of Haiti.

And once we got there, the devastation was beyond my powers to describe. Either you were there, and you know; or you were not there, and you will never know. Port-au-Prince, the city that had so awed me in my youth, was no more. In its place was a horrendous world of shattered stone and twisted steel. The Cathédrale where I had gotten my passport was an unrecognizable pile of tumbled walls. The hospital where I had gotten my shots had simply ceased to be. The hotel where we had stayed was still standing, but one whole face of the building lay shattered in the street. And the control tower of the airport from which we had departed was tilted at an odd angle, its control lights all dark.

I speak of the ruined buildings because those are less painful to remember. The true damage is far more haunting: the people. The dead, the dying, the injured. The mourners, the frightened, the traumatized. Even the aid workers were haunting, their faces—*our* faces—haggard and dirty and empty of hope. Oh, never when we were helping people: I noted with pride how we all kept smiles and positive attitudes and a cheery calm when dealing with the victims. But after, when we would return to our own temporary shelters after a long day of work, I would see the upbeat masks fall away, replaced by exhausted frowns and sometimes tears.

Father and I were in a strange middle ground in the aid crews. We both knew a little first aid, but we mostly did hard heavy lifting and carrying; but because we spoke Creole, we were in demand in the work crews. Any time a crew needed to coordinate a complex task with local crews, Father or I would be called in to help. Today I think that made us lucky: we got more work with people who could speak. Living people, in other words. We saw less of the dead than other crews did.

But we saw the dead. Far too many times, we dug through rubble hoping to find survivors, only to find crushed bodies instead. Far too many times, we helped carry the dead from the clinics to the streets—for the morgues had filled up before we even landed. Soon the dead became a health hazard, one the city couldn't afford. When the government decided they had no choice but to bury the dead in mass graves, we got the unfortunate task of trying to explain to protesting relatives. In Vodoun, such burial is unconscionable. I tried to console the survivors, explaining that the lwa would know this was the only option; but I doubt I was convincing.

And we saw the sick, and we helped care for them. On the ship, we had received instruction on the risks and prevention of cholera. In Port-au-Prince, we hauled and dispensed fresh water. We helped the people to understand the importance of washing hands and boiling water. We helped dig latrines, and we taught the people how cholera was spread and how to avoid it. Sometimes we got our message across, I hope, but not often enough.

We dug and hauled rubble. We helped to raise shelters. We

carried supplies. For the first time, I saw signs of Father's age. Oh, he was as strong as me, as willing as me; but he tired more quickly. But tired or not, we worked from sunrise to sunset, the days blurring into weeks. We worked so long, I almost forgot what life was like outside of the relief effort. And we were just two of thousands of aid workers from around the world.

And perhaps the greatest horror I took from Port-au-Prince is this: despite all that work by all those volunteers and military troops, the city was still in ruins more than a year later. Despite our best efforts at sanitation and education, cholera swept through the country late that year, claiming another three thousand victims. Despite our efforts at finding shelter, around a million Haitians still live in temporary tents. I know how hard we worked, how much we did; and the horror is that the destruction and suffering are so much greater than our greatest efforts. Haiti, never a rich country to begin with, won't recover fully in a generation.

Some fourteen weeks after we arrived, we had a break. It wasn't that the work was done, of course, but simply that we couldn't continue at that level. So, when new aid workers arrived, we volunteered for a team that would check conditions in remote country—including our village. In the face of so much human misery, we hadn't had time to think of Mama and Grandpa; and seeing what we saw, we were afraid to speculate about them. If I brought them up, Father would say that he trusted Grandpa to watch out for Mama. And then he would change the subject. But I don't think he ever stopped worrying about them, and I know I didn't.

Six of us set out in two Land Rovers stuffed with meal packs, bottled water, and other relief supplies. Each Land

Rover pulled a sturdy trailer with more supplies. As we drove north and east out of Port-au-Prince, conditions slowly got better. The epicenter had been southwest of the city, but that wasn't the only reason. The region we drove through was also less densely populated, so there were fewer potential victims. And even though the area was poorer and the improvised buildings more prone to collapse, those same buildings did less damage when they fell. Tin and plywood and thatch that falls a single story is not as hazardous as stone and steel that falls from the sky. And unlike in the city, most of the villagers grew their own food. So, there was poverty, but not the same overwhelming degree of suffering.

When the Land Rovers pulled into our village, we were greeted by curious children and weary adults. I honestly couldn't tell if the village had been damaged by the earthquake at all. Some buildings were damaged or even collapsed, while others showed signs of recent patchwork; but both conditions were part of the normal course of life in our village. I had been gone over a decade, long enough for almost the entire village to fall to pieces and be rebuilt.

After arranging to meet us in two weeks, our teammates dropped us off, along with half a trailer of relief supplies (more than warranted for the size of our village, perhaps). The villagers eagerly gathered around for the supplies. At first, I didn't recognize the two who hailed me, then I realized it was Georges and Alain, now grown to strong men. They both wore remnants of military uniforms. We swapped warm greetings and a few stories. They had both fought in the revolution, and had battle scars to prove it, but they were among the survivors. Talking with them, I felt a mix of guilt and relief that Mama and Father had sent me to New York.

I put Georges and Alain in charge of distribution, then Father and I set off for Mama's house. Word of our arrival must've run ahead of us. As we drew near, I saw Grandpa standing by the water trough, looking older and smaller but still standing straight. Next to him, Mama bounced up and down in excitement. I ran up and hugged her.

"My son ... My baby ..." She cried, and I cried. After so much ugliness, I hadn't realized how much I needed Mama to comfort me. "You're so *big!* I have to reach up to hug you."

Through her tears, she kept repeating these words or variations of them. Behind her, Father and Grandpa shook hands and clapped shoulders like long-lost friends.

"Joseph, it is good to see you. Haiti welcomes you back."

"I'm ... sorry this is what brought us. But it's good to see you, Thierry."

Finally, Mama let me go, and Father hugged and kissed her. "Chantale, you're all right!" She stood stiffly and tolerated his touch, but she didn't return it, so he quickly backed away.

Then we went into the house, and Mama served up a meal. She asked me a million questions, things I had told her in my letters, but she insisted on hearing them again. She asked me about New York, and school, and girls. Especially girls, but I assured her I hadn't met a girl who could cook like her.

Grandpa, meanwhile, asked Father about the earthquake and about the conditions in Port-au-Prince. He seemed well informed about the general situation in the country. He claimed the lwa told him, but I was sure his information came from gossip and from the crank radio I'd sent him.

Finally, I pushed my plate away. "I'm sorry, Mama, I can eat no more. I think I ate an entire goat."

"And how often do you get goat in New York? I doubt they even know how to prepare it. But you must have room for *Pen Patat!*"

"Mama! I'm going to burst!" But I had missed Mama's *Pen Patat* for a decade, and the smell of sweet potato and cinnamon was irresistible. I found room. For the first time, I also shared a bottle of kleren with Grandpa and Father. Mama frowned her disapproval but didn't say anything.

Mama went to bed when it got dark, but Grandpa and Father talked late into the night. The kleren and the tropical air made me feel warm, and soon I found my old bedroom. I no longer fit in the bed, so I rolled up the blanket as a pillow and curled up on the floor.

I woke to a soft knock on the door. I stretched, stood, and went out into the main room. I found Father at the door, speaking to Madame Vincent, our nearest neighbor. When she saw me, her eyes lit up. "Is that Patrice?"

"Mama Vincent!" I hugged her, careful because of how frail she had become since I last saw her. She had been practically a second mother when I was young, always looking after the neighborhood children. She had no children of her own, but all the kids knew she had cakes and cool drinks any time you knocked on her door. "You're as beautiful as ever."

"And you're still a charming rogue, I see. Come, you must tell me about your life so far away in New York City."

So, we invited her in, and Father and Grandpa cooked up another meal. Mama came in from the yard with three large eggs for the meal, and she and Madame Vincent took turns grilling me for more details.

Finally, when breakfast was done and the day was getting warm, Madame Vincent rose to leave. Father escorted her to the door. Before she could leave, he pulled two meal packs from his duffel bag and gave them to her. "Please, Madame Vincent, take these."

She smiled. "If you insist. Thank you, Joseph. And Patrice, you be sure to come see me before you leave Haiti again."

After she left, Grandpa turned to Father. "That was kind of you." I didn't understand. There was some part of the conversation I was missing.

Father sighed. "She didn't want to beg, of course. And she shouldn't have to. We brought more than enough meal packs for the village. Something's wrong. Patrice, let's go talk to your friends."

When we got to the village, Georges and Alain stood vigil behind a large crate stuffed with the meal packs and the water. Villagers were coming up in ones and twos and adding to the crate.

Father was ramrod straight, suddenly every inch the corporate attorney. "What's the meaning of this? These are for the village."

Georges looked down, ashamed, but Alain looked Father in the eye. Almost. "We understand, Monsieur Hudson, but the bokor has told us to bring them to him."

"What?" I stood in front of the crate, blocking access. "Alain, why would you do that?"

A voice came from the tree line. "Because I told them to, Little Pat." The figure who stepped from the trees was barely recognizable as Yann. Where Georges and Alain had grown hard and scarred, he had grown soft, if not fat. Yet he was still the tallest among us, and imposing. He wore a white hat and trousers, and his shirt was bright scarlet. Amid all this poverty, his impeccable tailoring bordered on obscene. "The bokor speaks to the lwa, and they tell him what is best for the village. And they say: 'Bring these riches to your manor, where you may keep them safe from robbers. You can give them back to the village as they are needed.'" He had the same smirk as when he was young, but his voice was deeper, more persuasive.

But Father was no stranger to performance, and he wasn't swayed. "That's not necessary. The people can have their supplies and can protect their own. They don't need your 'bokor' to take care of them."

Yann drew himself up straighter, but instead of answering Father, he turned again to me. "Be careful, Patrice. We know your Father does not respect the lwa, but you know better. You know the powers a bokor wields. Or have you forgotten, safe and sheltered in far New York? Perhaps you need a reminder?"

And for the first time in my life, I didn't let Yann's taunts and tricks persuade me. In fact, my reaction surprised even me: I laughed—not in humor, but a harsh, acrid laugh. Yann actually looked startled at first; but then his look turned to boiling anger.

Finally, I stopped laughing, and I explained. "You threaten me? You threaten me with your bokor and the lwa? You can't imagine how little you scare me. *I* have seen Port-au-Prince. Have you?"

I paused for breath, then continued: "I buried nine children in a mass grave, then got up the next day and buried ten more. I held a man down while doctors amputated his leg. I dug a latrine while the piss and shit flowed in around me." I laughed once more, one dry chuckle of pain. "I have seen Port-au-Prince. You think I'm afraid of your powders and poppets?"

"Enough!" Yann's face trembled with restrained anger. "I will teach you to respect the bokor. I will teach you *true* fear!" Yann reached into his pocket. I couldn't guess what was within.

"No, Yann." Grandpa had grown older and slower, but he still moved quietly, and he still liked to make an entrance.

"Nothing has changed. The bokor will leave my family alone. *You* will leave my family and this village *alone*."

Yann grinned. "Old man, you defy the lwa."

Grandpa grinned back, larger. "Little boy, I defy *you*. The lwa and I are just fine." He held the grin, face to face with Yann, unblinking.

Finally, Yann flinched. "As you wish, old man." By that time, most of the village had gathered, though not too near. No one wanted to get caught in a duel between the houngan and the bokor sur pwen. Yann climbed upon a rock and addressed them. "People of our village, the lwa have spoken. They decree that they have blessed these foods and this water and made them safe. They are yours. Take them and enjoy with the blessings of the lwa and the generosity of the bokor."

That was all the encouragement they needed. They rushed the crate; and once again, Georges and Alain kept order as the supplies were parceled out.

As Yann climbed down from the rock, Grandpa spoke again, so low that only Yann and I could hear. "You speak very freely as the voice of the lwa. Very freely, considering I did not hear them speaking at all."

Yann smiled so that no one would note the venom in his quiet response. "You win today, old man, but things are changing. The bokor *will* rule this village, and you cannot stop that forever. The bokor will deal with you at a time and place the lwa choose." Then with a friendly wave to the crowd, he retreated into the jungle.

The rest of our two weeks passed without event. Father and I made repairs around the house and the yard, and also at Madame Vincent's. I helped Mama with the chickens and the goats. Georges and Alain and I drank and talked all through one night. The people of the village stopped by for news from Port-au-Prince and elsewhere. Mama was still cold to Father; but even so, we ate all of our meals together as a family, and the house was far more peaceful than it had been before I left.

When the aid team returned, Mama clung to me as Father packed our bags into the Land Rovers. Finally, she gave me one last hug and kiss. "You take good care of yourself. And watch out for those girls in New York City."

I climbed into the Rover, and Grandpa reached in and shook my hand. "You make us proud, Patrice, all of us. Someday, you'll come back and make all of Haiti proud."

You seldom know when your last conversation will be. A month after that, Father and I left Haiti. There was still more aid needed, as I said, but we had no energy left to give. Father had to return to work, and I had a new semester starting. So, I had been in New York for nearly two months before I knew those would be the last words I would ever hear from Grandpa. That was when I got the letter from Mama.

Your Grandpa has passed away. Madame Vincent and I buried him today. The people of the village tell me the bokor poisoned him and told them to show him no respect, so they did not hold a funeral for him. I do not see how he could be poisoned and not me, as we ate all of our meals together. But a bokor can ask the lwa to poison a man from the inside, so perhaps that is what happened.

As always, he was thinking of you at the end, Patrice. Honor him with your studies, and someday you will become a great advocate for Haiti.

Madame Vincent has agreed to move in with me and help me with the farm. It will do both of us good to have some company. So, don't you worry about me. My Daddy raised a strong daughter.

Love, your Mama

I wept all that night. I considered going back to Haiti, but it was pointless. As slow as mail is from Haiti, Grandpa's grave was a month cold by the time I got the letter. It wouldn't matter if I visited now or in the summer. And Mama was independent. She and Mama Vincent would manage the farm. I needed to concentrate on my studies to catch up for lost time. I had made promises to Grandpa.

Three weeks later I got the second letter from Mama. *Your Grandpa's grave lies empty. The bokor has taken him.* And this time I had to go back.

After emailing Father, I called my advisor again. She expressed sympathy, but she said it would be much more difficult for me to leave school and return a second time. I pleaded and I told her my Mama might be in danger, so she told me she would do what she could. I didn't mention bokors and Vodoun, of course. On a bright fall day in New York, that would make no sense at all.

Father called me back as soon as he got my email. "Patrice, I'm sorry. Mama sent me a letter, too, and she begged me to keep you away."

"Father, I'm going. Don't try to stop me."

"Stop you? Patrice, you're a man now. You don't need my permission to do anything. And I know my son, so I know you'll do this, because it's right."

I paused. Finally, I said, "Yes, thank you. I have to do this, Father."

"I know, just like I have to help. It's the right thing. If you can give me a couple of days, I'll get you the money for the trip."

And that was how it went. Father had to sell some stocks. I'm sure he took a loss with the market down so far, but he wouldn't discuss it. He just handed me cash and a debit card and a ticket, and he drove me to the airport. My passport and inoculations were all up to date from our trip earlier in the year, so I was easily cleared for travel.

I flew into Cap-Haïtien International. By that time, Toussaint Louverture was once again accepting passenger traffic; but it was still operating under makeshift procedures, and it was over-crowded and slow. Besides, Cap-Haïtien was much closer to our village.

But almost immediately upon landing in Cap-Haïtien, I started to doubt my decision. The airport was under the control of UN aid troops from Chile. I speak no Spanish and their English was weak; and something about me inspired their distrust, so I was treated with rudeness and suspicion. I had friends at Toussaint Louverture, friendships forged through weeks and months of shared hard work. I wondered if my arrival would've been easier if I had landed there.

When I finally got into the city, things turned even worse. I had never been in Cap-Haïtien before, and I didn't know my way around. Trying to get to my hotel, I boarded a tap tap, a private bus service common in Haiti; but I misread the directions, and I ended up in the wrong neighborhood as dusk was falling. While I searched for another tap tap, five young men came down the shabby street. They were in their middle teens, and they were brash and loud. After my time in New York, I knew the type, and they meant trouble.

When they approached me, the largest smiled and said in broken, accented English, "Welcome, rich American tourist.

You come to see poor in Haiti? We are poor. You see us? Give us aid?"

I answered in Creole. "I'm not American, and I'm not a tourist. I am Haitian."

A smaller youth answered, also in Creole. "Oh, Haitian. Friends, he is Haitian. One of us, eh?" The others laughed. "But look at his clothes, look at his bags. You are a very rich Haitian, and in a very poor neighborhood. Haitians must stick together, yes? All these foreigners, they come in with aid they say, but we're still poor. They only help the businesses. We Haitians must help each other. Share with each other."

The big one smiled again. "You want to share, yes?"

I assessed the youths. They were younger and smaller than me, but not by much. There were five of them, and in a neighborhood like this, they were probably armed. I had been in my share of teenaged fights in New York, as well as a few incidents while working in the relief effort, but I was hardly a skilled combatant.

I sighed. I wasn't ready for violence; it would only slow me down. Reluctantly I handed my suitcase to the large one.

But I had misjudged them. Oh, they were happy to rob me, but they *wanted* violence. It was sport for them. While I was handing over the suitcase, the second youth kicked me in the knee, knocking me to the ground. Another punched me in the head. Before I knew what was happening, I was flat on the ground, and they were kicking me and hitting me with clubs of some sort.

Before I passed out, I heard some sort of whistling. It might've been a police whistle.

I woke in a bed in a dirty neighborhood clinic. My injuries weren't lasting, but I had to spend two days there. An officer named Lieutenant Tomas had rescued me. He returned to the clinic on the second day, but he wasn't encouraging.

"I'm sorry, Monsieur Hudson, but there's no chance we can recover your belongings. Cap-Haïtien has a hundred such gangs, maybe a thousand. Your belongings were likely sold or traded ten minutes after they fled the scene."

"I know. That's how it works in New York, too."

"Yes, New York. I see that you traveled from there, but your passport says you're a Haitian national. So, you understand the way things work here."

Yes, I understood. Many of the police were nothing more than hired security for the wealthiest citizens, or for local criminals. Honest men like Tomas were overworked and unable to curb such small and common crimes. I was lucky he had been around to hear my attack. "I understand."

"You had poor fortune to run into such a gang alone. At least they ran away before they could get your money. But I would be careful, monsieur. Cap-Haïtien is a very rough city, and very unforgiving. It is not a place for those with poor fortune."

I thanked him for his time, for his rescue, and for his advice; but I didn't really believe in poor fortune, just poor choices. I would indeed be more careful.

But the days that followed could make anyone begin to believe in poor fortune. Every move I made seemed to take longer and cost more than I expected.

I had to pay a large share of my remaining money to the clinic. I thought of haggling with them; but I saw the work they were doing and the poor people they were serving. I remembered the aid clinics in Port-au-Prince, and I didn't have the heart to haggle.

I bought a few changes of clothes and a duffel to carry them. The prices I paid were far less than I would've paid in a tourist market, but I still felt overcharged. This time I did haggle, but not very successfully.

I booked a room in a local hostel. It was a relative bargain, but still it exhausted my debit card.

I went to a local market, and I asked about to see if anyone planned to travel in the direction of my village. It took three days before I found a farmer and his sons headed that way. Monsieur Pierre agreed to give me a ride at the end of the week —for a fee, of course.

And before the week was out, my room at the hostel was robbed. Gone were my duffel and my spare clothes.

Monsieur Pierre and I spoke for hours as he drove across the country. When he learned I was a law student in New York, he grew suddenly interested. Not long after, he casually mentioned his daughter Astryd, and suggested I should meet her. But before he could work his matchmaking magic, the truck got stuck in deep mud. Monsieur Pierre's sons and I clambered out to dig and push and pry the truck out. By the time we were done, we were all mud from head to toe, and my shirt was torn in two places.

And on the next day, the truck got stuck again. This time our efforts to dislodge it ended with a broken axle. Monsieur Pierre was an honorable man: he offered to give me back half the money I had paid, since we hadn't yet reached my village. But I knew he would need that money to repair his truck, and he would likely lose time and money getting his next load to the market, so I insisted he keep it. He smiled and gave me a small pouch of food, and he reminded me to come visit him and

Astryd when I got a chance. I promised to come by when I could, and then I set off on foot.

Later that day I was able to hitch a ride for a few miles. The day after, I hitched two more rides. Each time I paid the drivers for gas.

The second day after, there were no rides to be found. There were none on the third, either. One truck slowed, but when the driver got a look at me, he sped back up and pulled away. I imagine I looked a little rough after so much travel.

On the fourth day I got one more ride; but I also shelled out the last of my cash. I resigned myself to walking the rest of the way.

The fifth day I was nearly out of food, so I stopped at a farm and bartered some chores for some food and water. This slowed me further, but it kept me fed. I did the same on the sixth day.

On the seventh day, finally, I walked into my village. By that time, all vestiges of New York had been stripped from me. With my muddy clothes and torn shirt, I might easily be mistaken for just another villager, and a poor one at that. People stared at me as I passed through, but none seemed to recognize me.

When I reached the farm, I was struck with a mix of rage and fear. The farm had been destroyed.

The chicken coop lay in ruins, feathers and bones and wood strewn about. The feed bin was smashed open and all the feed was gone. The well cover had been ripped off and dumped into the well. The water trough was in pieces. The planks had been torn from the goat barn.

And the house ... I ran up, shouting, "Mama! Mama!

Where are you?" The walls lay tumbled, the porch torn up, the roof in shreds. This was old damage, and I couldn't see any sign of anyone alive.

Alive? I ran to the old family graveyard on the edge of the farm. There was a new grave with a broken, tumbled wooden marker. The grave had been re-excavated sometime back, and now the edges were crumbling and loose dirt covered the bottom.

As I stared numbly at the grave, I heard a shout. "Patrice!" I turned, and Mama ran up and threw her arms around me. She just held me and hugged me and cried, and I cried, too.

Madame Vincent came up behind Mama, and with her help I coaxed Mama back to Madame Vincent's house. It was immediately clear from the clothes hung about that they both lived there now. As Madame Vincent prepared lunch, I calmed Mama down and dried her tears. Finally, I got her to talk.

"Oh, my baby ... Oh, my boy ... I knew you would come. I shouldn't have told you; I knew you would come."

"I had to come, Mama."

"I know, I know. But you shouldn't have! Madame Vincent and I are all right, but you won't be safe here! Oh, I prayed, I prayed to Ezili Dantor. I begged her: *Please, Ezili Dantor, great mother of the lwa, please stop my Patrice. Please keep him away from this village and the anger of the bokor.* But she didn't listen."

But then for just a moment, I wondered if she had. Oh, not fully. I had long stopped believing in Ezili Dantor and lwa and Vodoun. But disbelief from the comfort of modern New York is easier than disbelief when you stand in a poor Haitian village. And I thought of all the trials I had faced since landing in Cap-Haïtien, and just for a moment I wondered: *Was Ezili Dantor trying to turn me away?*

But then the moment passed. I might look like a poor

Haitian villager, but I was still a New York law student. Vodoun no longer had a place in my world. But now was not the time to discuss that with Mama, so I changed the subject. "Mama, what happened to the farm?"

That was a bad choice for a new subject. Mama started crying again and became incomprehensible. Finally, Mama Vincent brought over our lunch, and she answered the question. "It was the bokor. He wasn't satisfied with Thierry's death. Word spread that he wanted to punish the whole family for your grandfather's disrespect. He even wanted to punish *you*."

I was surprised at that. I understood that in some way I had been a pawn in the bokor's rivalry with Grandpa, but I only met him that one night. What was I to him?

Mama Vincent continued. "And so, one night, we heard commotion in the yard. We looked out, and the coop was under attack. By ... by zombies."

"Mama Vincent!" Somehow, I had always seen her as the wise, rational lady of the village. I hadn't expected such nonsense from her. Zombies!

"Hush, Patrice, show some respect. I know what you're thinking, but I know what we saw. And I never saw anything so terrifying in my life. These were the walking dead. I gathered up Chantale and we went back to my house. Chantale hid, but I watched as the zombies slowly tore the farm apart. They left the house for last, and then faded into the jungle before dawn."

I didn't know how to respond to that, so I ate the rest of my lunch in silence. Under the circumstances, I could think of no way to ask about Grandpa's grave without making matters worse. Mama stopped crying but also remained silent, occasionally reaching out and patting my hand. Mama Vincent made the silence unanimous.

After lunch Mama insisted I change into clean clothes. She

had salvaged some of Grandpa's, and they fit me surprisingly well. When I stood before her dressed in Grandpa's best outfit, she burst out crying and hugged me again. "My baby ... My baby boy, all grown up ..." Yet strangely I didn't feel grown up. I felt like a child again, like a child wearing grown up clothes to pretend to be grown up.

Then I went back to the farm. I dug through the rubble of the house for almost an hour before I found what I was looking for: Grandpa's cabinet, tipped over but not broken. This cabinet contained all his dearest possessions. It was an eclectic mix of the practical and the superstitious: hand tools and nails right next to Vodoun powders and pwen. I took out a hammer and a saw and a jar of nails.

And then I began repairs. I started with the goat barn since it seemed the least damaged. I found most of the planks to be serviceable, though many had split. Slowly and methodically I began hammering them back up.

By nightfall both the barn and the coop were functional, though they still needed a lot of work. Mama Vincent came out to the farm and summoned me back for dinner. It was too dark for me to keep working, so I followed her back. Maybe I could start on the house the next day.

In the night, I woke to a light touch on my shoulder. Mama Vincent leaned over me, a finger to her lips. "Shhh! Do not wake Chantale, but you need to see this, Patrice."

"What is it?" I whispered as she had.

"No, first you must promise not to get involved. Chantale would never forgive me." I started to object. "Promise!" I nodded. "Then follow me outside."

We went outside, and Mama Vincent pointed across the

field to our farm. I would've broken my promise, but she held me back. Three large men were busy tearing apart the chicken coop and the goat barn.

I yanked my arm free from her grasp. "I have to stop them!"

"No, Patrice. You promised me. Besides, there are three of them, and they're larger than you."

"I can go get help! We have to put a stop to this!"

"No!" In her agitation, Mama Vincent grew louder. Then she whispered again. "No, you cannot. Chantale will never forgive me if anything happens to you. But you have to understand. You have to remember: *this is Haiti!* This is not New York, and the rules here are different. You really need to understand that. So here is what you will do: you will hide in the shadows, and you will get closer to the farm, close enough to see what evil you face. *And no closer!* And then you will understand, and you will accept the fact that the farm is a lost hope."

"All right. I promise; close enough to see, but no closer." I didn't want to upset her; and besides, my experience in Cap-Haïtien had made me cautious. Three large men, possibly armed, were too much for me to handle. I would have faced them if they threatened Mama, but not just to defend a goat barn.

I crept through the fields in the moonlight, much as we had on childhood adventures. I crouched low to get cover from the tall grass. The night was filled with familiar animal and insect noises. The moon, the grass, and the noises all worked together to drag my brain back ten years, back to pre-teen life in the Haitian countryside.

So perhaps my brain was suggestible that night, or perhaps childhood stories and memories had primed me to see what couldn't possibly be. Whatever the reason, when I got close enough to see the first man in the moonlight, only one word echoed through my mind: *zombie.*

The man was tall, with muscles that were thin and wiry and stood out against the bone beneath. His hair sprouted in spare patches. His clothes were tattered, and he didn't seem to notice that he wore only half a shirt. The back of the shirt was torn off, revealing a back covered with scars and creeping with insects and grubs. Some of them squirmed in and out of gaping holes in his flesh.

The second man was taller, with one arm missing. This one pulled and pulled on the planks I had spent all afternoon nailing up. No man should've been able to remove those planks without tools, but this ... this creature did.

And then the third came around the corner of the barn and looked in my direction. I don't think he saw me amid the grasses. But I got a good look at his emaciated face, and ...

I barely remember running back through the field. I remember collapsing on Mama Vincent's porch, gasping for breath. Mama Vincent brought me a drink, just as she had when I was young, and then she rocked silently in her chair as I sat and drank and shook.

We didn't talk. I couldn't tell her—couldn't tell myself, even —that I had seen zombies. I refused to admit the possibility. And I certainly couldn't tell her that one of the zombies had been Grandpa.

By morning I had stopped shaking and had managed to sleep a little. With the sunrise my sanity had returned. Zombies? Nonsense!

When I looked out at the farm, though, I knew that the attack at least had not been nonsense. The barn and coop lay in ruins once more. That only made me more determined than ever. I would rebuild them stronger than ever; and then I would watch for the attackers—the *human* attackers, I was sure of that —and stop them once and for all.

But for that, I would need assistance, and I knew where to find some. I went into the village and tracked down my old friends, Georges and Alain. They had small neighboring farms on the far side of the village, and I found them both at work in the fields. They hailed me, and we swapped greetings much as we had three months before.

Finally, I found a chance to explain my plan. Their response surprised me. Alain was the first to answer: "No, Patrice."

"What? This is my Mama, and our farm! We need help, and who else can I turn to?"

"I'm sorry, Patrice," Georges joined in. "If these were bandits, we would help you. We faced worse in the revolution, and we still have our guns. But this is Vodoun."

"Nonsense! You're grown men. Don't fall for children's tales!"

"Vodoun is *not* a children's tale!" Alain had grown fierce. "It's well for you, Patrice, that you can leave Haiti behind and go to the great land of New York, where the lwa are silent and the bokor have no influence. But we live here, in the true Haiti, the Haiti that you have forgotten. And here, the lwa are everywhere, and the bokor bargains for their favors."

"And the bokor has declared war on you and your family, Patrice." Georges had lowered his voice as if afraid the bokor and an army of zombies might appear from nowhere. "Somehow your grandfather angered him, and he wants revenge on all of you. You must leave Haiti."

"What?"

"Yes." Alain nodded. "Leave Haiti. Take your Mama with you. Leave and never return. You will both be safer in New

York. There is no place in Haiti for you anymore, not with the bokor as your enemy."

I tried a while longer, but they were adamant. Finally, I gave up and returned to Madame Vincent's. As I passed through the village, people got out of my way without meeting my eyes. Behind me, they whispered about the bokor.

The bokor wanted war? Fine, I would show him that one man in Haiti did not fear his juju.

Or maybe ... Maybe I could use his own superstitions against him. I didn't really have a plan, just a stubborn insistence that I would beat him even if I had to use his own tools. I had a vague idea, and an impulse to follow it. I borrowed an envelope from Mama, and then went back to Grandpa's cabinet.

And then I set out into the jungle. It was time to face the bokor.

When I pounded on the door of the manor, I wasn't surprised to see Yann open the door, but I was disgusted. He wore the same outfit he had worn on our last encounter, white and scarlet; but in the intervening months, while Haiti suffered and children starved in Port-au-Prince, he had actually gained weight. He was vile.

But he feigned warmth as well as he ever did. "Little Pat, come in! Welcome! Come to pay your respects to the bokor at last?" He let me in and closed the door behind us. Immediately the smells of smoke and incense took me back to my first meeting with the bokor. Then I remembered the attacks and my purpose here. I was twelve no longer, and I wouldn't let old memories make me afraid.

"Respects? Ha!" I spit on the floor, and Yann scowled. "I

have no respect for the bokor. Bring him to me, Yann. I will speak to him about this 'war' he has declared. Bring me your master."

And then Yann laughed, surprising me. He laughed for many seconds. Then finally he called out: "Valery! To me!" And with that, he went to the far corner where the same metal chair sat beneath the same elaborate tapestries, all clean and well maintained as if no time had passed since my last visit. Yann sat in the chair, crossed his legs casually, and smiled.

A deep voice came from behind me. "You called me, bokor?" I turned, and a tall, muscular man stood in the hall entry. He carried a large machete.

I turned back to Yann, and he laughed again. "Yes, Valery! My friend Little Pat has come to speak to the bokor. Make sure he doesn't try to leave."

"What? The bokor? You—"

"Ah, Little Pat, the surprise on your face is delightful. You didn't suspect, and your grandfather didn't suspect. The old bokor, he died in the earthquake. Well, with a little help." He laughed again. "I am no longer the bokor sur pwen. *I* am the bokor asogwe, and I have been for nearly a year!"

My head spun, and it wasn't just from smoke and incense. "What? I don't understand. Yann, if you're the bokor now, why does the village think you're at war with me?"

Yann glared. "I *am* at war with you, Little Pat. With you, and your grandfather, and your whole family."

"But we were friends!"

"Friends? We were never friends. You were a tool, and I used you for my amusement."

"That's a lie! We played games. We built a fort!"

"And who won all the games? Me. And who did all the work on the fort? You. A bokor has no friends, he has the lwa! He has power! And with his power, he should have *respect!* But your grandfather, he never respected my master. He certainly never respected me. And he never taught you respect. And then you left Haiti, left your people. You went off to grand New York and abandoned the lwa and Vodoun. You abandoned me! What sort of respect is that?

"But now the time has come. The lwa demand punishment."

"All this trouble because I didn't cater to your whims even more? Because I don't pay obeisance to your stories, your lwa? I don't believe it!"

"You believe *nothing!* And that will bring your doom. You turned your back on the lwa, Little Pat, but your belief in the white man's ways is too weak! You doubt, you think you may be wrong, and you fear the lwa may punish you! You have no belief, so you stand alone, no power, no defenses. You're still twelve years old and afraid; and this time, there's no one here to rescue you. You have no beliefs, and so you are alone."

The smoke stung my eyes, and the scents made me dizzy. He was wrong. He had to be wrong. I didn't want to believe him. I didn't ...

"But me, I *believe.* I serve the lwa, and they reward me. The bokor does not command the lwa, he propitiates them and asks for their gifts. And with those gifts, he can command others. Even the dead."

He waved his hand and crooked a finger, a most casual summons; and I heard a noise behind me. I turned, and I saw a ragged figure shuffle from the shadows. It was the same as I had seen the night before. It was ... It was ...

"And what the bokor commands is *respect.* Those who do not give him respect in life, them shall he choose to respect him in death. Your grandfather defied me and my master too many times. Now he shall serve me until he rots and can no longer serve. And then, Little Pat, then I shall grind what remains and use it in rituals that will bind his soul to the Petwo, who will torment him with the memory of what he has done in my service. Including killing his grandson."

And Yann laughed as Grandpa's corpse advanced on me. I backed away, but without a plan. I could elude him easily, for he had not been quick even when alive; but where would I go? There was no exit save one, and Valery blocked that one.

As the corpse drew closer, I could more clearly see Grandpa's face. The jaw hung slack, tongue lolling around with each shambling step. The face bore scrapes from some unspecified trauma, but with no bruising or bleeding, for no blood flowed in that body. The white hair, once thick and bushy, was pulled out in patches. The eyes ...

The eyes ... Something wet in those dark, hollow eyes. Something still—if not alive, something still aware.

"I believe ..." I stopped backing away. There was something there, something that reached me somewhere below my rational brain. "I believe ..." I took a step forward. "I believe in Grandpa."

The corpse raised its arms, not as if to strike, but as if to grab. To crush. To ...

"I trust you, Grandpa. I believe in you."

Arms wrapped around me. The smell of rot and earth mingled with the spices of the bokor's potions. Clumsily, the cold, swollen hands patted my back. I returned Grandpa's embrace.

"I believe you, Grandpa. Family is stronger than juju." I pulled back, and Grandpa pulled back as well. Then I pulled out the small white envelope and ripped it open. Grandpa half-nodded, and I poured the contents into his gaping mouth. From somewhere he summoned the will to close his mouth and swallow the salt.

"No!" The bokor rose from his cushions. "No! I can't reach him. Kalfu has sundered the link!"

Valery shifted uneasily. Grandpa started toward him, and the guard slid away from the door.

"Stop them!" Yann flashed his knife. Valery flinched but shook his head.

"He knows." I unlocked the door and opened it for Grandpa. "He knows that Grandpa has eaten the blessed salt, and now must return to his grave. He knows he cannot stop Grandpa. He's afraid to try. He believes too strongly."

"But he can stop *you*. Stop him!"

Valery raised his machete and took a step toward me. Grandpa turned his head toward him, glared with those dark dead eyes. The guard dropped the machete and fled down the hall.

"Kalfu is disappointed in you, Yann. He gave you power, and you failed. The lwa are closed to you."

"I still have my knife." But I could see the fear in his eyes.

"You don't believe in the knife. You don't believe in yourself, Yann, and you never have. If you had had the strength to fight your own battles, you never would've turned to the lwa for power."

"You take that back! Take that back, Little Pat, or your mother will have another grave to dig. Or maybe I'll curse her first, let her suffer and fail and die while you watch." Yann laughed, the laugh of a man trying to bolster his courage. "And *then* if you give me a baseball, perhaps, I'll kill you quickly."

I stopped, but not because of Yann's words. I stopped because Grandpa had stopped in front of me. Slowly, silently, he turned back. And when Yann saw Grandpa's glowering face, he screamed.

I turned back to Yann as well, but Grandpa laid a cold hand upon my shoulder and turned me back toward the door. He waved the other hand toward the outside, and I understood. What followed was a Vodoun matter, and I was not a part of it.

I exited through the door, and it slammed behind me. I hurried into the surrounding jungle, and then I turned back.

At first, I heard nothing. Then I heard Yann chanting; but his voice faltered, and that's never a good thing in a Vodoun ritual. And then I heard a strange, hissing laughter shake the walls of the manor. At the same time, an unearthly red light arose in the windows. It was not the red of flames, but more like the deeper red of hot coals.

And then I heard screaming and shouting, all from Yann. And I heard the laughter change to a voice, speaking loudly and clearly but not in a language I knew. I started to feel the heat from the walls. The stones themselves glowed with a dim red light.

The door opened again, and Grandpa shambled out. Behind him, I saw the deep red light, and also tinges of white, and some sort of smoke or fumes billowing though the manor. Through the fumes, I made out vague shapes, serpent-like but shifting, sometimes almost human. And I saw the shapes pulling and tearing at Yann as he screamed. Then the door slammed shut again, though I saw no one to slam it.

Grandpa stumbled past me, no longer noticing me. I fell in behind him, just like I always had when I was young. We crossed the jungle in silence that was briefly broken by the sound of crashing stones.

When we reached the village, the sun was rising over the hills; but the doors and windows remained closed to us. I could see a few shutters part and eyes peer out, but no one dared approach us.

When we reached the family graveyard, Grandpa knelt by his grave. Rain and erosion had filled it partly, and he started clumsily scooping it clean. I grabbed our old shovel and started to help. Soon we had dug so deeply that there wasn't room for both of us to work. I stepped down into the grave, and Grandpa laid down next to it. Now that Yann was gone, Grandpa's vitality was fading. If he weren't compelled by the blessed salt, he might have simply fallen apart already. Or maybe he was driven by something stronger than juju.

When the grave was completely excavated, I stood, my back aching from the work. To my surprise, Mama stood there, a clean sheet in her hand. The salt compelled a freed zombie to return to his grave and bury himself, but that wasn't good enough for Mama. She had prepared a new shroud. She spread it upon the ground, and Grandpa showed his understanding by crawling into the shroud.

Mama began to sew the shroud shut, but Grandpa's dead hand stopped her. He clasped her wrist until she stopped. Then he gestured to me.

"He wants to say goodbye," Mama said. "He never got the chance the first time."

I climbed out of the grave and over to Grandpa. On my knees, I leaned over him. He weakly reached up his arms, and I leaned further into his embrace. He patted me twice on the back, and then his arms fell to his sides.

Was he dead? What did that even mean in his condition? But he had stopped moving, and that was dead enough. I helped Mama to sew up his shroud. Then I climbed back into the grave, and Mama helped me pull him gently in. I set him down upon the rocks, and then I climbed out and began shoveling.

Before I finished filling in the grave, Georges and Alain joined me with shovels of their own. Madame Vincent stood beside Mama, holding her hand. By the time we were done, the entire village had gathered. They gave Grandpa the funeral they hadn't given him the first time, and they helped me and Mama to draw vèvès and sprinkle a circle of salt.

And over the next day, the funeral turned into a full-blown celebration of Sèvis Lwa, with rituals and drumming and songs. During the height of the songs, a lwa possessed Mama; and from the glow of her face, I knew it was Ezili Dantor who rode her.

I didn't actually believe it. After what I had seen, I didn't know what I believed or didn't. But Mama believed it, and so I was happy for her.

ABOUT THE AUTHOR

Martin L. Shoemaker is a programmer who writes on the side ... or maybe it's the other way around. He told stories to imaginary friends and learned to type on his brother's manual typewriter even though he couldn't reach the keys. (He types with the keyboard in his lap still today.) He couldn't imagine any career but writing fiction ... until his algebra teacher said, "This is a program. You should write one of these."

Fast forward 30 years of programming, writing, and teaching. He was named an MVP by Microsoft for his work with the developer community. He is an avid role-playing gamemaster, but that didn't satisfy his storytelling urge. He wrote, but he never submitted until his brother-in-law read a chapter and said, "That's not a chapter. That's a story. Send it in." It won second place in the Baen Memorial Writing Contest and earned him lunch with Buzz Aldrin. Programming never did that!

Martin hasn't stopped writing (or programming) since. His novella "Murder on the *Aldrin* Express" was reprinted in *The Year's Best Science Fiction: Thirty-first Annual Collection* and in *Year's Top Short SF Novels 4*. His work has appeared in *Analog, Galaxy's Edge, Digital Science Fiction, Forever Maga-*

zine, Writers of the Future 3 1, *Year's Best Military and Adventure SF* 4, *Avatar Dreams,* and select service garages worldwide. He received the Washington Science Fiction Association Small Press Award for his Clarkesworld story "Today I Am Paul," which also was nominated for a Nebula award and appeared in four year's-best anthologies and eight international editions. The story continues in *Today I Am Carey,* published by Baen Books in March 2019. His novel *The Last Dance,* published by 47North, was in the top 30 paid eBooks on Amazon for the month of October 2019.

Learn more at http://Shoemaker.Space.

IF YOU LIKED ...

IF YOU LIKED TODAY I REMEMBER, YOU MIGHT ALSO ENJOY:

Selected Stories: Science Fiction, Volume 1

by Kevin J. Anderson

Avatar Dreams

Edited by Kevin J. Anderson, Mike Resnick,

Dr. Harry Floor, and Ray Kurzwell

Racers in the Night

by Brad R. Torgersen

OTHER WORDFIRE PRESS TITLES BY
MARTIN L. SHOEMAKER

On Being a Dictator

with Kevin J. Anderson

Our list of other WordFire Press authors and titles is always growing. To find out more and to see our selection of titles, visit us at:

wordfirepress.com